G000094184

About the Author

Strawberry Fields is Ross Mooney's second novel. He has degrees in History and Security Studies. Born in the United States, he currently lives in England.

Strawberry Fields

Ross Mooney

Strawberry Fields

Olympia Publishers
London

www.olympiapublishers.com
OLYMPIA PAPERBACK EDITION

Copyright © Ross Mooney 2022

The right of Ross Mooney to be identified as author of this work has been asserted in accordance with sections 77 and 78 of the Copyright, Designs and Patents Act 1988.

All Rights Reserved

No reproduction, copy or transmission of this publication may be made without written permission.
No paragraph of this publication may be reproduced, copied or transmitted save with the written permission of the publisher, or in accordance with the provisions of the Copyright Act 1956 (as amended).

Any person who commits any unauthorised act in relation to this publication may be liable to criminal prosecution and civil claims for damage.

A CIP catalogue record for this title is available from the British Library.

ISBN: 978-1-80074-390-8

This is a work of fiction.
Names, characters, places and incidents originate from the writer's imagination. Any resemblance to actual persons, living or dead, is purely coincidental.

First Published in 2022

Olympia Publishers
Tallis House
2 Tallis Street
London
EC4Y 0AB

Printed in Great Britain

Dedication

For Alexa

Acknowledgements

Thank you to my father, for the long days of helpful research.

For in the end, it is all about memory, its sources and its magnitude, and, of course, its consequences.
— Elie Wiesel

Prologue

What hope did we have… those of us born into madness?
    -Eliana

You must understand… I am not like the others…
    -Sascha

1
Eliana

In the summer of 1960, my husband asked what I remembered most about my childhood. I told him, the taste of strawberries.

I was born in Weimar, Germany in 1927, though I am not certain of the exact date. I have no official documentation. In truth, I am unsure of anything before the camps. I have obtained the facts of my youth and family from others, as though attending a series of history lectures, and I have had many teachers: those who fled before the war, like my uncle, Efrayim; those in the camp who knew my family, like Gershom, the doctor who delivered both my sister and I; and those who survived, like Golda, who found me amongst the other refugees after we were liberated by the Americans. The lessons themselves never varied much. My parents' names and professions were always the same, for example, my father, Askel, was a professor of mathematics at the University, while my mother, Mira, worked occasionally as a seamstress. When memories turned to finer points of physical appearance or personality, accounts invariably diverged. Golda likened my mother's hair to the color of ripened wheat, while Efrayim assured me her curls always turned a dark amber in the evening light. Gershom knew my father to be a fastidious man, the consequence of a mind devoted to mathematics, I suppose, and yet Golda recounted his playful nature, pretending to be a horse while I sat upon his shoulders twirling a stick like a knight. Golda laughed when she told me this, noting that Illa, my elder sister, was always more interested in playing the princess, and inclined to learn my mother's talents with a needle. I was pleased to run about, soil my shoes and dresses, or call out boisterously for no particular reason, even when we attended temple. Though our personal traits were dissimilar, Illa and I, despite being two years apart, were often confused as twins, Golda remembered; our noses, hair, lips, and eyes were identical in almost every way.

But I have no recollection of any of this.

I have no photographs of my family, only a decaying hyalotype given to me by Efrayim of him and my father from when they were young men. I have my father's face, dark eyes and high smooth cheek bones. I look in the mirror sometimes and talk to my sister, to the woman in mirror. I tell her about my life, that I am married now...

Three days before his death, Gershom said I was a gift from God. My mother's first pregnancy with Illa had been difficult, nearly claiming both their lives, he said.

"I told her it would be impossible to conceive again," said Gershom between coughs. "So, when you arrived two years later, I knew you were sent by God... that your life is blessed and holds a great purpose."

Gershom lies on a filthy straw mattress, just one of hundreds crowding the tiered wooden bunks, his listless eyes draining into his skull...

I woke, my face covered in sweat. I've been dreaming of Gershom lately. I don't know why. His death was peaceful compared to the others. I left Jacob in bed sleeping soundly, slipped out of my night gown and stood naked next to the open bedroom window, staring out at the dark sea beyond Jaffa's dim lights. A warm summer breeze washed over me, bringing with it the honeyed smell of eucalyptus from the garden. I lit a cigarette and took a slow inhale. The warm smoke filled my lungs. I let it linger there, imagined it was Zyklon-B... I remembered the smell of burnt almonds choking the air around the medical cantonments.

"Can't sleep again?" said Jacob, turning over onto his back, resting his head upon the pillow.

"The heat."

"I can see that."

I turned around. The breeze cooled the sweat on my back. I joined him in bed, lending my cigarette to his lips. Jacob ran his hand down my back and inner thigh, then came up, stopping to play with my belly button. I laughed, and he kissed my shoulder, giving the cigarette back to me.

"We've only been married four months," he said. I felt his hand pressing against my belly.

"It took Chaya and Peter nearly a year after their marriage," he said, kissing me again.

"Yes, I know," I said, returning the cigarette to my lips. I took the ashtray from the bedside table and placed it on my stomach, so he had to remove his hand.

"I'll see about getting a cooling unit this weekend."

"Aren't we going to Haifa for you mother's birthday?"

"I can go to the market in the morning before we drive up."

"All right," I said, holding the smoke in my lungs as long as I could, then exhaling. "You should pick your own birthday."

"I was given January 1st when I arrived."

"Wouldn't it be funny if you were actually born on

January 1st?"

"Yes... very funny," I said, putting out the cigarette.

I put the ashtray back on the table and got out of bed. "Where are you going?" said Jacob.

"Shower. If I'm awake, I might as well get an early start at work."

"Darling, it's four in the morning. Why would a secretary need to be in so early? You know I'm on deployment starting Monday... wouldn't it be better to spend the day together instead?" said Jacob with a smile, intending that we should spend the day making love.

"Captain Nazarian," I said, turning on the shower, "are you ordering me to forgo my duty to the nation?"

"I know better than to give you any orders, darling... think of it as a strong suggestion," he said.

I looked back at him; the light from the bathroom cut him down the middle. I could see his bright green eyes and auburn hair. When I met him a year ago his hair was longer, naturally full, and wavy.

Returning to duty after our marriage, Jacob cropped it short to the army's liking.

"My work is important... even if I'm just a secretary," I said, leaning against the door frame.

"I never said it wasn't," he said, studying my naked body. "You devastate me..."

I laughed.

"Did you learn such romance from the army?"

I turned and stepped into the shower's cold water, remembering the echoing sound of water dripping from shower heads in that dark, cavernous, concrete tomb full of dead test subjects.

By the time I'd dressed, morning light was beginning to strike Jaffa's rows of white limestone homes. Walking down the street, I studied the painted clouds stretching to the horizon where the sky met the sea; my eyes followed the blue-green waves back to the shoreline. I took the bus into Tel Aviv. The road was lined by cypresses, looming like pillars of ruined temples. I sat next to an open window, the air streaming through my hair. I could smell the bakeries coming alive with babka, challah, laffa, and pita. We neared central Tel Aviv. The roads and sidewalks were mostly empty, a few idling taxis, and street cleaners with brooms. I leaned my head against the window and watched the wakening world rush past.

The Office never closed. Though it was quieter in the mornings, the Office's various departments were never empty; always a lonesome body or two, hunched over a desk, a silver ribbon of cigarette smoke rising up to the churning ceiling fans.

I made it to my desk. Across from me, Zvi looked like he'd been working all night, dark circles cradling his old eyes. I clicked on my desk lamp. Offended by the light, Zvi turned away.

"Long night?" I asked.

"You could say that…" he said, taking off his glasses and rubbing the bridge of his nose.

"Did something come in after I left yesterday?"

"You could say that…" Zvi smirked, furrowed lines running across his balding forehead. "Why didn't you call me back in?"

"Didn't want to take you away from that beautiful husband of yours…" said Zvi, handing me the stack of papers he'd been studying.

Flipping through, my eyes latched on to what was important.

Operation SCYTHE... East Berlin... Dr Oscar Koenig...

I checked the information's date. "It's two months old..." I said.

"Yeah," said Zvi, leaning back in his chair, patting himself down in search of his cigarette packet. "Becoming harder to get information out of the East."

"Still don't believe the reports about the Soviets and East Germans planning to build a wall?" I asked.

"After what I saw in the war, I believe the Russians are capable of anything. They're as smart as they are stupid."

"Same as the Americans?" I laughed.

"The Americans are worse... as stupid as they are smart, God help us," said Zvi, locating his cigarettes in his trouser pocket. He took the crumpled packet out, slipped a ragged cigarette between his lips. "Now where the fuck is my lighter?" he mumbled, beginning the search all over again.

"Koenig was last reported in Budapest... now East Berlin," I said, pulling my lighter out of my purse and handing it to Zvi.

"Mmm... thank you," he said, leaning forward, "Yeah... upstairs wants to know why East Berlin, and how long."

"How long has he been there?"

"No..." said Zvi, lighting the cigarette, and handing me the lighter. "How long will he stay..."

"He was born in the Pankow district of Berlin... could just be visiting family for all we know."

"Yes, Nazi missile scientists have families too, I'll remember that... want some coffee?" said Zvi, rising from his chair slowly.

"Tea, if it's there," I said, laying out the files on my desk. I began to go through the intelligence more thoroughly.

Accompanying the written reports was a series of blurry black and gray photographs. I sorted through them one at a time. Each photograph showed a man, assumed to be Oscar Koenig... sitting on a park bench... another of him walking down the street with a bag full of food... another of him across the street from the Russian embassy...

"Looks like he's moved in," I said to Zvi, as he placed a steaming cup of tea on my desk. "The food?"

"Yeah, doesn't look like a man in town for a vacation."

"The agent was able to follow him to a row house on Danziger Strasse," said Zvi, picking out one of the photos I'd yet to see.

"That one there, number 47," he said, pointing to a tall, thin structure.

Number 47, Danziger Strasse was an old brick street house, three stories, and an attic. Two steps led up to the front door, two windows per floor, and a single port hole fitted with a joist cantilever for the attic. The curtains were all drawn. Number 47 was attached to house number 46, but house number 48 was gone, a pile of rubble, obliterated by the war, most likely, and yet to be rebuilt.

"Not a very nice house for such a prestigious man," I said. "His hair is long, almost unkempt, same with his beard. He looks thinner compared to the last photos we had of him; I think."

"Perhaps he started working for us..." said Zvi, running his fingers through the last gray hairs still left on his head

"Have we misjudged him?"

"How so?" said Zvi.

"Koenig was one of the lead design engineers for the V-2's engine and gyros. After the war, the Russians relocated him to the USSR until 1953 when he was released... seven more years now... not all men can keep pace... maybe the Russians wrung out all his knowledge, then threw him onto the trash heap."

"Why?"

"If the Russians are done with him... could make him desperate."

"How responsive is the agent?" I asked, looking through more of the photos.

"Deichmann says it's touch and go... it's the timeliness of the information, as you already noted."

"Because," I said, handing Zvi the photo of Koenig across the street from the Russian Embassy, "the agent took this photo of Koenig, making sure the Russian embassy was clearly in the frame."

"So? He had likely just come from the embassy," said Zvi assuredly.

"I can think of four possibilities... the agent didn't annotate in the report that Koenig exited the Russian embassy, so we can't be certain that's where he came from... so first, either he did come from the Russian embassy, and the agent failed to mention it, which means Deichmann needs to train his field officers to train their agents better... or the agent needed to take the photo quickly. Koenig is walking toward the agent, on the same side of the street," I said, handing the photo back to Zvi. "They probably passed right by one another."

"Yeah," agreed Zvi, shaking his head, angry at himself for missing something so obvious. "The agent must have been caught off-guard; crossing the street or turning around would have stood out."

"If that's true, the agent would only have an opportunity for one photograph... risking more would be foolish," I said.

Zvi looked up at me, his eyes bloodshot.

"Third?" he said, putting the cigarette back to his lips.

I walked over to the filing cabinet where maps were stored, opened the top drawer, and began sifting through the meter-sized maps of cities...Amsterdam, Antwerp, Barcelona... Berlin. I pulled the Berlin map out and laid it on the nearby coffee table.

"Maybe it's not where Koenig is walking from, but where he's walking to. What building is down the street from the Russian embassy... almost directly behind where the agent is likely stood when they took the photograph?" I said, pointing to a central grid point on the map.

Zvi came over, fixed his glasses, and bent over to examine the map. "Ben kalbah," he cursed. "The Egyptian embassy."

I sat back down in my chair, going through my purse for my cigarettes. Zvi looked up at me. "And fourth?"

"Fourth... well, he could just be walking down the street," I said, putting a cigarette between my lips and lighting it.

"I don't think upstairs will like option four," said Zvi, coming back to his desk.

"They're all still celebrating Eichmann; they won't notice something like this..." I said, referring to Adolf Eichmann, the so-called architect of the *Final Solution*.

Zvi laughed.

"You've still a lot to learn. Now that we've got Eichmann, upstairs will be wanting more, and more... if we can get Eichmann, why aren't we getting all the others?"

For the rest of the morning, I worked with Zvi writing up the report for Office leadership. When, finally, I looked up from my desk, I noticed everyone else had arrived. Every department was full and buzzing with phone calls and conversations. I took a moment to clear my eyes.

"Eliana Wasserman," said a toneless voice behind me.

I turned round to see Elon Redlich, deputy director for analysis. He wore his usual expressionless face.

"Yes, sir?"

"Come with me, please," he said.

"Where are we going?" I asked, standing up.

"The Director has asked for you."

"The Director?"

"This way, please."

I shot a worried glance at Zvi, who could do nothing but shrug his shoulders with confusion.

Redlich and I rode the elevator alone. He did not speak. The Director's floor was white and sterile like a hospital ward; none of the buzzing in the departments below. I followed Redlich down the hallway, his steps so heavy they drowned mine out. We passed through a heavy wood door and entered a waiting area with a conference room. Two female secretaries were sat on either side of the doorway leading to the Director's office. The secretaries, both older, didn't bother looking up when we entered.

"Wait here," said Redlich, who went to the Director's door and knocked twice. Redlich waited for a response before entering.

"Come," I faintly heard from the other side of the door.

Redlich opened the door and peered in. His voice was low, and I couldn't hear what he said. After a moment he turned to me.

"The Director will see you now," he said, opening the door and stepping aside to allow me in.

I entered. The room was dark and windowless, just two lamps on the Director's desk providing somber lighting. The Director, Isser Harel, was sat at his desk, pen in hand, feverishly scribbling on a notepad.

I could feel the deputy director enter the room behind me and shut the door. Harel glanced up, lamplight coloring his bald head. This was the first time I had seen him up close and was surprised to see such delicate, almost feminine features... pursed lips, soft cheeks, a thin sloping nose.

"Ms Wasserman, please come join me," he said, finally putting his pen down and sitting back into chair.

"Good morning," the director continued as I sat down.

"Good morning, sir," I smiled, looking him in the eyes.

"I have your file here. I've just been reading through it... been with us about three years?"

"Yes, sir."

"Do you enjoy your work?"

"Yes, sir. Very much."

"Good... attended Oxford after the war. Studied mathematics and history... quite the odd pairing."

"Yes, sir... my father was a mathematics professor, it seems to come naturally to me, so I continued with it."

"And history?"

"What's past is merely prologue, sir."

Harel let out a subdued laugh, as though clearing his throat.

"Very good, Ms Wasserman. I see despite having a new husband... a Captain Jacob Nazarian... you still go by your family name."

"Yes, sir," I said with pride.

"Is that because you're the only one of your family left?"

I felt my chest become heavy.

"Yes…"

"My condolences," he said in a warm tone. "I imagine you are wondering why I brought you here."

"Is it about Operation SCYTHE?"

Harel looked over my shoulder at Redlich, then back to me.

"No… although I'm kept well-informed of your work. No, I have brought you here for a different matter."

My mind raced; I tried to quiet it. Memories are like smoke; one should never try to hold on to them…

"You and your family were first taken to Buchenwald in 1937, where they perished. After six years in Buchenwald, you were transferred to Mittlebau-Dora labor camp… eight years in the camps, total… is that correct?"

I looked down. My hands were shaking. "Yes, sir. That's correct," I said.

2
Sascha

Everything has sound, light most of all. As a boy I discovered God speaks to us using light.

Sitting in the pew, my legs dangling above the floor, I watched the others close their eyes and bend their heads in prayer. I tilted my chin toward the light filtering through the gothic arches' stained-glass... the word of God, I thought.

I woke from a strange dream, more tired than usual. Down the hall I heard Rita's consumptive lungs slowly succumbing to tuberculosis. The apartment building was never without sound: Rita's drowning coughs, wailing infants, mothers weeping, the fathers' percussive violence. The building vibrated with sound, as though a living thing. But its organs were failing: the mechanical lift had broken and seized between the third and fourth floors; pipes moaned and belched brown water; lights buzzed and flickered; the wood floors creaked and bowed; paint flaked off walls like leprous skin. The building, and all those within, were dying.

I lived in a single room. A bed, chair, and waist-high dresser upon which I kept a wash bowl.

Each floor shared a toilet and sink. I rose from bed, slowly, and stood over the wash bowl. I dipped a rag, and used it to wash myself... face, chest, armpits, genitals. I broke into a fit of coughing. My lungs, what was left of them, burned. I spat out a mouthful of blood and bile into the wash bowl. The fit continued, my body shook uncontrollably. I sat down in the chair beside my bed, its cracked leather scratching my bare back.

I sat awhile, recovering; I looked at the beam of morning light coming through my window. My reflection was in the dirty window. I looked an abstraction, like the work of one of those modern artists in the West. The face drooped like a bead of water; the nose a pumice stone; the left eye disfigured and milky; lips swollen and cracked; cheeks sunken...

I dressed and put what money I had and my passport in my left coat pocket. I opened the dresser's bottom drawer, took out a small flat bronze box, the size of a book page, and put it in my right pocket. I had kept it safe all these years. Not much longer now, I thought.

I swept my hair back and put on my flat cap, made the bed, and placed my apartment key on the dresser. I lingered in the doorway a moment, one last look. I closed the door behind me and went and knocked on Rita's door.

"Five marks for a fuck," said a haggard voice.

"It's Sascha," I said.

"Sascha? What do you want? A free go?"

"No, I haven't had a hard-on in years. I'm leaving. I wanted to check on you first and say goodbye."

"Always a kind heart, Sascha... have any schnapps?"

"No, no schnapps today."

Rita let out a sigh.

"Bring some back, will you," she said between coughs.

"Yes, I'll do that," I lied.

Hobbling to the bus station, I stopped every half-block or so to catch my breath. I could hardly stand up straight these days. I often stooped, as though orating from an unseen lectern. My disfigurements drew stares. I often remind myself that I was not always like this; before the war, I was handsome, not remarkably so, but I believed I would find a kind woman to marry one day.

I have always been well-aquatinted with loneliness. A child of devout Catholics, my upbringing was not one of sport and mischief like other boys, but faith and scripture. I did not attend the summer youth programs in the mountains, the neighborhood children all returning home with tanned faces and bright smiles, instead I memorized scripture and read about the lives of saints.

That is why... yes, I remember now, that is why my mind took so naturally to the study of medicine, the rote memorization of the body's thousand parts, and the various chemical compounds to treat it. My faith brought me to medicine, for we are made in his likeness, and so to examine the body, its organs, tissue, muscles, tendons, and skin... to do such work is to become closer to God.

Waiting in the ticket line at the bus station, I took my cap off and used my coat sleeve to wipe the sweat from my face.

"Which bus goes to the West?" I asked the ticket clerk.

"Number nine," he said. "Departs at noon."

"How much?"

"Fifteen."

"Fifteen marks?" I said with surprise. The clerk was stoic.

"Ja, Ja... fifteen marks," I grumbled. "You know I could get three fucks for fifteen marks..."

I boarded the bus and found a seat in the back, away from everyone. We did not depart on time.

There was no driver. We waited. A quarter past. Then half past. The other passengers did not stir or complain, just waited.

I buried my coughs in my handkerchief, careful to wipe the blood off my lips. I began to sweat. The sun was directly above. I looked out at the bus terminal. Nothing cast a shadow. Light was everywhere.

The driver arrived at a quarter to the hour. Even from the back of the bus I could smell the schnapps on him. The bus's heavy diesel engine turned over. We pulled out into the street and turned west. At the border we stopped and waited in a line of vehicles. Each vehicle was inspected by border guards. We presented proper documentation; our passports were stamped. After rolling through a razor-wire fence, we arrived at a customs post, manned by smart-looking West Germans. They boarded the bus, completing the same checks as their eastern counterparts, but did so with a smile.

Waiting for the border guards to complete their checks, I stared out the window at West Berlin. I had imagined it looking different after all these years, grander I suppose. In truth, it did not appear dissimilar to the East. Its streets were lined with the same trees — linden, maple, and oak; war memorials were surrounded by well-tended flower beds; men wore drab suits; women, knee-length dresses; children ran about in summer clothes, same as the boys and girls in the East.

"Hey, Opa," said a guard looming beside me.

Startled, I turned and looked up at him. He was a young man, clean shaven, with soft cheeks and a delicate face.

"Passport, please," he said.

"Yes, apologies, young man," I said, reaching into my pocket. I broke into a fit of coughing.

The guard stepped back as my whole body constricted violently a dozen or so times. I held the handkerchief against my mouth and nose.

"Are you all right, Opa?"

"Yes... yes," I managed between gasps.

I handed the guard my passport, my hand slightly shaking. He examined it, applied a stamp and handed it back to me.

"Take care, Opa," he said.

"Yes... thank you, young man."

The guard was about to turn when I spoke up. "Might you help me a moment?" I asked.

The guard stopped.

"It has been many years since I was in the west, can you tell me the best way to Uhlandstrasse?"

"Uhlandstrasse?"

"Yes." I nodded.

"The walk is not far, but for you, Opa, best to hire a taxi," he said.

I nodded and sat back. I began the day with twenty marks. I only had five left.

After arriving at the station, I began to walk, asking for directions to Uhlandstrasse now and again. Many ignored me, but a few were kind enough to point the way, though all were unwilling to look me in the eyes. By the time I reached Uhlandstrasse, daylight was fading. I feared the consulate would be closed. I was very tired, and out of breath, when at last I sighted the flapping red, blue, and white of the British Kingdom. There was a guard stood beside the door. I went over to him and asked in broken English if the consulate was still receiving visitors. I believed the guard answered with, "Whom do you wish to visit?" I wasn't quite sure, honestly. All this time, and I had never thought about exactly who I should contact.

I took off my flat cap, slicked back my ruffled hair,

cleaned the sweat from my face, and presented myself as best as I was able.

"Mein Name ist... my name is Dr Sascha Ziegler, Schutzstaffel Sturmbannfuhrer, Buchenwald concentration camp." The guard looked at me with a blank expression.

"Very good... but who would you like to see, sir?" he said.

I shuffled my feet about and thought a moment. I looked up at the sky, burning with every color of the setting sun... the word of God.

"Is there someone...who would know...what to do with an old Nazi war criminal?" I asked.

3

Stanislav

Everything they told us was a lie. Party political officers who said no German would set foot on Russian soil were the first to run when Stuka dive bombers screamed across the summer sky. Red Army officers adorned with medals and ribbons who said the Motherland would never surrender were the first to lay down their arms when the columns of German tanks appeared on the outskirts of Orsha. As for the rest of us, boys from villages without names, we fought with old rifles and rusted machine guns in hastily dug entrenchments...

The German army was not prepared for so many prisoners; they didn't know what to do with all of us. Those not shot outright were herded into massive makeshift barbwire pens. A small contingent of Germans remained to guard us while the rest of the army continued its advance toward Smolensk. For two days, we heard the war rumbling in the distance like thunder. German supply columns passed soon after. The next morning, trucks arrived with men wearing black uniforms who carried large ledger books. I thought they looked like accountants as they searched the pens for Jews and Party commissars, who were loaded into awaiting trucks.

We lingered in the pens for a week; men began to grow ill and die. We'd hardly anything to eat or drink; no place to shit or piss. At night, we slept side by side with the dead, their rot attracting hordes of black summer flies.

I can't be sure, but perhaps half the soldiers who entered the pens never left. After three weeks, the Germans marched us west. Prisoners too sick or weak to walk were shot. The farther we walked, the more frequent the executions became. One day I counted them, every rifle crack, precisely one thousand, six hundred and fifty-four. Of course, I could only count the shots in proximity to me. Our column stretched for miles. We trod along dust-choked roads and through fields of burnt crops. There seemed no end to the walking.

During the heat of the day, rainstorms would gather and loom in the distance like black curtains drawn across the horizon, but the rain never touched us — it tantalized, driving men mad with thirst. By now, our bodies had withered, our skin was no longer skin, it became like the bark of dead trees. We could no longer feel fly or mosquito bites, so they feasted on us... a slow-moving banquet.

All my life, I've felt close to God. As a young man, I yearned to join the church and become a priest. Even now, I sensed God was with me. While others around me died, one by one, I remained strong and healthy. God's grace fed and watered me. He must have a purpose for me, I thought, why else had I not perished?

We walked for weeks, it seemed. Men's feet swelled like balloons. Most could no longer wear their boots and continued barefoot. Infections and rot soon set in; feet became black and gangrenous like strange pieces of rotted fruit still clinging to vines. When we arrived at our destination, a large rail yard, there were only a few thousand of us left, gaunt, stick-line figures, our skin pulled taut over our bones.

The Germans loaded us into train cars, and we continued traveling west. I peered through a gap in the car's wood slats and watched the world change. Gone were the steppe's grass plains, replaced by dark forests and mountain ranges crowning valleys of wildflowers. One night, while helping to stack the dead in the corner of the car, I realized I could no longer smell death. I don't know how long we were on the train; strange, because there was little else to do but sit and listen to the wheels' rhythmic ticking as they rolled along the tracks like a well-kept watch... click-clack... click-clack... click-clack.

I became friends with another prisoner in the car, mostly because he was one of the few still alive. His name was Sergei. By chance, he had grown up not far from me in a village on the banks of the Volga, north of Kazan.

"What's your name?" he asked, lying on the wood floor staring up at the light filtering through the slats, painting the car's interior with tiger stripes.

"Stanislav Preobrazhensky," I said.

"What was your rank?"

"Yefreytor," I said.

"Good, I outrank you," smiled Sergei, a Junior Sergeant.

"Where do you think they're taking us?" I asked, peering out the gap between the slats.

"Prison camp... labor camp... some kind of camp."

"Do you think they will kill us?"

"Why ship us all this way only to kill us? They could have done that back in Russia. No, my guess is a labor camp."

I believed him. He spoke to me as though we were two old friends on an adventure. "I don't expect it to be any worse than the gulag," said Sergei.

"You spent time in the prison camps?"

"No," he said. "My father and brother did. My father said nothing about it. That's why I know it must have been bad."

"And your brother?"

"He never returned… killed in a mine collapse they said."

"I'm sorry."

Sergei shrugged his shoulders.

"My brother was an asshole. My father, on the other hand, was a son of a bitch, which probably is why the fucker survived," smiled Sergei.

The train began to slow. I peered out. "Another refueling stop?" said Sergei.

I saw rail signs written in German. The train reduced to a crawl. There was a barren expanse of what looked once to have been a dense forest, the ground dotted by rows of tree stumps. The men in the car became anxious, asking where we were and what I could see.

Suddenly, a sprawling labor camp came into view.

"There is wire fencing… guard towers… wood barracks in the distance, dozens of them…" I said.

"Do you see other Russians? Other prisoners?" asked Sergei, pressing his cheek against mine so that he could see for himself.

Before Sergei could get a good look, the train stopped abruptly. Dogs were barking and I could hear the doors of adjacent train cars sliding open, followed by a chorus of harsh German voices shouting orders. The bolt to our car door was lifted and the door slid open. Blinding sunlight flooded in. Germans holding rifles and truncheons ordered to us to get out of the car.

"Raus!" they said, again and again.

The first of us began jumping down, many tumbling awkwardly when they hit the ground.

"Steh auf! Sneller!"

Once out of the car, the Germans herded us through a large gatehouse with iron bar doors. It looked like the entrance to a sporting stadium or racing track. We arrived at a dirt parade ground of sorts, beyond which were the rows of wood barracks. The Germans used their rifle butts and truncheons to beat us into place in the center of the field. There was a line of wood desks set up. Each desk was attended by two men; one sat at the desk with a ledger, the other stood adjacent and wore a smock and face mask, giving them the look of physicians. We were put in long lines facing the desks and told to remove our clothes. One at a time we approached the desks and were inspected. The healthy went right, the sick left.

"Don't worry, my friend," said Sergei, who was stood behind me. "We are both fit and strong... good workers."

When it was my turn to approach and be inspected, I said a prayer to God, asking him to protect me.

The physician prodded me with a truncheon... shoulders, chest, thighs, genitals, feet... I bit my tongue to stop from crying out when he tested my feet. He tapped the truncheon on my chin; I opened my mouth. Initially, I thought he was examining my teeth, but realized it was a treasure hunt; the prisoner at the next desk was having his gold teeth pulled out with pliers.

The physician waved me right. Relieved, I hobbled toward the other healthy prisoners. I suddenly noticed a grand residence on the other side of the barbwire fencing... the camp commandant's home most likely. There were three individuals on the residence's terrace looking down at us like audience members at a theatre. On the left was a refined German doctor wearing a white physician's coat over his uniform. He stood calmly, hands clasped behind his back, swaying to and fro on his heels. Sat in a chair next to the doctor was a middle-aged German woman with a round, fat face wearing stylish sunglasses; her hair was the color of fire. I found the third individual, stood on the right, the strangest of the three; a little Jew girl with large brown eyes, her dark hair cropped just below the ears. She wore a tattered grey dress, a yellow Jew star stitched over her breast. I was transfixed by her; the Jew girl was a statue, her anemic skin white as marble. She was holding a white porcelain bowl out in front of her. The German woman reached her hand into the bowl and pulled out a ripe strawberry. She brought the fruit to her lips and took a bite; a line of juice raced down her chin, staining her dress.

4
Efrayim

Spring arrived, and after five years of inconvenience in the countryside, the women of Mayfair and Kensington were flocking back to London; city streets and parkways brimmed with vibrant parasols and children's laughter. Iconic buildings were shaking off the mounds of sandbags that once surrounded them; gone too were the ubiquitous signs indicating the nearest bomb shelter, along with the constant fear on people's faces, ears no longer attuned to the howls of buzzbombs and rockets.

I threaded through the morning crowds in Hyde Park on my way to an appointment with one Lady Sutcliffe and her friends: an important commission for me. I had spent the war mending government-approved utility clothes, hemming military dress uniforms, and refurbishing funeral attire; just enough for Zelda and I to pay rent and stave off hunger. Now, I hoped the spring's celebratory mood would carry on to summer, the season for balls and galas, a return to the time when an exquisite gown was the talk of Bayswater Road...

Before the war, I foolishly aspired to create my own high fashion house... imagine, the first in London run by a Jew. Unsurprisingly, every British bank I met with refused to invest. So, when the war arrived, bringing indiscriminate death, first the blitz, then the vengeance rockets, I decided I should be content just to be alive; yet how guilty that contentment feels now. Each day more news about the camps is unearthed, printed in the newspapers, or broadcast on the nightly radio program. Just last night, Zelda and I listened to a BBC correspondent interview an American colonel about the liberation of a camp near Weimar called Buchenwald.

"Buchenwald," I said, letting my chin drop to my chest.

"What is it, darling?" said Zelda.

"Buchenwald, it translates to, *beech forest.*"

"Like the forests near Weimar?"

"Yes, as a boy our family went on hikes and picnics there."

I reached Bayswater Road opposite Hyde Park. Resting a moment, I gathered my bearings, pulling a slip of paper from my coat pocket.

'Lady Sutcliffe, 27 Bayswater Road, eleven am'

Waiting for a gap in the traffic to cross over, I admired Bayswater's elegant Victorian residences, the light sharpening their white stones. After crossing the street, I stalked the sidewalk, checking off the house numbers, 55... 50... 48... I was careful to hold my equipment bag close to me, afraid I might accidentally brush past someone. My bag held the essentials: fabric samples, sketch designs, tape measure, shears, pencils, rulers; everything I needed, save inspiration. I had spent the morning considering whether Lady Sutcliffe would request something traditional — a formal gown with pumped shoulders or jacket perhaps — or would she wish to make a statement, something to dazzle, a three-tiered, full-length cocktail dress, a bit of a scandal for a woman of her age. But the war was over, and the world would be changing, born anew; how we talk and think, eat and travel, even how we dress would change; nothing would be as it was. That will be good, I thought. So much ugliness these last years, the past deserves to be erased.

I obtained the commission from Lady Sutcliffe purely by chance. Some weeks ago, the end of March, as I recall, when Germany's last rockets were falling on London, I was leaving an appointment in Knightsbridge. Hearing the air sirens, I dashed to the nearest shelter. The bunker was lined with people sat against its walls. I found a seat near the entrance, clutching my bag against my chest. Everyone was quiet. The rockets were striking far away from us for now. A young couple came running into the bunker; the husband in a black, double-tail tuxedo, the wife, a beautiful Grecian style satin dress in sea green, perhaps. The light was dim. The couple had nowhere to sit. I offered my place to the young woman, who hesitated, seeing the dirt and grime on the wall. The husband took off his tuxedo coat and began to lay it on the ground. I stopped him.

"Please, sir, allow me," I said, removing my coat; a grey two-button unbothered by such grime. "I wouldn't want to see such a fine coat dirtied and wrinkled."

The young man smiled.

"You're too kind. Perhaps I could offer you compensation," he said, searching his pockets for money.

"None required, sir," I said. The young woman smiled.

"Thank you, you're awfully kind. We were on our way to a friend's wedding if you can imagine," she said.

"Germans aren't very considerate when it comes to weddings," I said, doing my best to suppress my accent.

"The bloody Hun aren't very considerate of anything, why they haven't surrendered… its madness is what it is, pure madness," said the young man.

"Oh, darling," sighed his wife, inspecting her dress. "I've got a tear. It must have snagged a nail or something when we came running here."

She was very upset. In peace time, mending a satin dress would be little trouble; but now, with hardly a meter's worth of silk not already designated for the war effort, a simple mend could prove challenging.

I set my bag down and opened it.

"Do you mind if I have a look, miss?" I said. She looked at me rather queerly.

"I'm a dressmaker and tailor. Perhaps I can help."

The husband laughed. "That explains the desire to save my double tail."

"I don't like to see fine things damaged or made ugly, even if they're not mine."

"What're the odds, darling, running into a shelter with a dressmaker to save the day," said the woman.

I examined the tear and got to work quickly with a needle and thread. When I was done, only a close examination of the dress would discover there had been a tear.

"How marvelous," said the woman, admiring my work.

Her name was Elizabeth, and she happened to be Lady Sutcliffe's daughter. The next week, Elizabeth contacted me, commissioning a dress. At first, I believed it pity, but who am I to reject good work for a fair price at a time like this? Over the course of designing Elizabeth's dress, a simple pearl and floral tea dress, I found her to be genuine. It was not pity at all, rather a sincere thank you.

I arrived at 27 Bayswater just after eleven am. My tardiness was noted by the head maid, Beatrice, who took my coat and hung it in a closet adjacent the foyer.

"Apologies, the streets were mad this morning; made for slow going," I said. Beatrice was not amused.

"Lady Sutcliffe expected you at eleven, promptly. She's in her dressing quarters, along with the other ladies; Ladies Forsythe, and Winthrop.

"Yes, again, apologies."

"It's not me you should be apologizing to, dressmaker," said Beatrice as she began up the stairs which spiraled round a grand crystal chandelier recently rehung.

"Follow me," Beatrice snapped.

Before the war, there was nothing special about being a Jew; loathed almost as much in London as Weimar, or Berlin. Now, we're something of a rare jewel, at least in the minds of Lady Sutcliffe and her companions Ladies Forsythe, and Winthrop, who must have thought I'd come straight from a death camp.

"He comes highly recommended... by my daughter," Lady Sutcliffe explained. "He's a Jew, you know..." she said with a smile. "Beatrice, be a dear and bring up some champagne, the Moet... nothing wrong with a little fun early in the morning."

After introductions, Lady Forsythe studied me as I set down my bag and began taking out my materials.

"Have you come from the continent?" she asked. I stood attentively.

"Yes, Madame, but it was some years ago now."

"Oh, and Beatrice!" called Lady Sutcliffe suddenly, "do bring some strawberries as well, will you!"

Beatrice hurried back to the dressing room and performed a minor curtsy.

"Of course, your Ladyship," said Beatrice, who retreated downstairs once more.

"Strawberries! How wonderful," said Lady Winthrop.

"Where did you manage to find those?"

"Smuggled them from our country estate in Cambridgeshire. They grow wild there," said Lady Sutcliffe.

"And where did you once call home?" Lady Forsythe resumed her inquiry.

At first, I hesitated, weighing my answer. Of course, they would know if I lied. Certainly, Lady Sutcliffe would have checked my background before inviting me to her home.

"Germany, Madame, a town called Weimar," I said, a sudden pride filling my voice.

"Edyth, not only do you bring us a Jew, but a German Jew at that... you fled, then, before Hitler and his goons took power?"

"No, Madame, shortly thereafter, in 1935."

"What luck," said Lady Forsythe. "That you and your family escaped in time."

"If was only myself, Madame; my family, my parents, brother, and sisters, and their children, could not be convinced to leave, and I was unmarried at the time."

"How did your family fair during the war?" said Lady Forsythe.

"I don't know, Madame. I have received no letters or news of their safety in many years..."

Since August 1937 to be exact.

"Stop interrogating him, Abigail," said Lady Winthrop.

Lady Sutcliffe interrupted, having examined my fabric samples. "No satin or silk, I presume?"

"I am sorry to say, no, Madame."

"I had hoped a dressmaker such as *yourself* would have squirreled some away," she said, turning toward the dressing room entrance as Beatrice entered with champagne and strawberries.

"Wonderful, Beatrice... just there on the table, please," said Lady Sutcliffe.

Ladies Forsythe and Winthrop were quick to enjoy the champagne, ignoring the strawberries. "The rationing is likely to continue for some time, as I understand it, Madame," I answered.

"What good is winning the war if we continue to suffer so terribly..." sighed Lady Winthrop.

"Not all will suffer as we do. I'll tell you who will be thrilled is Agatha; her Reginald owns some of the largest government contracts for fabrics and textiles production in all of England," said Lady Sutcliffe.

"Edyth!" gasped Lady Forsythe, nearly spitting out a mouthful of champagne. Lady Sutcliffe turned on her heels.

"What is the matter?" she said in confusion.

"Have you not heard?" said Lady Forsythe, looking at Lady Winthrop as well.

"Heard what?" said Lady Sutcliffe.

"Of Agatha and Reginald. Do neither of you know?"

"What is it?" inquired Lady Winthrop, expecting a scandal. "Divorce? I knew Agatha was never good enough for him, was only a matter of time."

"No..." said Lady Forsythe, "they're both dead. I thought you both would have known. Such terrible news."

"What happened?" said Lady Winthrop.

"One of those ghastly German rockets fell right out of the sky and landed on top of their estate in Sussex."

"Oh my...," said Lady Sutcliffe.

"How awful," said Lady Winthrop.

I took a step back, clasping my hands behind my back and

bowing my head, hoping to appear respectful.

Lady Sutcliffe paused a moment, setting down her champagne flute on the table. She roamed pensively around the dressing room before coming back to the table with the fabric samples I had laid out. She picked one up, a square of crimson velvet, stroking its soft texture between thumb and forefinger.

Without looking at me she said, "No, satin you say, but velvet is in supply?"

I cleared my throat. "Yes, Madame, and in many shades."

Given her daughter's manners and kindness, I had presumed Lady Sutcliffe would be of a similar nature; I was mistaken. How a lovely flower such as Elizabeth came from such a poisoned root as Lady Sutcliffe, I could only guess.

I caught a bus to Lambeth and walked home. Rain began to fall. London's springs, I had come to learn, varied between squalls and sunshine. I raised my collar and continued on. The flat was not far.

Entering the building, I ascended the stairwell to flat 7, already able to smell Zelda's borscht. I took out my keys and entered.

"Hello, my love," I called out upon entering, setting my bag down. I took off my coat and shook off the rain.

"In the kitchen, Effy," said Zelda, her accent as thick as the borscht. "How did it go?" she asked.

I worked my way through the dummies and stacks of fabric rolls lining our dining room and entered the kitchen. I kissed Zelda on the cheek as she was chopping vegetables.

"What a frightful woman," I said.

"Frightful?" Zelda asked, still coming to terms with English colloquiums.

"Unkind," I said.

"But she pays?"

"Very well, if I can make something which pleases her..."

"You will, Effy."

I went to turn on the radio in the dining room to listen to the evening news program. "No radio tonight, Effy, please, it's too... frightful," said Zelda.

"Of course, my love, perhaps a record instead. Chopin?"

"You know my favorites."

I played Nocturne in E Flat Major. Joy and sorrow in so few keystrokes, one emotion sharpening the other. The rain fell harder, striking the windowpanes. Ten more minutes and I would have been soaked through.

I looked at the picture of my brother and I as young men. I often cannot recall his face. It scares me to think if I would recognize him now. Were we stood on a train platform shoulder to shoulder, would he be just another passenger? Is he even alive...?

"Zelda, my love," I said.

"Yes, Effy?"

"Shall I open our bottle of wine, a nice red?"

"Yes, Effy, a French red would be wonderful."

It was our nightly joke, discussing all the delicacies we couldn't afford. "Caviar?"

"Of course... the Siberian salmon?"

"Only the best for you, my love." Better to pretend than wallow.

I thought I heard a knock at the door, a single timid knock. I dismissed it. The rain. There it was again, subtle.

"Did you hear that, my love?"

"Hear what?" said Zelda.

"Someone knocking at the door."

"Who knocks at dinner time? Frightful…"

I tiptoed through the fabric stacks and dummies to the front door and opened it. I looked down at a young woman, chilled and shaking, wet strands of dark hair plastered across her neck, cheeks, and forehead. She wore no coat, just a faded blue dress, nearly transparent from the rain. Hers was a face I knew but could not place.

"Can I help you, miss?" I said.

"Who is it?" asked Zelda from the kitchen.

The young woman peered around my waist into our flat. I turned my head. She was looking at my fabrics and dress making tools.

"Are you in trouble, miss?" I said, turning back. She looked through me, a blank and distant stare.

"I have come very far to find you, uncle," she said.

5
Eliana

CLASSIFICATION: SECRET//EYES ONLY —
DEPARTMENTS 1,2

Born in Leipzig in 1913, the son of Dieter and Elsa, Sascha Ernst Ziegler advanced quickly in school, outpacing his peers to begin studying medicine at Leipzig University, age seventeen. After completing medical school, age twenty, Ziegler specialized in genetics and radiotherapy at Munich University, conducting research on cellular and chromosomal radio-sensitivity.

Scant records exist of Ziegler from 1931–1939. The official Nazi Party manifest indicates Ziegler became a Party member in Munich, 1934. According to documents found in military archives in Berlin, Ziegler was commissioned an Obersturmfuhrer (First Lieutenant) in the Schutzstaffel, 1937. It is believed, according to surviving documents captured by the American military in 1945, that Ziegler likely arrived at Buchenwald concentration camp sometime between July and September 1937, where he began work, with fellow doctors and chemists, on various toxic gases, including Zyklon-B; the preferred gas used by the Nazis to carry out their Final Solution. From 1939 through 1942, according to witness statements and captured records from Buchenwald, Ziegler experimented on camp prisoners, including studying the effects of acute radiation on reproductive organs and cells.

CLASSIFICATION: SECRET//EYES ONLY —
DEPARTMENTS 1,2

I was about to flip to the next page in the file when Director Harel interrupted.

"You see why you're here... did you know this man, Dr Ziegler, when he was at Buchenwald?" he said in a dispassionate voice.

I closed the file and looked up at Harel, instinctively mirroring his posture: I sat up straight, crossed my right leg over the left, folded my hands in my lap, relaxed my face to allow the corners of my lips to drop.

"Everyone in Buchenwald knew of him," I said.

"Of him?"

"Yes, Buchenwald was a small camp, compared to the others I mean — the death camps, Dachau and Auschwitz — everyone in Buchenwald knew the name Ziegler, even if we had never seen him."

"Would you be able to identify Dr Ziegler if asked?"

"Identify?"

"Were he sat before you, as I am now, would you be able to identify him?"

"I don't understand, sir," I said.

I could hear the deputy director's hoarse breathing behind me.

"It has been almost twenty years since last I saw Ziegler; he could sit down next to me on the bus home, and I might not recognize him..."

Harel looked at Redlich, who immediately spoke. "One

week ago, a man claiming to be Dr Sascha Ziegler surrendered to the British Consulate in West Berlin. British intelligence attempted to identify him. However, no known photograph exists of Ziegler, not even in his official military record."

"The official records would have been in Berlin…" I said, looking at Harel.

"Our intelligence exchange with the Russians regarding wanted Nazi war criminals occurred years ago… there's no reason to believe the Russians withheld Ziegler's photograph on purpose," said Harel. "But stranger things have occurred… nevertheless, we don't have any photos."

"And the Americans?" I said. "They liberated Buchenwald."

"They say no," said Redlich.

"So, I ask again, Ms Wasserman, can you identify Dr Sascha Ziegler?" said Harel, leaning forward.

My hands began to shake again…

"I don't know, sir… there must be others, other survivors who remember him more clearly than I… I was just a girl," I said, trying to calm my voice.

"Others… yes, but none of them work for state intelligence… after Eichmann, the last thing we need is a misstep," said Harel. "One victory must be followed by another… you do understand, Ms Wasserman? Because if this man is indeed Ziegler, the prime minister will want extradition… followed by a public trial, and a sentence of death. Memory is our people's most precious resource… Eichmann was a great victory, but the world forgets quickly… we do not have that luxury… so we must give the world constant reminders that Israel does not forget."

"Yes, sir… I understand," I said.

"Good…" said Harel, who opened a different file on his desk and handed me a black and gray photograph; a portrait of an old man stood against a bare brick wall.

"This is the man claiming to be Ziegler. The British passed it to us. So, Ms Wasserman, what do you think?"

I held the photograph gently, almost cradling it. He looked a lonesome old man: a milky disfigured eye, swollen nose, and crooked smile… the smile, sincere in a strange way, like a grandfather admiring his family…

"Ms Wasserman, is that Ziegler?" said Redlich in an urgent tone.

"I don't know," I began, "if it's him, he is much changed."

"Yes," said Harel. "I can imagine, twenty years is a lifetime… look beyond the disfigurements, beyond his age… is that the man responsible for murdering thousands of Jews, including your family?"

"I don't know, sir," I said, warm tears beginning to well in the corner of my eyes. I fixated on the smile…

I handed the picture back to Harel, "I don't know, sir."

"Does he bare a resemblance?" snapped Redlich.

"I do not want to accuse a potentially innocent man," I said.

"I understand, Ms Wasserman, but the fact remains… this man turned himself in, and says his name is Sascha Ziegler. Why would an innocent man do such a thing?" said Harel.

"I don't know, sir. Most likely if this man says he's Ziegler… then he's Ziegler," I said. Harel put the picture down.

"A team is being put together, individuals from a number of government ministries, traveling to Berlin to interview this man… I want you to be the Office's representative, along with

Deputy Director Redlich. Be prepared to leave early next week," said Harel, motioning his hand toward the door.

I stood to leave. "Sir," I said. "If it is Ziegler, what happens if the British, or the West Germans for that matter, refuse to extradite him?"

Harel sat back in his chair, the light draining from his face.

"If this man is Ziegler, he will be tried and executed, Ms Wasserman... not all trials occur in courtrooms, nor executions in a prison yard. Israel does not forget."

"I understand, sir," I said and left.

The next morning, after Jacob returned from the shops with a cooling unit, we drove north along the coast to Haifa. He tried making conversation: how the sea sparkled in the morning light, how much he would miss me while he was away, how I should be kind to his mother, especially on her birthday; all for a woman who believed I was not good enough for her only son. I retreated behind black sunglasses and watched the landscape change; sparse desert gave way to ancient cedar forests, which became thicker the farther north we traveled; lofty green canopies twisting in the summer wind.

"I thought Peter and Chaya were coming?" I said as we pulled into the Nazarians' empty driveway.

"Papa said they were," said Jacob, parking the car in shade of an olive tree. "They're probably just running late; you know how Chaya is with Izzy now."

"That grandchild is the only thing between me and your mother's constant scorn that I'm not pregnant."

Jacob smiled.

"Not for a lack of trying, my love..." He leaned over and kissed me on the cheek. "We could probably squeeze a quick one in... we're ten minutes early," he said, looking at his watch.

"Get out of the car, Captain Nazarian," I said.

We got out. Jacob opened the truck and took out our present to Miriam, a large abstract glass bowl.

"She's going to hate it, whatever it is," I said as we walked to the front door.

"She always loves our gifts," said Jacob.

"Our gifts, no… she detests everything I've ever given her… just be sure to say you picked it out,"

"Don't be silly," he said, thumping on the door with his knee while balancing the glass bowl. I removed my sunglasses, straightened my hair, and managed to hold a smile until the door opened.

"Hello, Papa," said Jacob.

Mr Nazarian, Isaac, still sleek and muscular for his age, embraced his son. He looked down at the bowl and shook his head, then he turned to me.

"Hello, Eliana, welcome my sweet child," he said, kissing me gently on the cheek. Isaac was always kind, treating me like a daughter.

Isaac, the old soldier; he looked the part: his was a face pulled from the kiln, tempered by age and desert sun, distinguished by furrowed lines on his forehead and cheeks. His bust would sit comfortably in a museum alongside the generals of antiquity, cropped wavy hair, a pointed chin, and his eyes… though sharp and green like Jacob's, they too, like his marble-cut forefathers, expressed a hollowness, I suspect on account of his past, the weight of his former responsibilities, sending so many young men to their deaths.

I knew only what Jacob told me of his father's life born on Crete, and a Zionist from an early age, he joined the resistance when the Germans invaded. After the war, with news of the death camps spreading like wildfire, he moved his young family to Jerusalem to help build a Jewish state; there, he fought the Palestinians for farmland, the British for control of Jerusalem's streets, and finally the Arabs for our right to endure. These last years, though, an old gift from the Egyptians had slowed him, a piece of shrapnel burrowing deeper into his hip bone. Six months ago, Isaac retired as a Brigadier, and though would never admit it, I could see the relief, finally laying down his sword after a lifetime of war.

"Where's Mama?" said Jacob, showing off the glass bowl.

"Where she always is on days like this, by the pool," said Isaac, shaking his head at the strange bowl once more.

"Your son picked it out, not me," I said.

"I thank God every day he found you, Eliana, a woman with sense. It looks like some kind of sea creature, an urchin or something."

"It's abstract," said Jacob. "You know how she likes modern things."

"Yes, I know," said Isaac, looking over his shoulder at the living room, decorated with various interpretative pieces of artwork. "We can put fruit in it or something."

I smiled at Isaac. I couldn't help but think of my own father... he would have been retired too now, I suppose, spending his days walking, reading, debating science and politics with other old intellectuals at a local cafe...

"Mama!" said Jacob, striding through the house toward the back courtyard. Isaac shut the door.

"How are you, my child?" said Isaac. "How was the drive up?"

"Wonderful," I lied with a smile. "The sea was beautiful.

Will Peter and Chaya be joining us? I'm surprised they're not already here since they live so close."

"Chaya called just a little while ago. Yitzak had a restless night, but they'll be here in an hour or so."

"Poor Izzy, I hope he's all right."

"He's fine, I think it's Chaya who wanted a little rest before facing Miriam." I couldn't help but smile again.

The Nazarians' matriarch, Miriam, wore no uniform, had no medals or battle ribbons, yet in a family of soldiers she was perhaps the most fearsome. Born in Anatolia to a small Jewish sect living on the outskirts of Smyrna, she came of age during the Ottomans' collapse and the ravages of the Greco-Turkish war. After the Greeks' capture of Smyrna, her body endured Turkish reprisals. Of these things, she does not speak. Her family — father, mother, and her two younger brothers — fled to British-controlled Cyprus. Shortly thereafter, her mother died of Spanish influenza. Miriam's father moved the family to Crete, working as a day laborer and indentured farmer. Miriam grew up destitute, living in a single-room stone house. Constantly hungry, she worked hard to help support her family. While at the market selling goat's milk one day, a young man lingered near her, smiling and asking many strange questions. She thought him a distraction; in any case she had not bathed for a week, why would any man pay her attention? The young man, named Isaac, was a soldier in the army, on leave visiting his home nearby.

"I have not bathed for a week," Miriam told Isaac without looking at him. Isaac simply smiled.

"You are beautiful even when covered in goat shit." They tell this story at nearly every family gathering.

After a few glasses of wine, Isaac invariably says, after

each recounting, "The army didn't teach us how to talk to women, and I didn't care that she was covered in goat shit, she was still the most beautiful woman I had ever seen."

Isaac and Miriam wed in 1928, having Jacob the following year. In the spring of 1941, Miriam watched from her kitchen window as thousands of silken white parachutes deployed across the sky. All able-bodied men fled into the mountains, including Isaac, who was made captain of a group of eighty resistance fighters. In the towns and villages across the island, women and children were left to fend for themselves.

When Miriam arrived in Palestine, she told her husband she no longer wanted to live in fear; when the number of dead Palestinians, British, and Arabs began to mount, she never spared them a thought of mercy.

"My sweet boy," said Miriam, welcoming Jacob.

She was seated beside the swimming pool in the shade cast by a bright blue parasol. She wore dark sunglasses and a blue summer dress, no doubt selected to match the glimmering water and parasol. Miriam was exacting in every way, with her words most of all.

"Happy birthday, Mama," said Jacob, embracing his mother, kissing her on the cheek, and then presenting the abstract glass bowl.

I studied her face as she in turn studied the bowl; lips pursed at first, she did not frown. "Eliana wants you to know that I picked it out, in case it's too garish," smiled Jacob with a sarcastic tone.

"Garish?" said Miriam, a smile immediately forming across her chin. "It's beautiful, my sweet boy. I love it."

"We can put fruit in it," said Isaac, limping toward a sun

chair beneath the parasol beside his wife. "Come, come... we already have drinks and refreshments out."

Miriam put the bowl on the table and leaned back in her chair.

"Let me get a look at you, my sweet boy... are you eating enough? Have you lost weight?" Miriam's comment was not directed at her son, but to me.

"Hello, Miriam," I said walking up to her, kissing her on the cheek, "happy birthday."

"Eliana, darling, I didn't see you there... are you feeding my Jacob enough?"

"Mama, the army feeds me most days," said Jacob, pulling out a sun chair for me before seating himself. He poured us drinks.

"Why isn't the army feeding our boys?" Miriam said to Isaac.

"What do you want me to do about it?" said Isaac, half-smiling. "Your son can take care of himself."

Miriam sighed and turned to me.

"Eliana, you must see to it that he is well fed. I know the food the army gives our boys, and it's no good."

"I will, Miriam," I said, taking a sip of my cocktail: bits of orange, lemon, and pomegranate in sparkling white wine.

"So... when am I getting my real birthday present?" said Miriam, staring at my belly from behind her sunglasses.

I feigned a polite smile.

"Good things come to those who wait," I said.

"I'm an old woman, how much longer can I wait?" shrugged Miriam. She turned to Jacob. "I should be surrounded by grandchildren by now."

"Mama, you're not even sixty, and I promise we're

working on it… day and night," smiled Jacob with assurance.

"Maybe you need to see a doctor, then… both of you, both young, both healthy… as far as I can tell, it should not take so long. Your father and I conceived you on our wedding night."

"And what a night it was!" toasted Isaac.

"As I recall," said Miriam, you did your job and were fast asleep, all in under a minute." I let out a sharp laugh.

"We should all admire such efficiency," said Isaac. "It's no matter, God decides such things, there is no rush, life is life, it is to be enjoyed… and now that I'm retired, a little peace and quiet is not so bad for once. Scores of grandchildren can come later."

"Peace and quiet… I have to repeat everything I say three times he's so deaf," said Miriam. "I've become a broken record."

"It's just quiet then," mocked Isaac. "I'm still waiting for the peace after thirty years." Just then the doorbell chimed.

"I'll get it," I said, standing quickly. "Must be Chaya and Peter."

I opened the door.

"Chaya… Peter," I smiled, kissing each on the cheek. "And little Izzy… how are you?"

"Eliana," said Chaya, "it's so good to see you, I hope you haven't been here long, alone with mother."

"We've only just arrived."

"Sorry we're late. This one was crying all night," said Peter, holding nine-month-old Yitzak, in his arms.

"Crying as if there's no tomorrow," laughed Chaya. "Finally gets to sleep, and then is up at dawn, crawling around the house like mad."

"He no longer sleeps in the bassinet?"

"Oh, he sleeps there when he wants but can already climb out of it. We find him in a different spot in the house every morning."

"Yitzak!" I smiled, caressing his head with the palm of my hand. "A famous mountaineer in the making."

I let Chaya and Peter come in and put down their things. "Everyone's by the pool."

Chaya called out, "Mama... Papa... we're here."

She took Yitzak from Peter and brought him out to meet his grandparents. I could hear everyone fawning over the child, the beautiful boy, hair dark as a black cumin seed. Peter rested a moment, sleeplessness in his eyes.

"Can I get you a drink?" I offered.

"Maybe an espresso or two," he smiled. "Let's see what we can do."

For lunch, Isaac and Jacob grilled tilapias filled with lemon slices, and lamb cuts rubbed with harissa and rosemary. Chaya and I prepared a large vegetable salad of diced tomatoes, red onions, cucumbers, peppers, artichoke, parsley, and mint, mixed with Isaac's favorite Greek cheese. Chaya cut a fresh lemon in half, squeezed the bright juice over the salad, careful to catch the seeds, then splashed olive oil over top. I could smell the mint, and the biting lemon. Peter kept an eye on Yitzak as Miriam played with him in the grass beside the pool.

"He'll be walking soon," I told Chaya.

"God help us..." said Chaya, finishing the salad and cleaning her hands in the sink. "How many times today has mama asked you about when you're giving her another grandchild?"

"It was the first thing she said to me, after hello," I said, looking out at Yitzak in the grass.

Sat in the grass with the child, Miriam had removed her sunglasses; her eyes glowed with happiness.

"Take your time... enjoy being married for a while. Peter and I hardly see one another since Yitzak came... when he's at work, I'm with Yitzak, and when he's home and watching him, I'm cleaning, getting food, or just trying to get some sleep... not to mention the sex, that's the first thing to go."

"Chaya..." I smiled.

"I can't give Mama another child at the moment, one is enough. And Peter is starting a big project at work, which will have him traveling."

Chaya carried the salad outside. I brought more sparkling wine.

"What project?" I asked, trailing Chaya. I could smell the cooked rosemary in the air.

"Peter, darling, tell everyone about your big work thing, and how you'll be leaving me all alone for the next year."

"Leaving her? Peter?" said Miriam.

"Your daughter, my lovely wife, exaggerates, Miriam, as she tends to do... I'll have to make a few trips, mostly down to Jerusalem every other month or so."

"What is it you'll be doing?" I said.

Everyone gathered at the table. Peter bounced Yitzak on his knee as Isaac and Jacob plated the fish and lamb.

"I was contacted by the curators at Yad Vashem about some research and cataloging, it's nothing special," said Peter.

Yad Vashem, from the Book of Isaiah, *to give a place and a name to those without*; it was the nation's center remembering the Shoah, or what the rest of the world was beginning to refer to as the Holocaust. I had never set foot on its grounds.

"It's more than that, darling," said Chaya with pride. "He's leading a team of at least twenty archivists, going through original documents recovered from the camps just recently turned over to us by the French, British, and Americans. Enough to fill an entire warehouse."

"Like I said, research and cataloging," said Peter with a half-smile, holding Yitzak tight again his breast.

After completing his mandatory service, Peter pursued a life in academia, earning doctorates in History and Cultural Studies, focusing predominately on Europe, the rise of National Socialism, and Orientalism. Peter had a keen mind, but never portrayed himself as such. He was quiet. I mostly admired his endearing love for Yitzak; I saw his soul's devotion to fatherhood.

"It's important work," said Isaac. "If they'd had their way, each one of us would have been gassed and burned. God chose us to survive; we will never know why. But that's what all this is for now… we're together, in the land we've always called home, and those who could not see this beautiful place, like Eliana's family, all taken from her, each of them lives in us now, in this place. And they will live in the generations to come." Isaac looked at Yitzak. "What better memorial could there be… we are alive, and together."

Everyone was quiet; I heard the song of a kingfisher nesting in nearby tree. Miriam sipped her cocktail.

"How was it you were chosen, Eliana?" said Miriam. "Sent to live with your uncle in England, yes? Just before the war… what a lucky girl."

"Mama," Jacob interceded.

I looked down at my plate, the lamb's charred skin.

"It's all right," I said. "I have few memories from that time."

We finished lunch. I hardly ate. Chaya was falling asleep and went inside the house to take a brief nap. Jacob helped his father clean the dishes. Peter looked after Yitzak, whose boundless energy had him crawling around on the beds of grass in the garden. Miriam sat comfortably under the parasol watching Yitzak, drinking more wine.

"Please don't think me cruel, Eliana," said Miriam suddenly. I looked at Miriam, her eyelids becoming heavy.

"I don't."

"It's all right if you do… when you're a mother, you'll understand."

"I suppose it will change everything," I said.

"Yes, it does," nodded Miriam. "I know that you make my son happy… perhaps that is all a mother can ask for these days, for her family to be safe and happy… I believe that is why God saved you, why your family sent you away to England…"

Miriam reached for the wine bottle, knocking it over. The bottle shattered into many pieces.

"Stupid Jew girl! Look what you've done!" said Frau Koch.

Startled, Miriam bent down to pick up the shards.

"Miriam, no," I jumped out of my seat. "I'll get it…"

Miriam clumsily grasped a jagged piece, cutting her palm. She cried out in pain. I grabbed a cloth napkin from the table and pressed it against the wound.

"Miriam, it's all right," I said. "Let's get you inside to clean it." Miriam sobbed softly.

"I'm sorry," she said.

Peter stood up and came to help Miriam into the house. "I'll take her. Watch Yitzak, will you," he said.

"Yes, of course."

Isaac and Jacob came out to see what all the commotion was about, accompanying Peter and Miriam back into the house. Yitzak was on the grass crawling after a blue and white butterfly. I smiled. Beautiful boy. For a moment, I thought it wonderful to have a child of my own one day.

I began to pick up each piece of glass, cradling the sun-streaked shards in my hand.

"Dirty Jew girl! Clean it up before I have you beaten!" said Frau Koch.

"Yes, mistress..." I said.

Splash.

I picked up the last shard, holding it between thumb and forefinger. Its jagged edge hovered over my opposite arm's wrist, just above the light blue artery trapped below my pale skin.

"Eliana," said Peter from the doorway to the courtyard, 'where's Yitzak?"

"What?" I said, turning and standing up.

I scanned the garden's grass. Yitzak was not there.

Peter strode out, head and eyes swiveling, sure that Yitzak had crawled under a bush. "I was just picking up the glass... I only turned round for a moment," my voice shook.

"Yitzak," Peter called out wishfully.

The garden was empty. I took a step toward Peter. Something danced across the bottom of the pool; Yitzak, distorted by the light on the water's rippling surface. I dropped the shards.

Peter looked at me, then down into the pool.

"Yitzak!" Peter jumped into the water, diving down and bringing his child up to the surface.

"No!" I screamed.

Isaac and Jacob came out of the house. "What's going on?" said Jacob.

"Oh my God..." said Isaac, hobbling toward the pool.

Peter laid Yitzak on the brickwork surrounding the pool, then climbed out.

"He's not breathing," said Peter, turning Yitzak on his side, slapping him on the back, trying to jumpstart his breathing.

"What happened?" said Jacob as he kneeled down next to Peter.

"I was picking up the glass, I only turned round for a moment..." I said, my voice shaking.

"Hold him up by the feet," said Isaac. "We must drain the water from his lungs."

Peter held Yitzak up; dangling, he struck his son's buttocks. "Breathe, Yitzak!" said Peter.

Chaya came out of the house.

"Peter, what's going on?" she said. "Peter... is that Yitzak? oh God, Yitzak," she cried, running over.

"Again," said Isaac, instructing Peter to strike his grandson.

"Give him to me," demanded Chaya. "Give him to me!" She snatched her son away from Peter, and cradled him against her breast, bouncing him up and down.

Splayed across his mother's arms, Yitzak was blue and listless.

"Yitzak, come back to Mama," said Chaya. "Please, Yitzak. Come back to Mama..." Chaya wailed. Yitzak, her beautiful boy, was dead.

"Chaya?" said Miriam in a tender voice.

I looked up at Miriam, blood dripping from her palm onto the brickwork.

6
Sascha

I hadn't eaten so well in years. Three meals a day, plus tea and cake in the afternoon. I couldn't believe it. All this for a Nazi war criminal. Had I known such luxury awaited me, I would have surrendered years ago. I told this to the two British fellows who questioned me each day, in German, thankfully. I still had the lingering taste of ginger cake on my tongue when I told them, "I had crepes this morning," taking a sip of my afternoon mint tea, "with bits of chocolate in them. Cooked right into the crepes. Wonderful. In the East, I normally just have a plate of boiled potatoes at night, if I'm lucky."

They didn't tell me their names, nor what state ministry or organization they worked for. One was tall and thin, with blonde hair, a nose like a snipe's beak. The other was older, shorter than me, round too, bald but trying to conceal it. Their words were too barbed to make them diplomats, so I presumed they worked for British security services, spies.

I suspect they thought the food would loosen my lips, but I was happy to talk no matter what they fed me. How often in life does one have such a captive audience? We talked, or, I suppose, I talked, for hours every day, in-between my coughing fits and breakfast, lunch, afternoon tea, and supper, of course. After a few days of questioning, I began to wonder if they were ever going to ask me anything new; it was the same questions again and again.

The short bald one asked questions, like, "When and where were you born?" My responses, I confess, were operatic, as I do love Wagner.

"My birth is a very interesting story. I was born on the twenty-second day of May 1913, exactly one hundred years to the day of Wilhelm Wagner... who was also born in Leipzig. Growing up, my papa always reminded me of that. What a special little boy I must be... but you know, all I could ever think was, little boys are born all the time. There must be many others born in Leipzig on the twenty-second day of May 1913, the same as me. Aren't they special too?"

I laughed at the memory.

"Our mamas and papas always expect the best from us, yes?" I said. "Ah, well, Leipzig was a beautiful city... a beautiful cathedral too. My parents were devout Catholics. I'm not sure if you knew that. God always came first in our family. God and scripture. Every so often, after mass, we would go for a hike or picnic in the woods near the city. I would sometimes wander off... the woods there are special you see, long arcades of leafy canopies extending like a cathedral's nave... God's church, the sunlight piercing the canopy as though it were stained glass."

I took a sip of tea to try and stave off a coughing fit, but it did not work. I placed one hand on the interview table to steady myself, the other I used to hold a handkerchief against my mouth. I could taste blood. I spat into the handkerchief. The two British fellows were statues, watching me cough so terribly I was bent over, face flushed red, eyes watering, beads of sweat gathering across my forehead.

"How long have you had that cough, Herr Ziegler?" the short one asked.

"The cough?" I growled, trying to clear my throat. "Since the camp, I suppose. The winters there were terrible."

"At Buchenwald?"

"Buchenwald? No, no... life there was wonderful. The prison camps in Russia... after the war. How do you think my face got like this?" I twirled my finger, circling my disfigurements. "Eight years in Russian labor camps. God's grace any of us survived..."

I started to tell them how I was captured by the Russians while attempting to escape west in the back of a truck carrying fat pink and gray swine, but the tall one interrupted me. "Let's not get ahead of ourselves, Herr Ziegler," he said. "I want to go back, before the war. When did you begin your medical training?"

"Medical training? I suppose at a very young age, now that I think back on it. God formed us in his image; to understand ourselves is to better understand God, and though blighted by sin, we are the Lord's most perfect creation."

The tall one appeared displeased with my answer. "When, specifically, did you begin your formal medical education?" he asked.

"Formally? Well, let me think, I was maybe sixteen or seventeen, at Leipzig University. I was much more advanced than my peers. I had few friends because of it. But it was something I was used to... I had a lonely childhood, no brother or sister. But none of that mattered when I arrived at university. There, it was about the pursuit of knowledge. Cadavers became my companions, along with the authors of medical textbooks and journals. It's amazing how much one will talk to a cadaver. I always thanked them. I did the same with all the Jews, Russians, Poles, and Roma sent to my research laboratory. I thanked all of them, each one, sincerely."

The fat little one leaned forward in his chair, elbows on the table. "Is that what you thought it was? A research laboratory?"

"Yes, of course," I answered. "My assistants and I worked rigorously to ensure the highest standards of empirical research and cleanliness. What else would I call it?"

"Have you considered, torture chamber?"

The next morning, after a breakfast of oatmeal with honey, diced melon, eggs, and bacon, the questioning began again. The same two British fellows, asking the same questions.

Where was I born? When was I born?

What was my father's name? What was my mother's name? What primary school did I attend?

What year did I become a member of the Nazi Party? When did I join the Schutzstaffel?

When did I arrive at Buchenwald concentration camp? How many Jews did I murder?

And on and on and on, until lunch... which was a tasty sandwich with thick cuts of ham, spicy mustard, and tomatoes on toasted rye bread, served with a side of diced fruits, and a glass of lemonade with ice cubes. After lunch, the questioning began again. Although now there was an additional man sat across from me at the interview table; he had black hair laden with pomade, stringently parted to the left like the creased corner of a book page. This man, Hans Schwarzkopf, funnily, introduced himself as a representative of the West German government. He made it clear to me, and the two British fellows, that he would have arrived much sooner had the British government promptly informed Bonn of my surrender.

I smiled at him.

"Well, you are here now, young man. What would you like to know?" I said.

"Actually, I would like to speak to this gentleman in private, before any further questioning," said Hans, looking at the two British fellows.

Once it was just Hans and I, I leaned forward and whispered, "Do you know their names? They won't tell me. I think because they are spies, yes?"

"Herr Ziegler, if that is your name... I..."

I interrupted Hans. "Why does no one believe I am who I say I am? All these questions, it's so strange to me. My name is Dr Sascha Ernst Ziegler."

"Herr Ziegler," Hans began again, trying to calm me, "the West German government is petitioning London to have you released immediately into our custody. As a German citizen, it isn't prudent for you to be held by the British Government, particularly given the accusations against you."

"I surrendered to the British hoping they would be able to expedite my extradition to Israel for trial."

"You wish to be extradited to Israel?" said Hans.

"Yes, of course," I nodded.

"To be put on trial?"

"Yes, to clear my name... all these years having to look over my shoulder, it became tiresome.

"I've thought about it for a very long time. I considered Russia, but I believe I will be treated more humanely in Israel. Russia, well... I have spent enough time in Russia. And I cannot predict the future, but at least Israel is warm; better to have sun on one's face than snow, eh?"

"Herr Ziegler, you must understand that you can request

political asylum in West Germany. You would not have to be extradited to Russia or Israel."

"Would I be put on trial in West Germany?" I said.

"If claims against you proved true, there would certainly be an investigation, and proper legal protocols would be followed."

"If I asked for asylum, to stay in West Germany, where would I be held?"

"I can't be certain, but I believe you would be placed under house arrest while the government and security authorities conducted a thorough investigation into your background and claims."

I nodded.

"What sort of food would I be given?"

"Food?"

"Yes, the British have fed me very well, what food could I expect from you?"

"I don't quite know, Herr Ziegler. I'm sure it would be satisfactory," said Hans with a shrug of the shoulders.

"This worries me, it worries me very much, Herr Schwarzkopf. I had chocolate crepes just the other day for breakfast. Can the government of West Germany guarantee chocolate crepes?"

"Herr Ziegler, you're accused of the most severe crimes: genocide, and crimes against humanity. I do not think you should be worrying about chocolate crepes at a moment such as this."

I leaned back in my chair.

"My boy, this is exactly the time to worry about chocolate crepes."

"From what I understand, your identity is still being

confirmed. So, you have time to reconsider, Herr Ziegler."

"Identity... I've answered all their questions, produced my passport, surrendered myself, what else do they want?"

"Nazi war criminals simply don't turn themselves in, Herr Ziegler. Surely you understand there would be questions?"

"Questions, yes, but not about this... I have a passport, proof."

"An East German passport, Herr Ziegler. Authenticity can again be questioned by some," Hans nodded towards the door.

"They want proof, then? Should I have walked in holding the bones of my mama and papa?"

"Herr Ziegler..." said Hans.

"They want proof... I'll give them proof. When I arrived, a small bronze box was confiscated from me. Go talk to the British fellows, the tall one with the bird nose, and the short, fat, bald one, tell them to bring me the box. Proof of who I say I am is in the box."

"Herr Ziegler..." began Hans, but his eyes dimmed, resigning himself to my demand.

All three men returned. The bronze box was placed in the center of the table. "I assumed you opened it. Examined the contents, yes?" I said.

"Yes," said the short one.

"Then what more proof do you need?"

"Herr Ziegler..." said Hans, reaching out and taking the lid off the bronze box, "it is the Bible, a very old copy."

"Yes," I said, "and you found what was inside it?"

"I..." said Hans, his eyes darting over to the British fellows.

"Open it to second Kings, chapter twenty-three," I said.

Hans took the book out of the bronze box, his fingers

clumsily flipping through the pages. "I'm sorry, I'm not a religious man," he said, not knowing where to open the book.

"Just flip through the pages, you won't miss it," I said.

Hans ran his thumb over the pages, zipping through them, suddenly stopping. "That's it," I said, "second Kings, chapter twenty-three."

Hans removed it from the Bible.

"It's a flattened flower... a rose? My daughter does the same, using her picture books to flatten spring flowers... forget-me-nots, or edelweiss we collect on hiking trips."

"Look more closely, Herr Schwarzkopf. It's no rose bud," I said. "Amazing, after all these years, that the color should remain so enticing."

Hans held the flower up against the light by its stem; his eyes began to narrow, focusing on to the dozens of tiny yellow seeds embedded in the dry, velvet red strawberry.

7
Illa

I became a woman on a Wednesday in the autumn of 1936; so, said my mother after I stained my dress at school. I cried for hours, curled up on my bed, head tucked beneath the pillow. The next day, 15 October 1936, the Ministry of Education forbade all Jewish and non-Aryan peoples from teaching in public schools. That night, mother and father didn't speak during dinner. Eliana hummed a lullaby while stabbing at her food with a fork. Later, after mother put Eliana and I to bed, I heard arguing downstairs. Father told Mother to stop crying. Lying in bed, I thought they were fighting because I had become a woman. My heart filled with shame.

Across the room, Eliana slipped out of bed, came over and tried to crawl under my blanket with me.

"Go back to sleep, Eliana," I pushed her away.

"Why are Mama and Papa fighting?" she asked, the moonlight painting her white nightdress silver.

"They're not fighting. Go to sleep," I said.

"I want to sleep in your bed," she said. I turned over, my back to Eliana. "Sleep in your own bed."

Eliana whimpered.

"Go, Eliana... now."

When I woke in the morning, Eliana's bed was empty. I lifted my blanket up and checked whether there was blood.

Clean.

Was I a woman no longer?

I washed my face, dressed, and went downstairs to prepare for school. Mother wasn't in the kitchen, neither was Father. I called out. No one answered. The house felt empty. I ran to each room.

"Mama?" I said, standing at the doorway to their bedroom "Papa?" I said, standing at the doorway to his study.

I began to panic. "Eliana?"

I was alone.

I ran back to the kitchen, my heart racing.

I heard noises outside, like the sound of a truck engine sputtering, three loud pops in a row. I went to the window. Pushing up onto my toes, I pressed my nose against the cold glass and looked out at the street. The sky was full of thick, smoky grey clouds. The trees lining the street were bare, save a few lingering red and yellow leaves. I heard shouting farther down the street. A woman's scream. Then another sharp pop.

I went to the front door and carefully stepped outside. A rush of cold air stung my face. I'd forgotten my coat, but I didn't turn back. I went down the stairs and hid behind the tree closest to our front door. Peering down the street, dozens of people were standing against the houses and shops lining the sidewalks, their arms raised like pinned vines trained to climb walls. Policemen in black uniforms walked up and down the street, shouting angrily. Mr Dresler's butcher shop had been vandalized, the shop front's glass shattered. The police must be looking for the criminals. Who would do such a thing?

Two policemen dragged something large out into the street. For a moment, I thought it was one of the animals hanging in the back of Mr Dresler's shop, where he would slice away fur and skin, exposing the fibrous pink muscle and streaks of white fat. The two policemen went back into the shop and dragged out another thing... a woman. I could see her face, glassy blue eyes wide open. I knew instantly it was Mrs Dresler. She was dead, a bullet hole in her right cheek.

"Mama... papa..." I said, looking around, my fingernails digging into the tree's dry bark. I felt as though I were adrift, clinging to a jagged piece of flotsam.

Another policeman pulled a pistol from his belt, pointed it toward the sky and fired.

"Go home, Jews!" he shouted as the gunshot dissipated down the narrow stone street and alleyways.

The people scattered. The elderly hobbled away as fast as they were able with their canes. But it was not fast enough for one policeman, who battered an old man across the back with a truncheon. "Faster!" he demanded. The old man fell to the ground, breaking his head open, blood frothing out like popped champagne. The policemen all gathered round him, stomping on him with their boots.

I saw Mother and Father running toward me. Father was holding Eliana tightly against his breast. "Mama!" I cried, running toward her.

"Illa!" she said. "Get in the house!"

"Mama! What's going on?" I started to cry.

Mother's arms swooped down and gathered me up as though I weighed nothing. She carried me into the house and set me down on the kitchen table. Father came running in, still clutching Eliana. He jostled her across his chest and, with his free hand, bolted the door shut.

"What happened? Where were you?" I cried.

"Quiet!" he shouted at me, which made me cry more. Mother brushed my tears away with her fingers.

"What's going on?" I said.

"Quiet, Illa!" instructed Father. He placed Eliana down on the table next to me.

I looked at Eliana through my tears. She was wearing a mask of blood, its tendrils running down her neck, staining the nightdress' white collar.

Father began spending nearly all his time in the study. I sometimes heard him sleeping in there. Mother stayed in the kitchen, cooking, or sat at the table sewing, repairing local women's dresses. When not in school, I would sit at the table watching her fingers move so quickly the needle seemed to be flying through the air, piercing the cloth as easily as a bullet does flesh. Mother gave me scraps to practice with... cross-stitch, double stitch... in time, as my fingers grew stronger, I finally understood the fluidity of my mother's work, the unending repetition... stitch... stitch... stitch. We worked in silence.

"Does Papa no longer work at the university?" I asked one morning while sitting at the kitchen table.

Mother's head dropped slightly. She brought the cloth closer to her eyes.

"He's taking a sabbatical, which means he's resting. He'll be tutoring some local boys and girls at their homes for now," she said.

She didn't look at me. Stitch... stitch... stitch...

At night, my parents' fighting became louder and more frequent. Eliana stopped asking to climb into my bed, not since the day Mr and Mrs Dresler were shot. She didn't cry any more, not just at night, but altogether; just last week, when mother opened the stove door and a glowing piece of coal fell out and skittered across the floor, Eliana picked it up as though plucking a flower. The coal sizzled in her palm. She did not

77

cry, or scream, nor when mother placed her hand in a bowl of ice water.

By winter, there was less food in the house, and I would grow hungry at night. Mother and Father fought during the day now too. One afternoon, in late January, my mother's sister-in-law, Golda, came to the house, and they sat together in the kitchen, drinking tea and sewing. Golda brought Eliana and I pieces of caramel candy.

"Hello, my little loves," said Golda with a large smile.

A little later, Father returned home. He was angry and had a sharp smell about him. Mother pushed him into the study and slammed the door behind her. Golda took Eliana and I to our room. We sat on the floor in a triangle and Golda told us a story about a little boy and a little girl, brother and sister, named Hansel and Gretel, who one day wandered deep into a vast and dark wood. They came upon a witch's house made of breads, cakes, and sugar canes. The story made Eliana smile. I had bad dreams that night.

By mid-summer, I was hungry all the time. Mother scolded me when I complained. Things in the house like trinkets, picture frames, and vases started disappearing; then furniture, antique chairs, and books vanished. Mother no longer wore jewelry, including her favorite gold necklace which I had never seen her take off. Late one evening, while father was in his study and mother was heating water on the stove to bathe Eliana and I, policemen in dark uniforms came to our door, thumping with their truncheons. Father rushed out of the study. Mother knelt down, pulling Eliana and I close to her. I had on my nightdress; Eliana was naked.

"Upstairs!" said Father, peering out the window adjacent the door. The policemen thumped again.

"Open the door, Jew!" they demanded. "By order of the

Reich! Open the door!"

Before Father could answer, the policemen broke the door open and stormed in. I screamed at the sight of them, black nightmares come to life. A policeman in a long leather coat struck father in the belly with a truncheon, causing him to crumple to the floor.

"Why are you doing this?" said Father through a fit of coughing.

The policeman surveyed our home. "Askel Wasserman, professor at Weimar University..."

"I no longer work there..." Father coughed, trying to stand up.

"You have been identified as an enemy of the Reich, responsible for spreading fatalistic communist ideologies and propaganda."

"I teach mathematics...," said father.

The policeman struck him again, this time across the forehead.

Eliana and I were pulled from Mother's arms like teeth from a jawbone. I screamed and kicked. The policeman carried Eliana and I outside to an awaiting truck idling in the street. He put us in the back. There, under a tarp covering, many others were already sat, waiting; some stared at us with owl eyes, the rest, docile old men, looked down at the dark truck bed as though minding their own business on a packed rail passenger car. We were the only children. I held Eliana against me as tight as I could, tears streaming down my cheeks, dripping onto her. I realized Eliana wasn't crying, in fact she hadn't made a single sound.

They loaded Mother and Father into the truck. As we drove away, I watched our neighbors emerge from their homes like burrowed animals wary of predators, peeking their heads out to see what all the noise had been about, relieved the stalking beasts were leaving. Father was bleeding from his nose and mouth. Some of the others in the truck tried to help him. Mother collected Eliana and me into her arms.

"It's all right darlings... it'll be all right," she whispered in our ears, kissing us.

Father took off his shirt and used it to cover Eliana's naked body, then he slumped down, staring at the dark just like the old men.

The policemen stopped again and collected more frightened people. "When are we going home?" I asked.

My mother didn't say anything.

After leaving the city, we turned onto a dirt road and entered a dark wood. The truck's diesel engine growled as the road became bumpy. Suddenly, the city's lights disappeared; the only luminescence was in the arcade of leaves and branches above us, the waxing moon coating the canopy with its silver light. Warm summer air tangled itself in my hair; I swept it away from my face. Watching the vast woods flow past like a black river, I realized where the evil men were taking us...

"The witch's house!" I gasped. "Mama, Papa! They're taking us to the witch's house in the deep wood... to cook us in her big oven! Don't let them take us to the witch's house, please!"

Mother held me tighter.

"Shhh... Illa, be quiet, everything will be fine."

"But Mama, Aunt Golda told us about the witch's house in the dark woods! You mustn't let them take us!"

"Be quiet, Illa," she hissed. "There's no such thing as a witch's house. It's just a fairytale."

8
Uzi

Watching them dress was a kind of punishment I suppose. I couldn't help but study their skin in the bronze lamp light: birthmarks, scars, freckles, moles, stretch marks, bruises, blemishes… porcelain, cream, rose, auburn, sand, birch. Skin is a tapestry recounting the story of our lives; our ancestry, the children we carry, the pain we endure, the love we are shown. When skin is consumed by flames, the fat and water it holds flash boils, releasing jets of steam and smoke as though our souls are taking form to escape out the chimneys. When the moisture is burnt away, skin becomes like paper, charring black and crinkling as the flames build. I often linger in front of mirrors now, inspecting my skin; it is very much worn down, decorated by the scars of age and regret. It tells a long and pitiful story of abuse and loneliness, of too much alcohol and too little food; it says, this man is dying, not imminently, but that death will be welcomed on the day it finally arrives.

I put my wedding ring on. She sees me do so.

"My wife died many years ago," I said. "I still like to wear it."

She offered a polite smile, implying I didn't have to lie. Not to her. She sleeps with men for money, most of whom are married.

"Auschwitz," I said.

"What?" she said, finishing the buttons on the front of her

dress.

"Where my wife died."

"Was that one of the camps?" she said.

"Yes," I said, getting out of bed and putting my underwear on, "one of the camps…"

She noticed the tattoo on my arm and became anxious, grabbing her purse. She would only have been a few years old then, too young to remember.

"I'll get your money," I said, going into the living room and opening my briefcase. I gave her the money.

"Thank you," I said.

She didn't say anything. She checked her hair one last time in the mirror by the front door and left.

I went into the kitchen, searched the cupboard for a clean glass but couldn't find one. No matter.

When did vodka ever require a glass?

Out on the terrace, I leaned against the iron railing and looked out on the flickering glow of Tel Aviv in the distance. So bright were its lights, it obscured the night sky. Only the brightest stars were visible. Warm winds carried the sea's saltiness. I sat down and began my nightly routine of drinking until I blacked out, or fell asleep, whichever occurred first.

The telephone rang.

I ignored it and drank. The telephone rang again.

I leaned back in my chair and closed my eyes. When there were no passing cars on the street below, I could hear the sea's tides crashing along the shoreline.

The telephone rang a third time.

"What? What do you want at such an hour?" I asked. It rang again.

I drank more. It rang. "Shut up!"

Ring... ring... ring...

I put down the vodka, went in and picked up the receiver. "What is it? Who calls at such an ungodly hour?"

There was a muffled clicking, then a weak voice. "Hello... Uzi, is that you? Are you there?"

"Yes, who's this?" I said.

"It's David."

"David... I'm sorry to yell, how are you, my friend?" I said, picking up the phone and taking it outside with me.

I sat down.

"I apologize to call so late, Uzi... but I need your help."

"My help? Too many parking tickets?" I said, picking up the vodka bottle and setting it between my thighs.

"Are you still working at the traffic court? I thought I heard you'd retired?"

I picked up the bottle by the neck and began swirling the vodka until it became a whirlpool.

Charybdis...

I smiled and took a drink.

"Still at the traffic court. You should come by some time; we get some interesting cases..." I coughed.

"Uzi, how drunk are you right now?" said David in a worried voice.

"It's my first bottle of the night," I said, squinting at the amount of vodka left.

"Uzi..."

"David..."

"We had something different come in yesterday."

"And you thought an old, semi-retired traffic lawyer best suited for the job?"

"Best suited because of what you used to do."

83

"Oh? Did we finally find Hitler running a stop sign in Jerusalem? You can't find another prosecutor in the entire Ministry of Justice?"

"I don't need a prosecutor, Uzi... I need you to defend someone... a woman...from the camps."

"A woman?" I said. "A Kapo? You know I spent ten years prosecuting them."

"I wouldn't ask if it wasn't important, Uzi. She's state security. The prime minister wants it kept quiet."

"Prime minister? Why's he care, did he fuck her?" I laughed.

"I need someone I can trust, Uzi. Will you meet with her?"

"Why would I defend a Kapo? They were worse than the SS."

"Have you been keeping an eye on the news lately... about Ziegler..."

"The Butcher? What does he have to do with it?"

"Will you come in the morning, my friend? Come and meet her?"

"I still don't understand, David, why me?"

"Because, my friend, I think she's innocent."

I drank.

"Yea... I'll come, but make it the afternoon, will you."

"All right, Uzi... thanks. Come as soon as you wake up will you," said David.

"Yeah, yeah," I said, and hung up the phone.

I clinked my ring against the bottle.

"Remember the bells in Vienna? In the autumn for our anniversary. You wanted to hear the symphony... I don't know if you would have liked it here, my love. This desert..."

I woke late the next morning on the terrace, sat in the

chair, still only in my underwear. The sun was shining in my eyes. Using the railing, I pulled myself up.

Mrs Fishkin, the old widow next door, was on her terrace hanging laundry. "Good morning, Mrs Fishkin," I said.

"Good morning, Uzi," she said. "How are you, my dear?"

"As well as can be expected, Mrs Fishkin. I hope you have a pleasant day." She smiled and went back to hanging up wet clothes.

Once inside, I noticed my skin was tender and red. Even the desert's morning sun could burn. My flat was old. It exuded the sensibilities and lifestyle of its British constructors: wrought iron railing on the terrace, mock Victorian windows, a separate area for tea and drinks, an unnecessarily large foyer, and oddly low ceilings. So low, in fact, they reminded me of a medieval hut, when Europe's malnourished and underdeveloped population would have found such accommodations to be spacious. Nevertheless, hardly any of the flat's characteristics were visible, many of them buried or obscured by my work, stacks of boxes and documents forming odd little mountains ranges, some dating back twelve years or so to when I first arrived.

In the washroom I vomited into the sink. Turning on the tap, I drank like a nursling, then splashed water on my face and slicked back the hair I had left. I dressed in my brown suit, my only suit. In the kitchen I drank more vodka to stop the tremors I knew would come. I put a bottle in my briefcase, then thought: the walk to the station would be twenty minutes, the bus to Jerusalem over an hour, the meeting with David and this woman… anywhere between one to two hours perhaps… then the trip back; I grabbed a second bottle to be safe. I preferred Russian, but it wasn't always easy to come by; in a pinch I would settle for Newport, though, a cheap American brand.

The bus from Tel Aviv to Jerusalem was full of schoolchildren on a day trip to visit Yad Vashem. I sat in the back, hugging my briefcase. Every so often, I covered my face with my coat while swallowing a quick mouthful of vodka. I took the bus to its terminus in central Jerusalem. Outside the station, I vomited behind a row of palm trees, and used the inside of my coat to clean my mouth. I washed it out with vodka, then found a taxi and asked the driver to take me to the Ministry of Justice.

When I arrived at the ministry, I instinctively straightened my suit and tie, strode in and asked one of the receptionists to inform Deputy Minister David Abelson that Mr Uzi Willner had arrived for their appointment.

I took a seat and waited. The ministry was abuzz with comings and goings, the rhythmic click-clack of shoes on the polished floor. Out of that mirage of fleeting suits and skirts emerged David, my boyhood friend, whose family fled to Finland before the war.

"Uzi, my friend, how are you?" said David.

"David... well enough," I said, picking up my briefcase.

David embraced me. "Come, Uzi... let's get you some coffee... maybe some toothpaste too..."

"I'm sorry, my friend, the last few days..."

"It would have been your anniversary this week... I wouldn't have called unless it was important. Come, my friend. Coffee will help."

When next I vomited in the gentlemen's water closet at the jail adjacent the ministry where pretrial defendants were held, it tasted of vodka, espresso, and mint toothpaste. I rinsed my mouth out, wiping it clean on my jacket sleeve. I looked in the mirror, thinking over what David had told me about the young woman I was about to meet, Eliana Nazarian. I washed my mouth out once more, all the while using my thumb to push the wedding band on my ring-finger round and round. I often did this without thinking but was conscious of it now. I felt distant from her. The day she burned was hot and windy; her ashes would have been carried for miles, scattered across half the continent maybe. Sometimes I liked to imagine she never fell back to earth, but was carried up to the stratosphere, remaining there, free from all of the wickedness below.

"Obviously, I can't go in with you," said David.

We were standing at the gate leading to the prisoners' cells.

"You still haven't told me why, David? Why me? And don't say it's because you trust me, because while we'll always be friends, not all friendships are built on trust. I've wretched three times this morning... I carry bottles of vodka in my briefcase. I'm not a man to be trusted. And that poor woman in there, whomever she is, whatever her crimes, deserves better."

"Yes, she does, Uzi... but no one else will stand beside her, and a ministry-appointed advocate will only go through the motions. Are you a drunk? Yes. Will you embarrass yourself in court? Probably, but if you decide to accept her, I know one thing for sure; you'll fight for her, my friend..."

"Are you related to this woman, is she a niece or cousin? Why have you taken such an interest in her?"

"I'm tired, Uzi," said David, looking through the gate's metal bars at the row of cells. "I'm tired of going after our own... you read the file, yes? Well, the file isn't everything. Just listen to her."

"Tired of going after Kapos?" I said, the aftertaste of vomit burning my throat. "You weren't there, David. You are a dear friend to me. We are both Jews. We live in a nation built by Jews... but until our generation is gone from this earth, turned to dust and ash, there will always be a great divide between you and I; between all those who went to the camps, and those who did not."

"Then you may be the only one that can help her, Uzi... whether you hate her or not."

I handed my clearance paperwork to the guard on duty. She looked it over, handed it to the other guard who signed it, and filed it away. They unlocked the gate and I stepped inside.

"Follow me," said the guard, taking a ring of keys from her belt and unlocking the secondary gate leading to the prisoners' cells.

"Shouldn't you be taking me to one of the interview rooms?"

"The prisoner refuses to leave her cell," said the guard. "Don't worry, you'll be provided with a chair to sit on outside the cell."

"All right..."

I followed the guard through the secondary gate. We filtered past a number of cells, all holding female prisoners. I tried not to stare, but knew they were all looking at me. At the end of the hallway there was a chair facing a cell. The metal bars were painted white.

"You are not to pass the prisoner any materials and you are not to accept anything from the prisoner... I'll be watching," said the guard, who turned and walked back down the row.

I sat down. The bottles in my briefcase rattled and clinked.

The sound was unmistakable.

"Who are you?" said a soft voice from within the cell.

I'd only been looking at the bars. I refocused my eyes on the woman sat on the cell's bed, leaning against the white brick wall.

"Eliana... Mrs Nazarian," I began.

"Wasserman... it's my family name."

"Yes, Ms Wasserman... I'm Uzi Willner, a lawyer."

"Assigned by the ministry?"

"No, well, not exactly. I'm a friend of a deputy minister. He asked me to review your case, and to meet with you and see if we're compatible."

"Do you do this type of work often? Defend killers?"

"Alleged killer, Ms Wasserman. But I was a prosecutor for many years, normally on the opposite side of things."

"What do you do now, Mr Willner?"

"I work in the lower courts, traffic incidents mostly."

"Traffic? And before that you were a prosecutor?"

"Yes."

"Whom did you prosecute? Criminals?"

"War criminals... kapos."

"You mean the Jews that aided in the running of the camps?"

"Yes."

She nodded. She looked a fragile thing. Pale skin. Thin wrists. Dark brown hair falling to the shoulders.

"I wasn't a Kapo," she said.

"I know, I read your file; taken by the Gestapo to Buchenwald, age ten..."

"What do you see?" she interrupted. "What do you see when you look at me, Mr Willner?"

"I see... a young woman, one who could use some help."

"A bird in a cage."

"I wouldn't say that... you survived eight years in the camps, more than anyone I've ever met or known."

"Which camp were you in?" she asked, moving up and sitting at the end of the bed to get a better look at me.

"Auschwitz."

"Auschwitz..." she said slowly, almost singing the name. "What did you do there?"

"I worked in the crematorium."

"The crematorium... a friend of mine once said that to preserve their innocence, our souls will tear themselves from our bodies. Is that what happened to you... day after day, loading the bodies of your fellow Jews into the ovens? Is that why the smell of vodka spills off you? Do you ever wonder why you didn't jump into the flames yourself?"

I sat there for a time, silent; her eyes did not move away from mine. I pushed my wedding band round and round.

"Are you married, Mr Willner?" she asked, her eyes darting down to look at my ring.

"I was. No longer."

"Divorce?"

"She died in Auschwitz," I said, balling my hand into a fist.

"And that is your original ring?"

"Yes."

"How did you manage to keep it? Where did you hide it?"

I laughed. "I swallowed it before they put us on the train."

"And then?"

"And then what?" I said.

"After it passed through you, where did you hide it?"

"I swallowed it again," I said, pulling the ring from my finger, and holding up in the light. "I swallowed and shit it out and swallowed it again for three years."

"And your wife, what happened to her?"

"I don't know how she died; one day her body was placed on my loading rack in the crematorium. I remember I stopped working. The Kapo on duty beat me with his truncheon. One of the other men pushed her into the fire."

"You were one of the lucky ones then," she said.

"Lucky?"

"How many of us never got to see or bury our loved ones after they died."

"You know, no one has ever asked that about my ring... or ever thought to ask how I kept it."

"We choose not to notice a great many things," she said, balling her knees up against her chest and leaning against the brick wall again.

"Will you tell me what happened to you, Ms Wasserman? Tell me about your life."

"Would you be surprised or think me a liar if I told you I don't remember?"

"No... I wouldn't think you a liar," I said.

My hands began to shake. I put my wedding band back on. The back of my throat burned. "Can you tell me what you do remember?"

She sat there, staring at the brick wall, then the floor, and finally directly at my chest. "I remember the taste of strawberries," she began.

9

Tomas

It's unnatural to wake before the sun and prepare oneself in darkness…

Long ago, in the Garden, there was no light. The darkness reminds us of our fall from God's grace, denying us his resplendence. That is why depraved creatures — Jews, Bolsheviks, Roma and their ilk — are drawn to it. Righteous men, holy men, must cleanse the world of its darkness. And in doing so, we draw closer to God…

When I leave the barracks, it's still full of snoring SS. I walk under a blanket of stars. Cutting across the camp parade ground, I follow the barbwire fence past the Singing Forest and the fields of strawberries, until I reach the medical cantonment and enter the laboratory. I turn on the lights, straighten up a bit, then put on my smock and rubber boots.

I start each day by checking the cells. I oversee the removal of the subjects that expired during the night and transfer them to the examination room for dissection. The empty cells are disinfected. The remaining subjects are fed and watered. Doctor Ziegler, who prefers to forgo his SS rank, usually completes his dissections and cataloging by mid-morning, after which the scraps are taken to the crematorium for disposal. Once this task is complete, I normally attend to the doctor's dissection notes.

Originally trained as a typist for the 132nd Infantry

Division's command staff, I am well suited to this task; my fingers are long and nimble, briskly striking the typewriter's keys with the arrogance of a master pianist. Once I have typed and indexed the notes, I take my lunch, unless otherwise instructed.

Not being a member of the SS and working at a camp such as this has its drawbacks. My barracks-mates constantly play jokes on me, filling my bed with garbage. Last winter I found a frozen Russian under my blanket, his fingers, lips, ears, and nose black with frostbite. I suppose it was a reminder that I should be in Russia with my old division, but instead I'm here, sitting across from the Singing Forest, staring into the rows of beech trees, eating a lunch of stale rye bread topped with pureed meat and cooked onions from a can. Oil from the meat drips and stains my trousers.

"Damnation," I mutter, cursing my inattention.

I will have to scrub the stain out when I return to the barracks.

I can hear the SS completing their late morning's work. The Singing Forest is nearing its crescendo. The SS in my barracks always say the forest's pitch can use some *fine tuning*. In truth, the SS bewildered me. The time and effort they put into the Singing Forest... time that could best be used elsewhere. I pride myself on efficiency, a necessary trait of a typist, of course (the SS assure me it's women's work).

Today, the forest sings in Russian. Yesterday, it was Yiddish. Tomorrow, well, only the SS know what it will sing. I watch them go about their work. Instead of a bullet to the back of the neck, the SS take their time. The Russians' hands are tied behind their backs with rope. Another rope, which has been thrown over a branch high in the canopy, is then looped around the knotted restraints. The SS order some of the remaining prisoners to hoist their comrades into the air. The arms break, and shoulders dislocate.

This is why they call it the Singing Forest, filled with men dangling like forgotten Christmas tree ornaments; their agony serenades the camp.

On my way back to the laboratory, I come across a Jew crawling on the muddy spring ground toward the latrines. It is an old and sick thing.

"Hey, Opa," I say, greeting the Jew. "Need some help getting to the latrine?" It says something in Polish or Ukrainian. I can't understand it.

"What's that, Opa? Looks like you've shit your trousers," I say, pointing at his bony ass. "Come on, Opa, let's get you cleaned up, all right?" I smile and nod at him.

His eyes are like glass. I can see my reflection in them. I walk to one of the nearby workhouses and collect a wheelbarrow. I return, lift the Jew into the barrel and begin back towards the Jewish quarters.

"Which one is yours, Opa?" I ask.

He points.

"Number 4?"

He nodes his head. "All right, number 4 it is."

I bring the wheelbarrow up to the entrance of barrack number 4. I clean my hands off on my smock, then knock on the wooden door.

"Hello, is anyone home?" I say. "Hello?"

The door opens. A skinny man, his grey skin drawn taught over his skull, peers out at me. "Yes?" he says.

"Ah, hello, I found this old Jew crawling on the ground over by the latrines. Does he happen to belong to you?"

"Sir?" says the skinny Jew standing in the door.

"This one, does he live here at number 4?"

The skinny Jew looks down. "Yes, sir, he does."

"Ah, very good. Would you mind taking him inside. I would help but my nose, it can't handle the smell inside your barracks. You really should clean up, you know. You'll get sick otherwise. Well, have a good day," I said, and started back to the laboratory.

"Yes, sir, thank you, sir," said the Jew.

Back in the laboratory, I check the day's timetable to make sure I'm on schedule. During the next hour, I oversee the collection of specimens from subjects 1342 through 1358, all of whom had their reproductive organs exposed to three hours of direct electromagnetic radiation, X-rays, the previous afternoon. Each subject will need to fill a paper cup with reproductive cells. Doctor Ziegler's little princess, the Jewess, enjoys handing out the cups, always letting down a part of her dress, exposing her soft pale breast; for encouragement, I suppose. Those unable or unwilling to produce a specimen are compelled to do so by an electrified metal rod inserted into the rectum and pressed against the prostate. On days when the camp's power supply is acting up, repeated thrusts with a broom handle works well.

Doctor Ziegler is happy to see me when I deliver the specimens to his personal office. He informs me that subjects 1348 and 1349 are monozygotic twins from Krakow.

"As rare as diamonds, Jew twins," says Ziegler with a smile.

Just as I'm about to leave Doctor Ziegler's office, he turns to me and says, "Have Eliana come and see me, will you."

"Yes, Doctor," I answer, closing the door behind me.

I find the Jewess taunting one of the subjects, dangling a white rat by its tail over the head of a subject chained to a pole. The rat squirms and squeals, baring its yellow teeth and sharp claws.

"Jewess, Doctor Ziegler wants to speak with you in his office."

She drops the rat in its cage, leaves the examination room and turns down the hallway toward Ziegler's office.

I don't work solely for Doctor Ziegler, Sascha, although his experiments take a great deal more time and care than the other doctors. For the rest of the afternoon, I assist Doctor Sule, testing new vaccines on subjects 1309 through 1338. Sule prefers to dictate his notes to me while reviewing the subjects. Afterwards, I type up the notes and deliver them to his office. Sule, under the guidance of Ziegler, is working on vaccines for typhus and typhoid. Trials are not going well, although Sule assures me a great deal is learnt from failure. Of the twenty-nine subjects injected with the vaccines, thirteen have died, death is imminent for five, and the remaining are having severe reactions around the injection sites on their arms. Large red streaks have branched out from the injection sites on the shoulders and are traveling down the arms like the root system of an ancient tree. The skin is becoming necrotic, Sule believes. Wishing to examine one more closely, Sule asks me to retrieve the bone saw; he removes an infected arm, taking it with him to the examination room for dissection and analysis. The scraps are taken to the crematorium for disposal.

By now it is late afternoon. I see to the feeding and watering of the subjects again. It is not uncommon for Jews in the camp to volunteer as subjects; news of receiving plentiful rations is well known throughout the camp, and compared to laboring in one of the factories, or completing excavations at Mittlebau-Dora, life in the laboratory would be a fine choice for a smart Jew.

I complete the day by straightening up in the examination room and in my office area. I clean my typewriter, taking each key out, oiling it, and finally applying a new ribbon. I hang up my smock, take off my boots, and put on my Wehrmacht jacket. I bid Doctors Sule, Ziegler, and the others a good evening.

Before leaving, I see the Jewess stood outside one of the subjects' cells, singing to the subject in Russian. I pause a moment, listening to her voice, calm as lake water on a windless day. I didn't know the Jewess could speak Russian. She learns quickly.

The Singing Forest is quiet. The sun has slipped below the horizon, the western sky a contusion of darkening light. In the dining facility I enjoy an evening meal of sausages, boiled cabbage and carrots, and roasted potatoes with mint peas. If the SS do anything right, it's feed themselves well. There are more than one or two strained belt buckles amongst the officers, most of whom are already enjoying their cigarettes and glasses of peppermint schnapps or cognac from France. I'm tired, and none of the SS would ever have a drink with me, the Wehrmacht typist. I head back to my barracks. I like to read before bed. A book titled *The Count of Monte Cristo* by Alexandre Dumas has engrossed me these last weeks. I keep it hidden in my trunk and have replaced the cover with *Mein Kampf*. Of course, French literature, especially one by an author of dark skin, is forbidden by the SS. I found this copy in the luggage of a recently arrived Jew. They bring so many books with them. It's wonderful, like a traveling library! When

I'm finished, I simply throw the book into the crematorium along with the doctors' scraps.

I relieve my bowels, urinate, brush my teeth and wash my face. I do my best to clean the oil from my trousers, holding then under the faucet as I scrub with steel wool, but it is too late, the stain has set. I shuffle to bed, yawning as I go. I have a look around. The barracks is empty. I open my trunk and take out *Mein Kampf*. I shuffle to bed and pull back the top blanket and sheet. Lying on the mattress is a Russian's flayed face… one from the far eastern Steppe; dark skin and thin eyes, its features are like a Mongol.

"SS shitheads…" I mutter to myself.

I throw the Russian's face in the trash, get new sheets and a blanket from the supply room, then get in bed. I pick up *Mein Kampf*, set it upright on my chest and flip to the where I left off. Dantes had just arrived at the rocky island prison known as Château d'If.

10
Zelda

The girl, named Eliana, told Efrayim his family was gone; transformed into smoke and ash. Effy let out such a wail of sorrow that I raced from the kitchen to find him collapsed on the floor like a hatchling fallen from its nest. The girl, stood in the doorway, clothes dripping wet, didn't speak another word for weeks. I was much the same when I first arrived.

One morning, some weeks later, as I was sitting by the window sewing, repairing an old skirt Effy hadn't found time to repair himself, Eliana came and sat across from me. She stared out the window, the same as she did every morning since arriving. I think she was studying the world, watching the way women walked, how men dressed, how the people of south London went about their jobs and lives. When one has lived with death and darkness for so long, it can become like a blanket. Light and innocence, that which is clean, becomes dangerous, because for the girl, nothing clean and good survived long in the camps. From time to time, I glanced at her; her skin was so pale it seemed sunlight had never touched it. When sun beams coming through the window grew closer to her, she pushed away, as though she was sat on a beach retreating from a rising tide.

I had tried many times to talk to her, asking whether she was hungry or cold, tired or sick, never a reply. Her only form of communication, the only I could discern, were her eyes; that she looked at something long enough to indicate she wanted it; a glass of water, a piece of beard, a bowl of soup. Suddenly, for reasons I did not know, I told her about my life…

"I was born on the 27th of December 1909," I began, still focused on my needle work, "in a village on the outskirts of Kursk, near the Oskol River. Twenty years later, on my birthday, secret police dragged my father, younger brothers, and husband from our home and into a frozen wheat field. The police had gathered the villagers to watch. One of the policemen stood on a box and said, 'These men are counterrevolutionaries, waging war against our Soviet Socialist Union… all Kulaks are to be liquidated, their accumulated lands and wealth returned to the state for redistribution to its people and workers.'

"My father told my brothers to be brave. My husband said he loved me. One by one they were shot in the back of the head, but all I remember is their bodies bouncing when they hit the frozen ground. The police encouraged the villagers to clap. Their applause was muffled by the heavy winter gloves and mittens they were wearing. Our home was ransacked, anything of value stolen, including our menorah, and loaded into a truck. One of the policemen complained how cold it was, so he lit our home on fire. The smoke was blown sideways by an approaching storm. Soon, snow drifts arrived, mingling with the smoke and flames, and began to slowly bury our loved ones.

"My mother… she laid on the ground for hours, refusing to leave the bodies. So, I began stripping away my husband's clothes. My mother went mad, slapping me, saying I was defiling him. But we needed their clothing for warmth, and they no longer did. We were going to freeze to death. I took off my youngest brother's coat, he was just thirteen, and tried to make my mother wear it, but she would just push me away. She wanted to die with them, and so I let her... we cannot save those who do not wish to be.

"I was certain to die if I stayed with her," I said.

"Nothing is certain," said Eliana in perfect Russian.

Startled, I pushed the needle through the wool skirt deep into my opposite index finger. I pulled my hand away, and put my finger in my mouth, sucking on the wound.

"You speak Russian," I finally said in my native tongue.

"What did you do?" she said.

I resumed sewing.

"I huddled close to the flames to survive the night. In the morning, I found my husband's razor in the ashes of our bedroom and used it to cut off all my hair. I bound my breasts as tightly as I could and wore the clothes, coat, and cap of my youngest brother. I rubbed dirt and ash on my face, then started walking west."

"You didn't bury your family?"

"It would have been like digging through stone with a spoon. One needs a chisel, not a shovel, for the Russian soil in winter."

"How did you come to be in England?" she asked, moving away from the light once more. I stopped sewing and looked at her.

"I didn't stop walking..."

In the afternoon I went to the market. Eliana chose to join me, probably because the sun had disappeared behind a thick grey ceiling of clouds. She walked by my side, tentatively, her head constantly twisting around, drawn by sights, sounds, and smells: old men sat outside public houses drinking beer;

cavalcades of diesel truck engines thumped past on their way to reconstruction sites; the essence of approaching rain filled the air.

At the market, I moved quickly around the stalls and shops picking up essentials. No one seemed to know how long the rationing would continue, least of all the sellers and shopkeepers. Flour and rye were still difficult to find, as well as butter, and meat of any kind.

You'd think all the English kulaks had been shot...

"Eliana," I said, "what's your favorite meal?"

Turning around, I discovered Eliana had left my side. She was stood by the bakery, listening to a group of men talking. I went over to her.

"Eliana?" I said.

She didn't look at me, rather continued studying the men. "Poles," she said.

The men were speaking Polish, but I couldn't understand them. "You speak Polish too?"

"Yes..."

"How many languages do you speak?" I asked.

"Many... I suppose. They arrived from everywhere and I had to keep them company, keep them quiet."

"Keep who quiet?"

"The subjects."

Effy cleaned his face with soap over the wash bowl. I was already in bed watching the flickering candle on the bedside table and listening to the rain strike the windows.

"Did you know she speaks Russian?" I said.

"What, she started talking?" said Effy, drying his face with a towel before he applied paste to a brush and began cleaning his teeth.

"Yes... first Russian, then Polish. I think she speaks many more."

"She still didn't say anything about which camp she was in?"

"No, only that people arrived from all over Europe, and that she would speak to them."

"It's good she's finally started talking."

"What are we going to do, Effy?"

"I don't know," he said, spitting out the paste and washing his mouth with water. Effy sat down on the bed next to me.

"She was a little girl when they took her... now she's a woman. It's a miracle she survived at all."

"But how can we give her a life? Teach her to be a seamstress? Thank God she is still beautiful, perhaps we can find her a good husband."

"Her life is her own, she should be free to choose its course."

"No education, no husband... what will she do, stay with us the rest of her life?" I said.

"Perhaps Mr Epping on the first floor would meet with her, he used to be a teacher at a private school for boys before the war."

"Effy... she doesn't need to see that, not right now at least."

"Zelda, darling..."

"I know, Effy, I'm sorry, I don't mean it like that, it's just that my heart breaks every time I look at him."

The next morning, Effy went downstairs to speak with Mr Epping. Mr Epping lived alone and had few visitors that I knew of. When Effy had spare time and materials, he would make Mr Epping new pairs of trousers or coats. I don't know what Mr Epping looked like before the war; Effy assured me he was handsome, bright green eyes and dark chestnut hair. Much of his face was burnt away. A young schoolteacher in the '30s, Mr Epping joined the Royal Air Force, eventually becoming something called a pathfinder. A pathfinder flew ahead of the bomber groups at night to illuminate the way ahead and identify targets with bright burning flares.

The only thing I knew to be true of Mr Epping was his love of American jazz music. I heard it playing in his flat every time I entered the building. In the spring and summer, when our windows were open, the music would flutter in like butterflies. Effy returned from downstairs and spoke to Eliana, telling her she didn't have to meet Mr Epping if she didn't want to, but that he would be happy to tutor her in whatever subjects she liked. I saw Eliana smile for the first time. After the two of them went downstairs to meet with Mr Epping, I went into the kitchen and made some tea. I instead found myself drinking a glass of vodka instead. I worried for the girl.

Effy returned without Eliana. She stayed with Mr Epping for most of the day returning in the late afternoon as I was about to begin preparing dinner. Effy was sat at his worktable, applying the finishing touches to Lady Sutcliffe's ball gown. Eliana opened the door and stepped inside.

"Hello, my dear," said Effy, pushing away from his worktable. "How did it go?" Eliana said nothing. She stepped aside to let Mr Epping enter.

"Oh, Mr Epping," said Effy, standing up to greet him. "Thank you for showing Eliana home."

"Yes… sorry to intrude…" said Mr Epping in a wispy voice. The burns had damaged his throat.

"Not at all, please come in," said Effy. "Can we get you a drink? Tea? Something stronger, perhaps?"

"No, no, please, don't fret over me," said Mr Epping, who put much of his weight onto a thin wood cane.

"I wonder if I might speak with you and Zelda, if you don't mind," said Mr Epping.

I had come into the living room.

"Eliana, would you like some tea?" I asked. She shook her head.

Mr Epping managed a crooked smile toward Eliana, who turned and went into her bedroom.

We all sat down at the dining room table. Mr Epping let out a sigh of relief when he was finally able to sit down after refusing Effy's help.

"Again, many pardons for showing up unannounced. I don't wish to stay too long and interrupt your dinner," he said.

"Please... Mr Epping, you're always welcome here."

"Thank you, Efrayim, and please, just call me Tristan. Mr Epping is my father, as they say." Effy smiled. I loved to see him smile.

"Eliana and I talked for quite a long time," began Mr Epping. "I have to say, she's an extraordinary young woman. You mentioned she entered the camps when she was just a girl?"

"Yes," said Effy, glancing at me, "we think when she was about ten or eleven years old."

"Remarkable..." said Mr Epping.

"What did she tell you?" I asked.

"I took her through basic instructions. She's weakest in English composition, which isn't surprising. She may speak it fluently, but she's never had to compose it, I think."

"She speaks Russian too, and Polish," I said.

"Yes… and a great deal more it would seem," said Mr Epping.

"How many more?" said Effy.

"As far as I can tell right now, fifteen…"

Mr Epping took a strip of paper out of his coat pocket, and began reading, "German, Yiddish, English, Russian, Polish, Hungarian, Italian, French, Dutch, Romanian, Slovak, Lithuanian, Norwegian, Romani, and Greek."

"Incredible," said Effy. "We had no idea; she hardly speaks to us at all." Mr Epping tucked the piece of paper back into his pocket.

"She also has an advanced understanding of mathematics: algebra, trigonometry, calculus, and even physics."

"Well, that shouldn't be a surprise, right?" I said, "Effy's brother was a professor of mathematics."

"But she was only a girl. I mean, how many little girls, even my brother's daughters, were learning advanced mathematics that young?" said Effy.

Mr Epping leaned back in his chair, resting one hand on his cane, and for a moment his disfigurements disappeared, and he was a teacher once more.

"There are only two possible answers… either your brother indeed passed on his knowledge to his young children, or Eliana was able to somehow continue her education while a prisoner in a German concentration camp."

11
Golda

Anna was the first to hear them coming that morning. The female guards entered our barracks, accompanied by male SS and dogs. All the women between the ages of sixteen and thirty, to which Anna and I belonged, were marched to the camp's central courtyard. The wardress, a middle-aged woman with blonde hair and eyebrows, was stood in the center of the yard, accompanied by a young adjutant.

"What's going on? Why have they only taken the young?" said Anna, her hands shaking.

It was spring, though mornings at Ravensbrück, built just north of Berlin, were still bitter cold. "A new work detail?" I answered. "Something, only we can do…"

The wardress ordered us to remove our clothes, including headscarves.

Anna shook terribly as she slipped out of her tattered dress. I grasped her arm and brought her close to me, rubbing her back to try and warm her. A female guard struck my arm with a truncheon and ordered us to separate. The dogs wouldn't stop barking; large black and brown shepherds, their mouths writhing with rings of froth. Their SS handlers circled us, enjoying our naked bodies.

The wardress, accompanied by her adjutant, began inspecting us like a butcher does meat, judging our hair, faces, teeth, breasts, and buttocks. Every so often the wardress would point to a girl and say, "that one," and the adjutant would quickly snatch the girl out of the line and place her in the center of the courtyard. Nine women had been selected when the wardress began reviewing mine and Anna's line. The commonality amongst the chosen women was their attractiveness: thin nose, symmetrical face, high breasts, a feminine line... meat on their thighs and buttocks.

I didn't look at the wardress as she passed. "That one," I heard her say.

Anna was pulled from the line. She let out a sharp scream. I tried to reach out for her, but we were already too far apart.

The wardress turned on her heels and approached me. She examined my breasts, pinching one of the nipples, erect from the cold.

"This one too," said the wardress, letting go of my nipple

The wardress dismissed the others. She ordered us to dress, after which the guards led us to the front gate and loaded us into an idling truck. We were driven to the nearby rail yard.

"They're taking us to another camp," said Anna, as we jumped out of the back of the truck one by one.

"Why are they taking us to a new camp?" she said.

"Quiet!" yelled a guard, restraining a shepherd dog by its choke chain. "Get into the train car, quickly!"

Scrambling across the rocky ground, I climbed up the ramp into the car, then helped the others.

Once inside, we huddled together for warmth like blind, newborn sucklings. In time, after the initial fright wore off, we started falling asleep. It was afternoon by the time the train's wheels moaned and began churning. We gained speed quickly. I stood up, peeling arms and legs away from me, and went to the small window on the side of the car, pressing my face between its bars so that I might peer out. A forest rushed past; its evergreen branches painted by sunlight. When I first arrived at Ravensbrück, I was certain I would never leave it, fated to die like so many before me. Perhaps it was foolish to feel hope now, but I had found a strange peace in this new uncertainty. I told myself, nothing is certain... not life... not death; I breathed the rich forest air deep into my lungs and held it there as long as I could.

Our train journey continued through the next day, stopping at a number of yards, but our car door remained shut, and the train continued south. Some of the girls began to faint from thirst, the car warming in the midday sun.

"Where are they taking us?" said Anna, using her dress sleeve to wipe sweat from her brow. "They don't even give us a bucket to piss in."

"You complain about a bucket?" I laughed. "They don't give us water to piss out, who cares about a bucket."

Anna laughed. So did a few of the other girls.

"Maybe they're going to leave us in here... kill us slowly," said one of the girls, her face ridden with fear.

"If they were going to kill us, they would have done it at Ravensbrück. Why go to the trouble to send us hundreds of miles by train only to kill us then?" I said. "No, we are something special."

"What? What are they going to do with us?" said the girl.

I reached my hand and gently held Anna's chin between my thumb and forefinger. "See why they chose us? All young... all beautiful..."

"I don't understand," said the girl. "What do you mean?"

I spoke louder so everyone in the car could hear me over the wheels' metallic *click-clack*. "We have to prepare ourselves for what lies ahead… some of you may already be thinking it… others may not wish to think about it at all. Wherever they're taking us, when we arrive, we will all have to become whores."

Some started to cry as they realized the truth. "Resist and they will kill you," I said.

"Better to die than be a Nazi whore," said one of the older women.

"I will not tell you what to do with your own lives, but if they intend to make us whores, then they also intend to feed us, keep us clean, make us beautiful."

"How do you know?" said another.

"Because what man wants to fuck a dying sack of bones?" I said.

After the train, we were put in an open truck and driven a short distance through a dense beech forest on a dirt road.

Beech trees… are we near Weimar, near home?

The truck's tires kicked up a wake of dust. Soon, we began to pass large groups of Russian prisoners cutting down trees using long two-man saw blades. There were SS with dogs relaxing near the forest edge smoking cigarettes. A little farther down the road we drove past hundreds of dead and dying men dangling from the beech trees, rope tied around their wrists. The truck slowed, pulling into a clearing. It was a meadow full of wildflowers. The guards in the cab jumped out, slung their rifles onto their shoulders, and walked into the field. One of them was holding a wood basket like something you'd take on a picnic.

All the women turned and watched the guards lightly stepping through the field, every so often leaning down to pluck something and put it in the basket.

"What are they doing?" said Anna.

"Gathering wildflowers to give to their girlfriends?" said one of the younger women. In time, after maybe ten or fifteen minutes, the two guards returned.

"Nice and ripe," said the guard carrying the basket.

"My mama always made strawberry strudel in the spring," said the other.

Once in the camp, the SS spent a week fattening us up like pigs: meats, cheeses, and bread twice a day. Everyone ate, no one denied themselves food. They bathed us, gave us make-up, told us to make our hair look nice. Despite our preparations, none of us were ready for the first night. The camp's senior staff and officers, all middle-aged men, balding or with growing waistlines, entered our would-be brothel smelling of schnapps and cigarettes. The two female guards told us to stand in a line. The SS inspected us, smoking cigarettes, debating and joking about which one they wanted. The ranking officer chose first.

Anna.

He took her into one of the separate rooms.

One by one, the rest of us were chosen, and then raped. Sweaty, drunk, their mouths smelling of tobacco and ash, they climbed upon us, trousers around their ankles. Most had wedding bands.

One or two of the girls cried, even tried to fight back. The female guards beat them. The SS laughed, drank more Schnapps, smoked more cigarettes, then climbed upon another girl. They sang songs. After an hour or so, some rested, glistening with sweat, watching their comrades continue to rape us. They partook in menial conversations about the weather, the camp's poor food, or an incompetent junior officer. It continued like this until suddenly it was over; the SS, drunk and depleted, disappeared like wraiths, and we were left alone in terrible silence. The younger girls, those who'd been virgins, sobbed quietly. The older women began straightening up, knowing this was only the first night.

It continued each night for weeks, then months. When one of the girls was found to be with child, the female guards would take her away and have the fetus removed. When one of the girls, Matilda from Paris, died in her sleep, she was replaced by a younger girl, Fenna from Holland. In time, the SS officers began to have favorites, bringing their chosen girl gifts: trinkets, extra food, or a bottle of wine.

An officer named Ziegler took a liking to me. He was the camp doctor, the one who removed our children, ensuring Aryan blood wouldn't be corrupted with Jewish. Ziegler always brought a tube of lubricant. He only ever had anal sex with me, and always wore a condom. Afterwards, I would bleed when I defecated.

At the end of summer, the female guards took Anna away. She was pregnant with the SS chief's child. Hours later, when Anna returned, I brought her a washbowl of warm water and cloth. She was weak; her skin white as marble; even her bright blue eyes became grey and lifeless.

"You'll be all right, Anna," I told her, as I started to dip the cloth into the bowl and gently wash her body. "Ziegler is a monster, but he's a good doctor."

"It wasn't Ziegler," said Anna, her voice hardly above a whisper.

"What do you mean?" I said.

"It wasn't Ziegler," she said again. "It was a girl, a young girl, dressed up as a doctor... she did this."

"What? Anna?"

I looked down. Blood was leaking from between Anna's legs onto the bed. "Anna... Anna, you're bleeding," I said, trying to pull back her dress.

She started to convulse. Her eyes rolled into the back of her head. Anna died an hour later.

12
Eliana

We buried Yitzak the next morning in an unfinished wood casket, that the earth might reclaim him sooner, and return his body to dust. One of Chaya's nails was torn off as she raked the dry rocky earth with her fingers. She collected the dirt into her hands, then released the fistfuls over her son's small grave, burying him. Overtaken by grief, Chaya wailed. Peter grabbed her with both arms and pulled her away.

Miriam came next; leaning over, she gathered a single handful of dirt, stood up straight, and released the dirt from her hand as though it were an hourglass. Her eyes were hidden behind large black sunglasses, but I knew she was looking at me. A sudden wind swept over the grave, blowing the dirt Miriam was releasing onto me; the coarse grains scraped against my lips and cheeks.

Isaac, the old soldier, was unable to carry his grief. He fell to his knees so that he might crawl into the grave and lay at rest alongside his only grandchild. Jacob helped his father to stand. I was last to gather earth in my hands and pour it onto Yitzak. There was a hollow knock each time a small rock struck the casket, as though it were empty.

On the drive from the grave site to Jacob's parents' house, Jacob asked if I was all right.

"Yes, I'm fine," I said, looking out the window at a grove of cypress trees clustered just beyond the cemetery.

"It's not your fault, you know," said Jacob, his voice full of mercy. "It was an accident. A terrible, terrible accident. One that you can't blame yourself for."

"Yes, I know."

"I'm going to call Regimental headquarters, request a delay of my deployment... perhaps we can go somewhere, try and forget about all this for a few days. What do you think?"

"What?" I said, only half-listening to Jacob.

"A trip, what do you think?"

"No... you have your deployment. The men need you... anyways, in all the fuss I forgot to tell you I'm going on a work trip as well."

"When is it?"

"They said just to be ready... sometime early in the week."

"Where are you going?"

"You know I can't say... just like you can't say where you're going."

"Can you say how long it will be?" said Jacob.

He sat up straight, squaring his shoulders.

"I don't know that either. Not too long, I think. A week, maybe."

"I didn't know secretaries were required to travel."

I bit the inside of my lower lip until I could taste the iron in my blood. "I don't ask questions," I said. "I do what I'm told, just like you."

After returning home to Jaffa that night, Jacob turned on the cooling unit before getting in bed. He wanted to make love to me.

I didn't stop him; it was always like this before a deployment. He held me tight, savoring my body, the smell of my skin. Near the end, he became forceful. Perhaps he thought with Yitzak dead I would finally conceive a child to carry on the family name, a child to replace what had been lost, to fill the void in his family's heart. After Jacob finished, his face red and body covered in beads of sweat despite the cooling unit, I excused myself and went into the bathroom. I look in the mirror and fixed my hair.

Nothing is certain.

I went to the toilet and let Jacob drip out of me.

In the morning, I kissed Jacob goodbye. He told me he would write and try and call at least once a week. I always thought he looked handsome in his uniform, not the dress uniform, but his battle fatigues.

"Are you all right?" Jacob asked me again.

"Yes, I'm fine, Captain Nazarian. As much as I loved Izzy, he wasn't my blood; the grief is your family's. I should not revel in it. Poor Chaya. She and Peter wouldn't even look at me, and Miriam..."

"It was an accident."

"Yes, I know..." I said and kissed him on the check once more. "I need to get to work."

"I love you, Eliana," said Jacob.

I kissed him on the cheek again. "Be safe."

Zvi was already at his desk when I arrived.

"Ah, Eliana, did you have a good weekend?" said Zvi.

"Yes, it was fine," I said. "Jacob and I took a drive up the coast to Haifa."

"It's beautiful there," said Zvi.

"What about you?"

"I caught up on sleep," said Zvi with a smile.

"Anything come in?" I said, sitting down and getting my desk in order.

"A few reports. I'm going through them now. Here are the ones I've been through already," Zvi handed me a stack of documents stamped SECRET.

"Anything more pertaining to SYCTHE?"

"I submitted our report. Upstairs hasn't come back with anything yet. I never got a chance to ask what Harel and Redlich wanted, if you can say?"

"They're sending me on a trip."

"Somewhere nice, I hope," said Zvi, going back to skimming the reports on his desk.

"West Berlin... nothing to do with SYCTHE, if you're wondering."

"When you get to be my age, all you can do is wonder... actually doing things is for young people like you."

For the rest of the morning, I read over reports of Russia's latest Vostok missile test in Siberia. Zvi and I calculated the rocket's elliptical ranges, should the Russians ever choose to tip the rocket with a nuclear weapon. I included in the report that such a scenario was unlikely given the Vostok-K72K's payload capabilities, and Russia's recent advancements in weapons miniaturization. Too much rocket for too little weight, basically.

"Thirty-eight meters... that's a lot of rocket," said Zvi. "Almost three-times the original V-2. Can you imagine?"

"Can I imagine a rocket thirty-eight meters high, is that what you're asking?" I said in a sarcastic tone.

"Some have bigger imaginations than others," said Zvi.

"I remember the smell of the V-2s," I said without thought.

"What do you mean?" said Zvi.

Only Upstairs knew about my time at Mittlebau-Dora, the underground labor camp where German V-2 rockets were designed and fabricated. Because of my slight frame, it was my job to crawl inside the empty fuel tanks, later to be filled with liquid-oxygen, and a water-alcohol mixture, and scrub them clean of any contaminates. The fuel tanks were just big enough to fit two women, or three or four children. However, the German in charge of fuel tank construction preferred women... especially those who were once maids, housewives, or nurses; women with experience being on their knees and scrubbing.

"There's a job for every Jew," I remember him saying, "even stupid old Jew maids who only know how to clean a kitchen floor."

I looked up at Zvi, his large watery eyes studying me through his heavy glasses.

"After the rockets hit London, the smell of the amatol, the mixture of TNT and ammonium nitrate, it would settle in the bomb shelters..."

"What did it smell like?" said Zvi.

I said the first word that came to mind: *Sweet.*

That afternoon, a car arrived at my home. A man knocked on the door. He asked for my luggage. I looked down at a single suitcase placed near the door. He picked it up, put it in the car's truck, then drove me to the airport. Neither of us spoke. Once at the airport, the driver handed me an envelope. In it was a single ticket, direct to Berlin.

"Someone will meet you when you arrive."

"How will I know them?" I said.

"They'll know you."

In the waiting area, I recognized no one: businessmen in blue, gray, and brown suits, smoking cigarettes and flipping through newspapers; women with fashionable hair styles accompanying their husbands abroad; tourists with overstuffed backpacks looking in need of a bath. If there were any others like me on the flight, I didn't see them, nor did I wish to find them. It felt good to be alone, anonymous, safe... as it was those few weeks in the refugee camp before Golda found me.

There was a call to board the plane. Once seated, I asked for a glass of wine, then another, and again, until my eyes were too heavy to keep open.

I woke as the plane was descending into Berlin. I looked out the window; it was nearly night. The city's bifurcation was clearly visible from the air. The lingering scars of war blotted the east, as though the land was afflicted by some strange pestilence: razed street blocks, collapsed buildings, skeletal stone pillars. Hardly anything had been rebuilt.

I was happy to be on the ground. Taxing to a halt, I straightened my hair. Descending the stairs to the tarmac, the night air was warm, filled with the saccharine scent of jet fuel. Once in the airport, and having collected my luggage, I passed through customs.

The guard inspected my passport. She was old, as old as Miriam, judging by the number of lines on her face. No way to know if she'd been a Nazi or if the Star of David on my passport would upset her.

"Purpose of visit?" she said in English.

"Tourism," I answered in German.

She looked up at me with what appeared to be scorn. "Length of stay?" she said, returning to German.

"One week."

"Welcome," she said, "enjoy your stay in West Germany." She stamped my passport.

I didn't know what else to do but stand near the airport's exit and wait, for whom or what I was unsure. Suddenly, a tall woman stood next to me. She had long, red hair, and bright green eyes.

"Eliana Wasserman, welcome to Berlin," she said. I turned, somewhat wary at first.

"Hello," I said.

"The others are waiting. Follow me."

"Who are you?" I said.

"Marie Holmstadt, Ministry of Justice, and the only other woman on the trip." She smiled. "Come, you're the last to arrive; everyone's waiting at a cafe."

Redlich was there, sipping an espresso and smoking a cigarette. He looked odd in civilian clothes, like an actor about to go on stage. The others, Marco Espirito, also from the Ministry of Justice, had dark hair and Spanish skin; Benjamin Gudin, from the Prime Minister's office, was older than Redlich, more refined. He wore a tailored suit, and his hair was neatly parted.

We took taxis to the hotel. Redlich, Marco, and Benjamin in one, Marie and I in another. Marie rolled the window down to enjoy the night air. The city was full of energy: music drifting out of beer halls, restaurants and cafes full of patrons smoking cigarettes and laughing over bottle of wine and glasses of liqueur.

"So, you're the one who's going to identify this man," said Marie in Yiddish, still staring out the window.

"Yes…" I answered.

"You know him from the camps?"

"Perhaps... it was a long time ago."

"Yeah..."

"Were you in the camps?" I said.

Without looking at it, Marie pulled back her long shirt sleeve, revealing a tattooed identification number.

"Bergen-Belsen," she said. "I don't care if it's him or not if he's a Nazi we should hang him. They all deserve to die."

All the way to the hotel, Marie never stopped staring out the window, watching the Germans go about their lives: smiling, drinking, singing, like none of it had ever happened, as though blood no longer stained their hands.

Marie used the bathroom first. I opened a window and lit a cigarette. *"You must keep your hands steady, my petite princesse... do you see how very delicate it is..."*

"It's all yours," said Marie, coming out the bathroom and drying her hair with a towel.

I put the cigarette out on the brick windowsill and went into the bathroom. The steam settled on my skin as I undressed. I stood in front of the mirror.

"Illa," I said. "I'm back home now... I've come for work. Were we ever in Berlin? Are you someplace safe?"

I curled up on the shower floor, pulling my knees tight against my chest. I buried my face down into the darkness, the water striking me as though I were a stone at the base of a waterfall.

The British consulate was not far. We walked as a group; Redlich leading, followed by Benjamin and Marco at a leisurely pace, then Marie and I. Marie had become quite motherly, preparing me breakfast, helping me with my hair and makeup. I thanked her.

"It's not every day we have to face monsters," she said.

Once inside the consulate, we were greeted by two men calling themselves Mr Baker and Mr Smith, the latter being willowy with delicate wrists, the other, a short plump man with a receding hairline.

Benjamin did all the talking. His languid face barely moved as he set about charming the two British men; laying the groundwork for extradition, I suppose. We were taken to a small conference room and presented with tea, and a platter of biscuits. The others indulged. I remained still.

The tall one, Mr Baker, began, "We questioned the individual, the presumed Dr Ziegler, a number of times, alongside West German authorities who are currently offering political asylum to Ziegler as he claims to have fled the East to come here."

"His answers have remained consistent throughout our interrogations, when we can get answers out of him," said Mr Smith.

"What do you mean? Is he avoiding answering certain questions?" said Redlich.

"Not avoiding, per se," said Mr Smith, leaning back in his chair and resting his hands on his belly, "more like talking ad nauseam… giving such lengthy and wandering answers as to blind us to our question in the first place."

"For the purpose of obfuscation?"

The two British gentlemen looked at one another, then back at Redlich. "We think he just likes to talk," said Mr Baker.

"Are you saying he's genial?" said Benjamin.

"Quite," said Mr Smith. "And you should know… he's requesting extradition to Israel and wishes to stand trial."

"He wants to stand trial?" said Marie, nearly laughing.

"Yes, he's very adamant about that," said Mr Baker.

"Why?" I said.

Mr Baker looked at me, "Because he thinks he's innocent."

"Also," said Mr Smith, reaching into his coat pocket, "he presented us with this…" Mr Smith laid a Bible on the table, "… as proof of his identify."

"A Bible?" said Redlich.

"Yes," continued Mr Smith, "and that's not all…" he opened the Bible to a page with a fold in it, revealing a delicately flattened strawberry still attached to its twisting green stem.

"Is that a strawberry?" said Marie. "What does it mean?"

"We were wondering that ourselves," answered Mr Baker. "The presumed Herr Ziegler told us wild strawberries grew all around Buchenwald, and in the beech woods, surrounding the camp."

"Is that true?" Benjamin inquired, inspecting the Bible and flattened strawberry for himself.

"We were hoping you could tell us," finished Mr Baker.

Benjamin looked at me, "is that true?"

Messers Baker and Smith, Redlich, Marco, and Benjamin sat at the interrogation room's table waiting for Dr Ziegler to be brought to them. Marie and I stood in an adjacent room, watching from behind a double-sided mirror. Marie kept shifting her weight, crossing and uncrossing her arms. I looked over at her.

"Sorry," she said. "Is it true… what they said about the strawberries, did they grow around the camp?"

"Yes," I said, continuing to stare at the interrogation room door, waiting for it to open.

"So, it's Ziegler then?"

The interrogation room door opened. In stepped a British army soldier, followed by an elderly man, then another soldier. The intercom picked up the shuffling of feet. The elderly man, who professed to be Dr Sascha Ziegler, sat down in the chair opposite everyone. He smiled.

"Ah, new friends," he said. "Welcome. Where have you all come from? Not far, I hope. Traveling can be so tiresome. Have they offered you some breakfast, or refreshments...? I had raspberry scones this morning for breakfast, they were excellent. Perhaps we could have some brought in here, to snack on... yes?"

"My name is Benjamin Gudin, sir, I am a representative of the Israeli government."

"Oh, how wonderful... I'm Dr Sascha Ziegler. It's a pleasure to meet you Mr Gudin," said the elderly man.

Marie turned to me. I don't know why she whispered, but she did, as though not to startle me. "What do you think, is it him? Is it Ziegler?"

I took a step closer, my exhalations fogging the glass.

Is it him?

I began to study him, pull his face apart one feature at a time: remove the scar from his eye and give it color; replace the aging skin, full of freckles, blemishes, and scars, to imagine a youthful visage; reduce his weight; shorten the hair, fill it with color...

"Eliana..." said Marie in a hushed voice again, "Is it Ziegler?"

"Hello," said the Russian inside the cell. He wasn't

looking at my bare breasts, but at my eyes. "What's your name?"

"Eliana," I said.

"Eliana." He smiled. "I am Stanislav."

13
Sascha

I carefully spread the rich butter along the edge of the raspberry scone. Biting into it, I first tasted the milky butter, then the crumbling sweetness of the scone, followed by the tart raspberry jam coating my upper lip. How wonderful...

Enjoying the final mouthful of the scone, there was a sharp knock upon the door followed by jangling keys. The guard was searching for the correct key to open my door. I was not in a prison cell by any means, more a former janitor's closet with a folding cot bed. Either way, the accommodation was far superior from whence I came, though I'm sure the guards were growing tired of my frequent trips to the toilet; my bowels and bladder being far more active since arriving...

Four meals a day, what is an old man to do?

The guard entered. "Good morning," I said.

"Stand up, please," he said in broken German.

I was escorted down the hallway by two British soldiers. They were very young, clean faces that didn't require a shave.

"Very early for the interviewing to begin?" I said in English.

Normally, the interviews did not begin until at least thirty minutes after I had completed my breakfast.

One of the guards opened the door to the interrogation room and stepped in. I followed. Entering the room, I saw many new faces.

"Ah, new friends," I said.

I took a seat in my usual chair and asked whether anyone would like some scones.

"They're delicious," I said, "and come with very good butter... the trick is, I think, to get the right amount of butter around the scone while leaving the jam undisturbed on top."

Strangely, none of them were interested. Perhaps they had already had the scones.

A tall man with finely parted hair introduced himself — I didn't catch his first name — as a representative of the Government of Israel. The other two introduced themselves... Red something, the other, Marcus, I believe; my hearing is not what it used to be. I told them to speak up.

"Redlich," the man said firmly.

"Ah, pleasure to meet you, sir. And you, Marcus."

"Marco," he snapped.

"Right, yes, Marco."

Marco had dark skin, far darker than all the others, and black hair, the color of rich soil.

Mr Gudin continued, "We've arrived to consider your extradition to Israel. I come from the office of the prime minister, my associates, from the Ministry of Justice..."

"Just the men I wish to talk to," I interrupted. "I know you've been hunting me for years, vilifying my good family name... so when does the trial begin? I will want to serve as my own advocate if your legal system allows. I must admit, my understanding of jurisprudence in Israel is limited, but I know you will give me a good trial. If Jews are good at anything, it's adhering to regulations and ceremony." I smiled.

"There is still the matter of your identity, sir," said Mr Gudin.

"Identity?"

"Yes, the question as to whether you are indeed Dr Ziegler remains unresolved."

"My name is Sascha Ziegler. I have a passport proving so. Why do I have reason to lie about such a thing?"

"Why did you turn yourself in... after all these years, why now?" said the stern-faced man, Redlich. "Was it because we got Eichmann?"

"Eichmann?" I said. "Who's that?"

"Otto Adolf Eichmann, the SS commander."

"He also turned himself in?" I said.

"We captured him in Argentina."

"Argentina... no, I have never been to Argentina. Was this recently? News in the East... it is not always the best, you must understand."

"We cannot simply remove you from West Germany," said Marco. "For the West German government to approve extradition to Israel, your identity must be proven. You say you are Dr Sascha Ziegler, SS-Sturmbannfuhrer, Medical Officer, Buchenwald concentration camp, also known as *the Butcher of Buchenwald*. We may believe it, but the West Germans need proof... proof before they let another German be taken to the state of Israel for trial and execution."

"They call me *the Butcher*. I do not like this at all."

I looked at all their faces, quite dour. I nodded at the two British fellows.

"I don't understand, you showed them the strawberry, yes? The West German man, Frans... Hans, whatever his name, he saw it too... where is he? Bring him here and show him the strawberry again."

"Sir," said Mr Gudin, "Where were you born? What

year?"

"What?" I said.

"What were the names of your parents?"

"Oh no, not again," I sighed.

The questioning continued for hours, the same as it had done every day for the past week. Today, however, we did not stop for lunch, which I found completely intolerable. The same questions over and over; questions I had already answered a hundred times for the two British fellows, now asked by Israelis.

"Excuse me," I finally said, having grown tired, and hungry. "Had I known extradition would be so difficult, I would have just flown to Israel myself, but I only had enough marks for a bus fare. Perhaps one of you gentlemen would be kind enough to give me money for a plane ticket and I could walk out of here and head to the airport, yes?"

There was a sharp rapping on the glass mirror on the opposite wall. Redlich left the room abruptly.

"Who's... behind the glass," I coughed, which then turned into a fit. One of the British soldiers got me a glass of water.

"Thank you," I said, holding my handkerchief to my mouth, spitting blood into it.

I tried to take long slow breathes, but the fit continued until my face was red and I was sweating.

"Lung cancer... they say," I said through the coughs.

Everyone in the room remained silent; not a single kind word, not even, *bless you.*

My hand trembled as I brought the glass of water to my lips. It was room temperature. I prefer cold water, when possible, to sooth my throat.

The door opened and in stepped Redlich. He had a hushed

conversation with the two British fellows. I couldn't hear what they were saying. After Redlich was finished, the two Brits stood up and left the room. I frowned.

"Where are you going?" I asked them as they walked past me.

Redlich spoke with his colleagues, after which they too exited the interrogation room, closing the door behind them. It was only Redlich and I. He sat down and stared at me but did not speak.

"You've sent them all behind the mirror? Who was tapping back there?" I said.

"I understand Dr Ziegler, the real Dr Ziegler, could recite the Bible... word for word," said Redlich in English.

"What?" I said.

"Verbatim," he answered leaning back in his chair, his heavy shoulders slumping down, as though relaxing after a long day at work.

I looked at Redlich then at the mirror trying to see who was behind it, but there was only my reflection.

"Who's back there?" I said more forcefully now. "Who told you this?"

"Can you?"

I looked again into the mirror, studying my own deformed face.

Who was behind the glass?

"In the beginning, God created the heavens and the Earth..." I began.

For five or ten minutes I droned on. Suddenly, the door opened, and I stopped. A young woman was standing there, long red hair framing her face.

"Hello, young lady," I said.

The woman stepped forward and I saw another woman behind her, as though they were Russian babushkas, nesting dolls.

"Oh, hello to you, too," I said.

This other woman was more delicate: thick strands of dark hair fell upon high smooth cheek bones; pale, almost soap white skin; thin lips, though bright red like stripes on a piece of candy.

Both women entered, but only the delicate one sat down. The one with hair of fire whispered to Redlich, and they both left.

It was only the delicate one and I. "Hello," I said.

She didn't speak, instead she placed my Bible on the table, and removed the flattened strawberry, feeling its dry, wrinkled texture with her fingertips. She laid the strawberry down in front of me.

"Do you know where the strawberries of Buchenwald came from?" she said in German, pure German, not laced with a foreign accent. I found her voice familiar, lyrical.

"They grew wild, everywhere, in the forest, some even in the camp."

"But not always… they were brought there by a woman who loved them. To grow them in the camp garden so that she could dine on them every chance she had: strawberries for breakfast, with lunch, accompanying tea, as dessert following dinner, baked in pies, turned into jam, preserved in jars. She could never have enough. In time, because of birds or rats, or the guards shitting out strawberry seeds in the forests, they spread, becoming wild."

"Who are you, young lady?"

She stood. Walked over to me and lent down, her mouth

131

nearly touching my ear.

"The question," she whispered, "is who are you? Because you are not Sascha Ziegler..."

I pulled away, studying her face.

She stepped back and opened the door. A few moments later, Redlich and the others appeared in the hallway.

I looked at all of them. The woman stared deep into my eyes, then turned to the others, her voice strong and confident.

"It's him," she said, "Sascha Ziegler, the Butcher of Buchenwald."

That voice...

They returned me to my holding room. I laid down on my cot and thought about the woman.

Petite Princesse, is that you?

14
Askel

On 11 November 1915, I earned a Doctorate of Mathematics specializing in the field of differential geometry from the University of Weimar. Two weeks later, the acclaimed physicist, Albert Einstein, published his *Field Equations for Gravitation* in the *Proceedings of the Royal Prussian Academy of Sciences*. I took a copy home to my single room apartment above a butcher's shop on Kantstraße, just down the road from the university. That night, sat next to the few candles I had, I read the journal. Einstein's theory, which gave understanding and form to our universe, was set out in equations using the language of differential geometry. I did not sleep that night, for how can one sleep after the mysteries of the universe have been revealed to them; it is not time that moves us forward from one moment to the next, but gravity. The next morning, I returned to the university where I was still working as a member of the adjunct faculty, excited to discuss Einstein's theories with friends and colleagues. In my excitement, I arrived in haste; the halls, classrooms, and offices were still empty. My office, in the basement of the Science building, was little more than a closet; one must earn their place in today's Germany, and if Germany was not before, it certainly is now the center of the scientific world.

On my desk I found an official envelope from German Imperial Army headquarters; it must have been delivered yesterday after I'd left. No longer a student, the letter notified me that I had been selected for service in the Imperial Army and was to report to the central recruitment depot in Berlin in two weeks to begin training. I trembled so badly the letter flew out of my hands and landed atop the *Proceedings*, which I had placed on my desk, still creased open to Einstein's equations. I went home and lay in bed for days. Friends from work stopped by, concerned for my well-being. Some delivered food, but I could hardly eat; others a bottle of wine, but I would only retch it back up. I had no interest in war. In truth, I'd hardly thought about it at all; for so long it had been something in the distance. What a small thing it was when compared to the ticking clock that is our universe.

A few days later, after I was able to summon the strength to leave my bed, I walked to the university. The weather had suddenly turned cold, the fiery colors of autumn replaced by winter's slate skies. The beech trees lining the roads were bare now. I informed my superiors of the summons I'd received. A few were empathic, but most patted me on the shoulder. "Congratulations, young man. Were I as young as you, shoulder to shoulder, we would march into war for the glory of Germany!"

That night I ate dinner with my family. It was a quiet meal. I hardly ate any of my mother's rabbit stew. My uneaten portion was finished off by Efrayim, my younger brother. In the morning, I bid farewell to Efrayim, and my mother, who wept. My father walked with me to the train station and gave me all the extra money he had.

"For the journey, for food, so your mother knows you're fed," he said.

"The army will feed me now."

He nodded. "I suppose they must. You are smart, be sure to tell them that. They won't want to waste men like you in the trenches."

"Yes, Father," I said, feeling the weight of my suitcase in my hand.

My father opened up his shirt and removed a threaded necklace that he had always worn. Strung on it was a gold Star of David.

"This was once my father's, and his father's, now it is yours."

I went into the central station and boarded the ten o'clock train to Berlin. I sat in a seat next to a window and watched the winter forest go past as the train sped away from Weimar, from home. I was twenty-three years old.

My father was right, mathematics kept me away from front-line duty in the trenches. I was trained in artillery, first on how to operate field pieces: assemble, disassemble, clean, load, position, aim, fire, and to do so at an astonishing rate. The next phase of training concerned calculating trajectory, the flight path of munitions. I excelled at this, and after a number of times correcting our instructing officer on mathematical errors, I ended up reteaching a number of the lessons at night to my fellow soldiers.

Calculating trajectory is basic physics and trigonometry, for the most part. The variables, being the precision of the equipment, a worn-out barrel for example, and atmospheric pressure, the wind, all could send a shell off its calculated flight path. In the right conditions, however, we were able to fire at targets nearly ten kilometers away and come within ten meters.

After my training was completed, I was assigned to the

2nd Royal Saxon Corps in Belgium, near a town called Ypres, as a member of the field artillery regiment; one hundred and forty-four guns in all. When my comrades discovered me reading one of Einstein's publications in 1917, they started calling me 'Asbert Wasstein'. By mid-1917, I was commander of the regiment's sixteen-heavy artillery pieces, now famed for their precision. According to captured British and Canadians soldiers from the trenches opposite us, they called our heavy guns the 'angels of death'. I did not take joy from knowing this, the death I dealt out. I wanted to get back home to Weimar. Return to the university and begin a career in teaching and research as I'd always hoped.

In the evening of 6 June 1917, I was struck down by a terrible case of dysentery. I spent the night emptying myself into the latrine ditch. I woke around three o'clock in the morning, shaking and covered in sweat. I stumbled through the darkness toward the latrine, trying to undo my belt as I walked. It was then that I felt what could only be described as the hand of God. Unknown to us at the time, British and Canadians miners had spent months digging tunnels deep beneath our lines, the excavated pockets filled with metric tons of high explosives. I survived only because I was behind the front lines, yet the explosions' percussive force tore through me. My ear drums burst, and I coughed up blood. Towering fountains of fire ascended into the night sky. Moments later, the first of the debris began to crash down around me: dirt, rocks, bits of wood and concrete. Then came the shower of burnt bodies and limbs.

Trapped within this horror, I couldn't help but think of Einstein's equations. In the days following the ensuing battle, it was estimated the explosions killed nearly ten thousand

German soldiers, most instantly. When I did return home to Weimar to begin my work, I still dreamt of it, the thunderous rain... limbs and bodies crashing down all around me.

After the war, I lived quietly in Weimar. I would rise before the sun and walk to the university along empty streets, stopping at the local bakery and butcher shop to pick up items for my afternoon meal. During the morning, back in the basement as an adjunct professor, I continued my research. In the late morning, I would teach my first class of the day, followed by a break to eat, which I would usually take in the park. I liked to sit at the base of a tree, my back pressed against its board trunk, and look out at the world. I tried to look past all the discord gathering around me. Surrender had brought shame and hardship. On the Sabbath I wouldn't attend temple, instead I would go for long walks in the beech woods around Weimar. The forest was a different sort of temple, I thought. Walking, I would contemplate many things, the war, geometry, Einstein; but in truth, I tried to be quiet, to think of nothing and just place one foot in front of the next.

By 1923, my brother Efrayim, by then a master apprentice to the finest tailor and dressmaker in Weimar, convinced me to return to Temple with him after the death of our father who simply did not wake one morning. At Temple, I recited holy words, but only in mimicry. I listened to the rabbi, but only in placation to my brother and sorrow-filled mother. Afterwards, with everyone gathering outside to bid farewell or to make plans to meet during the week, a young woman approached me.

"Excuse me," she said.

I turned and met her eyes, hazel. "Yes?" I said.

"My sister is coming of age and could use a new dress for

her bat mitzvah. I was hoping you could help us?"

She was slight, but strong.

"My parents tell me you are a fine dressmaker…"

"Still an apprentice…" I suddenly said, not wishing to introduce her to Efrayim without talking to her longer.

"A master apprentice, that is," I continued. She smiled.

"My name is Mira," she said, "and that is my little sister, Golda."

On a spring day in 1924, under a beech tree in full bloom, Mira and I wed. It was the happiest I'd been, and since falling in love with her I'd stopped thinking of the war. The dreams began to fade. The next year, Mira was pregnant with our first child. I had become an associate professor in the mathematics department and was able to afford a new home in central Weimar near many of our friends and colleagues. The winter morning Mira went into labor, we'd run out of coal. I could see Gershom's breath as he knelt beside Mira who lay in our bed in a great deal of pain. The labor lasted three days, and on the third day, Gershom took me out into the hallway and told me the child was in breach.

"It is best for you to stay out here, Askel," he told me.

Gershom went back into our bedroom and closed the door. A minute or so later, Mira screamed. I could not remain in the hallway and so rushed back into the bedroom. Gershom had reached inside Mira and rotated the child. Blood poured from between Mira's legs as Gershom pulled the child out, a girl, Illa, steam rising from her head.

"Take the child!" Gershom ordered one of the midwives as he began working frantically to try and save Mira's life.

I held Illa in my arms; she was still naked, covered in blood, wailing. A midwife cut the umbilical cord, while another took her from me and began cleaning and wrapping her in a blanket. Mira survived but she was very weak.

"I do not know if she will last the night," said Gershom, exhaustion draining his eyes. "One thing is for certain, if she does live, she will never be able to bear children again. I'm sorry, Askel, there was nothing else I could do. It's in God's hands now."

"It always was, my friend," I said. "He worked through you to give us our daughter."

I lay beside Mira for a week as she lingered near death. At night, while sleeping, she struggled to breath. I would place my hand on her chest and feel her heartbeat. Illa would sleep between us. On the seventh day, Mira woke, color restored to her face, and for the first time she greeted Illa and held her in her arms.

Two years later, to Gershom's astonishment, on 6 October 1927, Yom Kippur, our second daughter, Eliana, was born.

"She is a gift from God," I told Gershom, holding Eliana in my arms.

Instead of atoning, we celebrated, just the four us: Mira, Illa, Eliana, and I, together.

We enjoyed the following years, but Germany began to change. Many of my Jewish colleagues at the university, and throughout the nation, ignored it, and to a great extent so did Mira and I. We had a happy and simple life. The girls grew quickly, especially Eliana, who, from a very early age, showed a keen ability to focus intensely. By the '30s, the rise of anti-Jewish, and anti-Semitic beliefs was becoming more blatant. On a number of occasions, students appeared in my lecture hall wearing the all-brown uniforms of the national socialists. They made it a point to denounce me in front of their fellow students before storming out. More and more, there were stories of Jews and political liberals being accosted in the streets. We all thought it would simply go away one day, and the Fatherland would return to its senses.

In 1933, after the national socialists came into power, they enacted the *Law for the Restoration of the Professional Civil Service,* which forbade non-aryans and Jews from working in the civil service. This included being professors at universities. I went home and told Mira I no longer had a job at the university. She wept all night. We made the decision not to tell Illa and Eliana that I no longer worked at the university. They would not understand anyways. The next morning, I began submitting applications to work at local primary schools. That night, I dreamt once more of the war, of body parts raining down upon me.

Later that year, after our mother died of influenza, Efrayim told me he was emigrating to England, and wished for Mira, the girls, and I to join him.

"You must see what is happening in the streets?" he argued. "It's every day now, one of us is attacked, and the police do nothing. In many cases it is the police threatening us. Besides, what German is going to buy a suit or dress from a Jew now?"

"We are all Germans, Efrayim. I fought for Germany."

"Perhaps we once were, but not any more, brother; now we are just Jews."

"We can't just up and leave, Efrayim. What about the girls? Losing my position at the university has greatly reduced my income; we barely have enough money to pay for our home and food as it is. How am I to afford travel to England, and with no work awaiting me there?"

"You will teach. You always tell me math is the universal language. You will learn English in time, we all will. Think of the girls, Askel."

"I am they and Mira are all I think about."

A month later, Efrayim left. He told me he feared it would be the last time we saw one another. I told him not to worry.

"We will be together again soon, here in Weimar, as always," I assured him.

He hugged me, kissed Mira on the cheek, knelt down and kissed the girls' foreheads, then departed on the next train bound for Hamburg where a ship awaited to take him to Denmark, then on to England.

Efrayim was right. Things only got worse, and by the time I realized it, we could not escape. I lost my job at the primary school. My dreams became incessant. I no longer slept, and if I did, it was during the day, while secluded in my office. The night the SS finally came for us, fear quickened my heart; it was pumping so fast I could hardly breathe. We were loaded into a truck and driven away from Weimar, deep into the forest. Illa wouldn't stop screaming, tears rolling down her puffy red cheeks.

Eliana, however, did not make a sound.

We arrived at what looked to be a large encampment, barbed wire surrounding dozens of wood barracks. The men, members of the SS, ordered us out of the truck. Their commander, and camp commandant, a man named Karl Otto Koch, was waiting. He was dressed in all black, and if not for the moon I wouldn't have been able to see him at all.

I held Illa in my arms, trying to calm her. Mira held Eliana. Koch stomped forward, berating the officer in charge of our round up. The young office snapped to attention.

"What is this? What have you brought me?" demanded Koch as he snatched Mira's arm and hauled her and Eliana over to the young officer.

"Sir, I...," said the officer.

"This is not a camp for women."

"Apologies, Obersturmbannführer!" said the officer, who pulled out his Luger pistol and shot Mira in the side of the head.

Mira collapsed to the ground, taking Eliana with her.

"Mira!" I cried, reaching out for her, but she was dead. Black blood leached from her wound into the soil. I gathered Eliana into my other arm and turned away so neither Illa nor Eliana could see their mother lying dead on the ground.

"Idiot! What are you doing?" said Koch.

"Ridding the camp of women, Obersturmbannführer," answered the officer. Koch stepped over Mira's body.

"Take them to the crematorium before you execute them," said Koch, shaking his head. "Now you'll have to carry this one all the way there. This will be an efficient camp, understood?"

"Sir!"

The SS officer ordered his men to seize Illa and Eliana, along with the other women that had been rounded up by mistake and take them to the crematorium.

"No!" I fought with the SS trying to take Illa and Eliana from me.

One of the SS struck me in the side of the head with the butt of his rifle. They tore my children away from me.

"Illa! Eliana!" I said.

"Papa!" wailed Illa.

The soldier carried them in his arms, heading toward the

camp's central gate. "What's all this commotion?" said a young, barbed voice from the darkness. Koch turned to see a woman stood behind him: his wife, Ilse.

"Darling, what are you doing out there?" sighed Koch.

"I wanted to see what was going on, it all sounded like so much fun. Are those little girls? Bring them here. Order that man to bring them here," she snapped.

Koch did as his wife instructed and the soldier presented Illa and Eliana to Ilse.

"Oh, look at these two little Jewesses, twins by the look of them. Aren't they just little birds? Look, this one is shaking. What were you planning to do with them?" Ilse asked her husband.

"Depose of them. There are no women in this camp," said Koch.

"These aren't women," said Ilse, leaning over and pinching Illa on the cheek. "Just little girls. And I need some little girls for the house. I'll train them right up, to clean, fold clothes, and polish the silver. Yes, these two will do nicely. Have them brought to the house at once."

Koch flicked his head at the soldier who picked up my daughters and took them away. Ilse followed, excitedly skipping into the darkness.

15
Peter

In a rarely visited corner of Yad Vashem, near the archival office, a wood slat, once part of a bed frame, hangs on the wall; it came from one of the prisoner barracks at Buchenwald concentration camp. A line of Yiddish is etched into the slat, the Talmudic words:

In all creation there is not a single thing to which God did not give purpose.

The inscriber, and whether they survived, is unknown; I pray they did, but each time I walk to the archives I find myself stopping to read the inscription. The wood itself is old and dry now, the etching slowly fading away. Study it closely and you will see the carver's blood staining the wood's grain, for whatever they used to etch the words also must have cut into their fingers.

It had been two months since Yitzak's death. Chaya was still lost in grief. Her soul was withering away, same as her body; she hardly ate, and when she did, she would drink wine until she blacked out.

When I stopped buying wine, she refused to eat at all. Before leaving for the airport, I took her to her parents' new home in Haifa. They would not live in the place where their grandchild died. Miriam prepared her daughter soup. Isaac put his hand on my shoulder.

"We will take care of her," he said. "Try to enjoy your trip.

Maybe tomorrow we'll take her to the beach. She's always loved the ocean."

"Keep her away from water, Isaac," I said. "It's not good for her."

"Yes, of course," he nodded.

The flight from Tel Aviv to Paris took six hours. I slept most of the way. When I woke, I smelled the lobster being served in first class, followed by the joyful 'pop' of a champagne bottle. I sank down into my seat, lit a cigarette and looked out the window. Below us were the Alps, dressed in an impenetrable shroud of ice and snow. When we landed, I put on my coat, the warmest I had, but Israel's winters are nothing compared to Northern Europe. I shivered waiting for a taxi, my fingers hardly able to change my watch to Parisian time.

"20 Rue Pascal," I told the driver.

It was evening, but the city of lights was obscured by a dense winter fog which soon became a misting rain as we traveled into the city's center. Entire buildings and avenues disappeared, defaced by the fog like worn tombstones. The streetlamps were ethereal, their radiant glow diffused, ensnared by the misting rain and fog.

We arrived at the hotel, and I paid the driver.

"Merci," I said, climbing out and retrieving my suitcase and briefcase from the truck.

The taxicab sped away. I pinched the collars of my coat together and quickly walked toward the hotel's entrance. I pushed the door in with my shoulder, shaking off the chill after I entered. The lobby was quiet and forgettable. I walked over to the woman sat at reception.

"Bonjour," I said, which was about the extent of my French. She looked up.

"Bonjour, monsieur," she said, gently putting her long cigarette down on the corner of an ashtray.

"Reservation… Wolfman, Peter," I said, handing her my passport. She took my passport and examined it.

"Ah, juif…" she said, which I guessed meant 'Jew'.

She did not turn me away, but neither was she pleased to give keys to a Jew. The room was on the third floor and had a single window looking out at Rue Pascal. Rain continued to fall. I opened my briefcase and took out a large folder filled with black and gray photographs. I sat down next to the window, turned on the lamp and settled in. The folder was labeled *Buchenwald, 1938-41*, and contained the many grotesqueries of Dr Ziegler's work.

In the morning, I woke to the sun shining in my eyes. I sat up; the photographs scattered all over the bed. I had slept with them, like a child with toys. I went into the bathroom and vomited into the sink but had nothing in my stomach. I rinsed out my mouth and washed my face.

I collected the photos, dressed, and put on my watch: 8:37. With my briefcase in hand, I went to a patisserie across the street and got some coffee. The streets were choked with people. It was not the typical crowd of a large city. They were all marching in the same direction, north toward the city's center. The crowd was young and multiethnic. They carried signs and placards, though I could not read them.

Some of the signs were the portraits of French President, Charles de Gaulle; red paint had been added, smeared over his face and hands. I took the red paint to symbolize blood. I didn't know France was so restless. I walked opposite the marchers like a fish going upstream. Threading through their lines as they chanted what I could only imagine were derogatory remarks, all I could think was that I was going to be late.

My hotel was in the Latin Quarter, and I needed to get to Saint Germain. A taxi would be pointless, and I found out the metro system had been shut down because of the protests. After buttoning up my coat, and with my hands deep in my pockets, I began walking southwest. Every so often I would step in front of someone, or a couple, point abstractly west and say, "Rue de Rennes?" Most brushed past me, others nodded, some took the time to explain in detail how to arrive at Rue de Rennes, but I didn't understand them. All I could do was nod politely and continue walking in the direction they had so effusively gesticulated.

After many wrong turns, I arrived at number 17 Rue de Rennes at 11:17. I could not feel my nose it was so cold. I rang the buzzer for apartment eight. There was no answer. I rang again. Still no answer. I thought about ringing other apartments to see if they might allow me in to get out of the cold, but how to communicate? I buzzed number eight one last time before resigning myself to return later in the afternoon and try again.

"Allo?" said a static yet feminine voice through the intercom.

"Bonjour," I said, somewhat startled. "Je... Je suis Peter... Peter Wolfman. Madame Lilien?"

"Hello, Mr Wolfman," the voice said in Yiddish.

"Ah, Ms Lilien, apologies for being so late, the streets are swarmed with protestors..."

"It's all right, come up, Mr Wolfman."

The buzzer rang, unlocking the front door. I entered. There was a short hallway with hooks for coats and a tall decorative vase for umbrellas. I undid my coat but kept it with me as I climbed the spiraling stairs to apartment number eight.

I knocked politely and waited. The door opened, slowly at first. The apartment was dark. A pale set of eyes emerged.

"Peter," said Ms Lilien. "You've come a long way."

"Good morning, Ms Lilien. Again, apologies for my tardiness. It is not a habit of mine. This is my first time to Paris, and I'm unfamiliar with it. The streets are overrun with people, protesting."

"Yes, come in," she said, closing the door behind me. "You can hang your coat up there. Would you like some tea... coffee, perhaps?"

"Tea would be wonderful if it's not too much trouble. I am also not used to this kind of weather," I said, hanging up my coat and rubbing feeling back into my nose.

"Paris is a beautiful city when it wants to be, even in winter," she said, walking to the kitchen of her small apartment. She filled a kettle pot with water and lit one of the burners on the stove. "It's de Gaulle, if you haven't heard."

"What is, Ms Lilien?" I asked, entering the sitting room adjoining the kitchen.

The apartment was lovely, but spartan; lived in, yet lonesome. There were no pictures or portraits anywhere on the walls or shelves, no reminders of family and friends. Instead, the walls, papered over with a design of yellow flowers, were adorned with reproductions of French artwork, probably from the Louvre's gift shop, and strange little impressionistic paintings one might purchase from a struggling street artist. She had surrounded herself with fabricated beauty; things others tell us are beautiful and so we accept that they are. The reproductions made her home feel all the more destitute of life somehow.

"The protests. They're about the President. Parisians are

generally a restless bunch, always complaining about something. But don't worry, it will calm down tonight when they all go home to drink and make love."

"I saw many signs and placards with de Gaulle on them, painted red."

"He visited Algeria last week, riots and street fighting ensued. Many people were killed, according to the papers. Hundreds, maybe. With so many colonies declaring independence this year, de Gaulle tried to draw a line in the sand as it were. But as life so often remind us, nothing is certain."

"Yes..." I said. I felt the sensation of Yitzak's listless body in my arms.

"I don't pay attention to it much. Sometimes I think the world has simply passed me by. That I'm supposed to be living another life somewhere else."

The kettle began to whistle. Ms Lilien put dark brown tea bags into cups and poured the boiling water on top.

"Do you like lemon, or sugar?" she said. "Although I'm not sure I have any sugar... I'm told its still being rationed in England."

"No, thank you, I'm fine with just tea."

She put the cups on a tray and came into the sitting room.

"I always like a little lemon in mine," she smiled. "Please, have a seat, make yourself comfortable."

"Thank you, Ms Lilien," I said, placing my briefcase on the floor.

"And please, no need to be so formal, Peter, I'm not that old. Please, just call me Golda."

"Yes, of course, Golda, thank you."

"You said during your telephone call last week that you

work for Yad Vashem, and that you're conducting interviews with survivors?"

"Yes, that's correct."

Golda squeezed a slice of lemon into her tea, then swirled it with a spoon.

"I feel privileged you should come so far just to speak with me. Certainly, we could have talked over the telephone."

"I'm interviewing many other survivors…" I lied, taking up the tea, blowing across its surface to cool it, and taking a sip. It burnt my tongue.

"I see… and what would you like to know?"

"Just your story, in your words, however you'd like to tell it," I said, putting the tea down, and picking up my briefcase. Inside was a tape recorder which I took out and placed on the coffee table.

Golda stared at it for a moment.

"To be honest, I try not to think about it," she said, still studying the recorder. "After receiving your call, I've had troubling dreams all week."

"I'm sorry, Ms Lilien… Golda, I certainly don't wish to cause you discomfort."

"Dreams are only dreams. The mind does what it wants."

"As I mentioned on the phone, recently, I've been looking into one particular camp, which you were held at, Buchenwald."

"Buchenwald," said Golda, her eyes tilting downward; she ran her thumb across the lip of the teacup.

"Some time in 1942, I can't remember precisely," she began, "a group of us, all women, were transported from Ravensbrück to Buchenwald. When we arrived, many terrible things were done to us."

"You do not have to speak of those things if you wish. And if you'd rather I didn't record you, I will put this away," I said, beginning to reach for the tape recorder.

"Whether I speak about what occurred, or remain silent, it does not change the fact that it happened; silence only allows others to forget, I suppose... you can record."

She swept a length of hair behind her ear.

"When I turn on the recorder, please just state your name, and then talk about whatever you wish," I said.

Golda smiled. I hit record. The twin tapes began to spin. "Do... do I just speak normally?" she whispered.

"Yes," I said.

"My name is Golda Lilien," she began, "I was born in 1910, in Weimar, Germany... I was taken by the SS to Ravensbrück camp in late 1940, where I worked fabricating German military uniforms. In 1942, I was moved to Buchenwald camp, which was near Weimar. At the time, I remember thinking it was funny to be so close to home... and yet so far away. I arrived at Buchenwald with a number of other women from Ravensbrück. Some were only just girls really. We were immediately taken to a specially built barracks. It was much finer than the others. The SS officers wanted it that way. Unlike the other prisoners, we were well fed, allowed to bathe... taken care of. We didn't have to cut down trees, build rail lines, or work in the munitions factories either... our job was to look pretty. Each night..." she hesitated, "most nights, the SS would come and have their way with us... raping us. Many of the women died from this, either due to infection, or getting beaten by an SS officer, usually because the officer was unable to... unable to perform sexually, and so took his anger out on us..."

Golda continued for at least an hour, recounting her, and

the other women's treatment at Buchenwald. That weeks before the Americans arrived, the SS stopped feeding them. There wasn't enough food to go around.

"When the Americans finally arrived, we were almost as thin as all the others... the dead were everywhere, stacked in heaps like autumn leaves. Bodies do not stack well... arms, legs, heads with tongues hanging out... to this day I can no longer eat meat. Walking by an abattoir... I suddenly feel sick... I'm rambling now, that's it, that's what I have to say."

I took the folder with the photographs out of the briefcase and laid it on my lap.

"Would you mind, Ms Lilien, if I asked you about Sascha Ziegler, the doctor at Buchenwald? You said you were familiar with him."

Golda's shoulders dropped.

"Yes, I am familiar with him. Before he left the camp, he would visit me at least once a week."

"Are you aware of his surrender and extradition from West Berlin to Israel?"

"No...," said Golda.

"I have some photos here. If you would be willing to take a look, could you identify Ziegler, and perhaps some of his accomplices?" I said, opening the folder, preparing to hand the photos to Golda.

"I'd rather not see him again," she said turning away slightly.

"Some of these other men, in the photographs, may still be free... to give them a name, well that would be a start."

"Start to what?" she said.

"Truth... justice," I said, extending the photographs toward her, forcing her to look upon them.

"Six million dead... there is no proportion of justice to

that; not even God can equal the scales. I had so many forced abortions I'm now unable to have children... how can that ever be balanced?" I did not take the photographs back but held them steady.

For you, my little Yitzak.

"Truth, then," I said. "Let it begin with truth."

Golda took the photographs and began flipping through: SS officers smiling, stood over dead bodies; doctors inspecting prisoners subjected to experimental gases; Ziegler bent over and examining a man's charred genitals, having been exposed to four hours of direct X-rays...

She's missed her in the backgrounds.

I bit my lip.

Golda came to a group photo of all the Buchenwald doctors standing shoulder to shoulder in the examination room, all smiling, save one.

She is stood beside Ziegler. Now a young woman.

"Do you recognize any of those faces? You see Ziegler, yes? Anyone else?"

Golda suddenly covered her mouth with her hand so not to gasp or scream. "Eliana..." she said, her voice shaking.

"You recognize the young woman?"

"My God, my god, my god... Eliana," she said, tears rolling down her cheeks. "What is Eliana doing in this photograph?"

"The young woman... her name is Eliana?"

"She is my niece, my sister Mira's youngest daughter... why is she here...?"

"She appears in many of the photographs, you see, here... here again... here, in the background."

"Eliana..." said Golda, clasping her mouth shut with her hand once more.

"Ms Lilien, this woman, your niece, Eliana Wasserman, is currently standing trial in Israel for crimes against humanity."

"What? What are you talking about? There must be a mistake. Eliana... she was just a girl, what did she do? She was a prisoner like all of us. What could any of us do? What do you want from me?"

"As far as I know, you are her only living relative, and with no photographs from her childhood, you are the only one able to identify Eliana in these photographs."

"I want you to leave, Mr Wolfman, immediately," she snapped, standing up and walking to the door. Golda opened it.

"Out!" Her whole body shook. "Get out!"

I turned off the tape recorder, collected it and the photographs and placed them in my briefcase.

After putting on my coat, I walked past Golda.

"I did not wish to upset you, Ms Lilien," I lied, standing in the hallway.

"Why did you do this, show me such awful things, so that I might accuse my own niece?"

"No... nothing of the sort, Ms Lilien... we need to know... my wife and I... to know who Eliana really is; we need to know who came out of that camp... and if that woman was capable of murdering our son."

I wandered back to my hotel. Later, I went out to get something to drink at a bar. Mostly wine, then absinthe. I met a woman; she was warming her feet, smoking a cigarette, and drinking wine after a long day of protesting in the cold.

"De Gaulle is a pig," she said.

We returned together to the hotel. I fucked her on the floor of my room.

I love you, my son.

16
Zoya

They called us Mountain Jews. For centuries we lived in the lands between the Black and Caspian Seas, where the rocky soil was good for goats and little else. I was born in 1915, the oldest of three, in a village over-looking the Samur River. My father didn't care I was a girl, I was the eldest, and the goat's needed protection. I first held a rifle on my seventh birthday when my father took me to the grazing fields north of our village.

We had been traveling the worn footpath all morning.

"The grey wolf is a devious hunter…" he said, every so often whistling instructions to our two dogs to keep the goats together. "It will live alone," he continued, "but hunt in pairs. When you see a grey wolf, remember, there is always another… hidden… waiting."

"Yes, Papa," I said. "I will remember."

We reached a grassy plateau a few miles from the village. Father was out of breath, but I was excited and did not feel tired at all. He sat down on a rock and took the rifle off his shoulder. For a time, we rested, watching the goats eat the tall spring grasses and wildflowers. There were no trees or thickets here; the mountain ranges were barren, undulating like giant green sea waves to the horizon.

"You see… no trees, no thickets… no shadows for the wolf, so where do they hide?"

I looked around, studying the plateau and nearby rocky slopes.

"They must hide where the eye can't see, Papa," I said finally.

"Good, Zoya, in gulches, crags, the crest of a hill, there is always somewhere to hide... the less cover, the more lethal the wolf must become to survive."

He picked up the rifle, cleaned it, then took a single bullet from the bandolier strung across his chest and loaded it in the chamber.

"There is a wolf hunting the goats right now, do you see it?" he said.

My heart raced. I began looking everywhere, my eyes darting from one spot to the next... nothing.

"Look too quickly, and you will see nothing," said Papa.

"Is it hidden, Papa? Behind a hill, in a gully?"

"We are on a plateau Zoya, there are no hills or gullies for concealment, so where must it hide then?"

"I don't know, Papa," I said, tears beginning to well in my eyes. I couldn't see the wolf.

Sat on the stone, Papa carefully rested the rifle on his knee and steadied his aim. He took a deep breath, exhaled, then fired. The shot scattered some of the goats; the dogs gave chase, returning them to the herd.

"Come, let's go see what we got," said Papa, standing up, and slinging the rifle back on his shoulder.

We walked across the plateau. I saw no wolf. Then my father stopped and pointed. "When there is only the land, the wolf will become the land," he said.

Father had shot it through the neck, severing the spine. The wolf, still alive, could not move, its back legs jerking, the muscles instinctively trying to run. From a distance, its thick, textured, grey-black fur looked like any other rock on the plateau. Papa killed the wolf with his knife and cleaned the blade in the grass.

"But Papa, where is the other one?" I said.

He turned and looked at me. That is when we heard a howling yelp. Papa ran back toward the herd. The other wolf had attacked, wounding a goat, and stealing another. The dogs chased after it. Papa knelt down, inspecting the goat. It was alive, its belly torn open.

"It's all right, little one," he said, stroking the goat's head.

He quickly took another bullet from his bandolier, loaded it, and handed the rifle to me. "Zoya, do it quickly, don't let him suffer," he said.

"Papa?" I said, looking into his dark eyes

He reached up and tilted my chin down so that all I could see was the dying goat. "Don't let it suffer, Zoya."

I placed the rifle against my shoulder, held it steady, then pulled the trigger.

After the fascists invaded, I arrived at the Central Women's Sniper Training School in the spring of 1942, a member of one of its first classes. I had previously been in a self-defense unit, digging trenches and providing supplies to the front. Upon our arrival at the school just outside of Moscow, our instructor, Major Tatyana Shylakova, inspected each woman's hands, fifty pairs in all.

The woman next to me was immediately rejected from the school because her hands were too soft.

"I don't need seamstresses!" said Major Shylakova.

She stepped to me, snatched both my hands and turned the

palms upward. They were blistered, scared, the fingernails worn down, ugly little things. "Grew up on a farm, yes?"

"No, Major. The mountains," I answered smartly.

"Where?"

"Dagestan, Major."

She let go of one of my hands and ran her fingers down my face, feeling its features. "A Mountain Jew?"

"Yes, Major."

"Can you shoot a rifle?"

"I've killed many wolves, Major."

She laughed.

"Good, Mountain Jew, let's hope you kill many more."

Major Shylakova and her officers first taught us to be soldiers; then marksmen; finally, hunters. Shylakova was middle-aged, her hair, always tightly kept under a cap, was the color of sunlight; she was mother to all, and to none. She hungered to kill fascists, and as training continued, we too soon became ravenous.

"You will hunt in pairs!" said Major Shylakova, stood on the edge of the training field — a large expanse with targets at the other end used to teach stalking techniques. "The spotter is the eyes, the sniper the fangs, you must both learn to work as one to kill fascists."

I was paired with Nina Vinogradova, my spotter. She was a few years young than me, a stout little thing from the Ural Mountains.

"Both women of the mountains," said Major Shylakova. "You must learn how the other one moves and thinks, let your shared upbringing be the start of this."

Nina looked at me, and I at her. "Goats?" she said.

"Yes," I nodded.

"Me too," she smiled.

Training together, I learned Nina could move like a mountain goat, gracefully climbing sheer rock faces to get a better vantage of the terrain; she could also be still as a grey steppe wolf when we were hunting.

After graduation in September, Nina and I were sent to the 1st Sniper Platoon, 184th Rifle Division, fighting in Stalingrad. Whatever Stalingrad had been, it was no longer, a city of sulfur and death. We arrived on trains and were loaded into boats that ferried us across the Volga.

"There are no mountains here," said Nina, looking at Stalingrad's ruins.

At either end of the ferry, Party Political officers shouted slogans and praise, exalting the undefeated Motherland.

"Aren't mountain goats just as nimble on rubble and ruins?" I smiled.

"You won't need a spotter in this. We will be fighting street to street," said Nina.

"Building to building, girl," said the ferry's pilot, who throttled down as we arrived at the riverbank. "Try and kill one or two Germans before you die," he said.

After months of fighting, we marched through fields of frozen Germans, tens of thousands, arms and legs frozen stiff, protruding into the air like strange flowers blooming in winter. The fascists were retreating. We chased them to Kharkov, then Kursk, and Smolensk, and on and on until we reached Berlin in 1945. By then, our fellow comrades had long ago stopped treating us like women or playthings; we were the one's sent ahead to scout, crawling into Berlin's smoking ruins to lay in wait. Now they nodded their heads when we passed, acknowledging us with a simple "comrade".

Nina was killed in the final days of the battle for Berlin. She threw herself on a German grenade, saving me. The grenade had been thrown by a little boy, a Hitler Youth, who stood in the street staring at me. I shot him through the eye.

Two days later, the crimson red Soviet flag was raised above the Reichstag.

"I fucking hate Berlin," I said, sitting next to the open window. "Fifteen years, and the air still smells of death and sausages. Fucking Germans."

It was nearly dusk, the sky beginning to darken in the east.

"Remember, they're West Germans now, boss. The good guys," said Gabriel, sitting at the dining room table reading a magazine.

"They're all Nazis," I said, lighting a cigarette, "every single of one of them."

"Even the kids?"

"Hitlerjugends, the little shits," I said, remembering Nina lying on the floor of an apartment not dissimilar to this one. "They looked like fucking hedgehogs, running around with all those grenades and panzerfausts strapped to them. We couldn't shoot the fuckers fast enough."

I looked down at my watch.

"They're late," I said. "What a fucking shit show of a day, eh?"

I walked past Aaron who was still finishing up the brief, adding the last photos of Hoffman. I entered the second bedroom. Esther lay on the bed covered in glaze of sweat.

"Still shitting your guts out, eh?"

Esther leaned over the side of the bed and vomited into a bowl on the floor.

"Ya…" I said, taking the cigarette out of my mouth, "next time you're on a mission, don't fucking eat meat sold by a guy with a cart. I'm surprised they didn't teach you that."

I went back to the window and checked my watch again.

"Take it easy, boss, we're lucky they're here at all," said Gabriel.

I looked over at Gabriel, a young man with smooth tan skin and curly black hair.

"Next time, you can be the boss and I'll sit around all day. What are you reading anyways?"

"It's a magazine," he said.

"I'm not fucking blind."

"It's full of luggage, see," said Gabriel, turning the magazine around to show me the glossy pages picturing different pieces of luggage. "I think they want you to buy the luggage and go on a trip, because every few pages there is an advertisement of a vacation destination. See here, this one, we can go to the Bahamas, or a place called, Barbados… good deal too."

"I've never seen the ocean," I said. "Only mountains…"

"Boss, you've never seen the ocean. Half of Israel is coast."

"I've only ever been in Jerusalem."

Gabriel shook his head, "I'm gonna buy you some luggage, boss, and you're taking this trip to the Bahamas after this."

I smiled and put a new cigarette in my mouth.

The buzzer to the apartment rang. Gabriel put the magazine down, sat up, and leisurely went over to the intercom.

"Yeah?" he said.

"I'm looking for Mr Winterbaum," said the garbled voice. Gabriel looked at me.

"Yeah, good," I said.

He pressed the intercom and replied, "You've just missed him, I'm his nephew."

Gabriel hit the buzzer to unlock the front door downstairs. He left the apartment and returned a minute later with the deputy director, the ever-serious Mr Redlich, and a woman, a little bird of a thing, brown hair, dark eyes, simple breasts from what I could tell, and pale skin that looked untouched.

"Director Redlich, this our Chief, Zoya Rasulov," said Gabriel. I blunted the cigarette and put it in my pocket for later.

"He knows me, Gabriel," I said, walking across the room. "Good evening, Director."

"Where's the girl?" said Redlich.

I flicked my head toward the bedroom door. Redlich took a couple steps and peered in. "Food poisoning." I shrugged my shoulders.

Redlich shook his head then came back into the center of the room.

"This is Eliana," said Redlich, gesturing toward the girl who hadn't moved or spoken.

"Good," I said, "let's begin."

Aaron took Redlich and the girl, Eliana, through the brief. His name was Hoffman, Matthias Hoffman, a West German Professor with doctorates in Mechanical and Electrical Engineering, selling gyroscope designs to an Egyptian national posing as a Spanish businessman. The Egyptian, Samir Hassan, was traveling in West Berlin under the name Edgar Marin. Aaron handed Eliana a grainy photo of Hoffman stepping off a plane in Stuttgart, then others of him walking

162

the streets of West Berlin.

"We don't know where Hassan is at the moment," said Aaron, circulating the rest of the photos, "but Hoffman... he likes to get drinks after work..."

"You've found him..." the girl, Eliana, suddenly interrupted.

"What do you mean?" said Aaron.

"That's not Hoffman...," said Eliana. "He may be calling himself Hoffman, but it's not Hoffman."

"Who is he?" asked Redlich.

"That's Wolfgang Linz, a Nazi rocket scientist. He worked with von Braun and the others at Pennemünde, the development and testing site for the V-2."

"How do you know this?" I said.

"I was at Mittlebau-Dora when Linz toured the facility with von Braun. I watched him, excited as a little boy, take pleasure in installing a gyro into one of the rockets himself."

The room fell quiet. Aaron looked to me. "Continue," I said.

"Yes, so, Hoffman, or Linz, likes to get drinks after work either at one of the beer halls or the bar across the street from his apartment. That's where you come in." Aaron looked at Eliana.

"Come in where?" said Eliana.

"Make contact with Hoffman," I said, looking in her eyes, studying her, "get him drunk, seduce him, lead him where his cock wants to go."

"What?" she said, looking at Redlich, then to me. "I do analysis, not operations."

"You don't have to fuck him if that's what you're wondering," I said. "Just bring him back here."

163

"Then what?" she said.

"Then nothing, you're done."

"What if he won't come back with me?"

"Get out of there, return here. Maybe then the Office will let us do it the easy way and I can put a bullet in his head," I looked over at Redlich.

"Interrogation first," asserted Redlich. I shrugged my shoulders.

"Why not just take him yourselves?" said Eliana.

"Kidnapping in public... never a good idea, especially in West Berlin. We don't need to be confused with Stasi, then everyone would be after us."

"Why me?"

"This one asks a lot of questions." I looked at Redlich and sighed. "Do you think Hoffman, or Linz, this man, does he like to fuck old Russian Jews? Does he prefer a cock up his ass maybe?" I pointed at Gabriel. "Our normal girl is in the other room, shitting herself all day. So, you're the closest, prettiest thing we have."

"I have no training for this kind of thing," she said.

"You have all the training you need," I told her.

"Because I'm a woman?"

I took the used cigarette out of my pocket and lit it.

"No, because you're a Jew, who survived the camps. Now, you need to go get cleaned up and dressed. Gabriel, make sure the dress shows off her tits."

While the girl got ready, Redlich took me aside. "Can this be postponed?" said Redlich.

"Sure, as long as you're the one explaining to the boss why Egyptian missiles are raining down on Jerusalem in six months, and not me. You want it to stop? It stops. You don't think the girl can do it?"

"Do what? Get him to want to fuck her? Any woman can do that, even you, Zoya. She just may not be in the right frame of mind."

"When's the last time any of us were in the right state of mind?" I said, blowing smoking out my nostrils.

"Just don't fuck up, Zoya."

"You know how this works, no one can promise that."

The girl came out of the bathroom, hair curling down the back of her neck, cheeks colored like pink roses.

I examined her. "Good," I said.

I opened the dress's top button, revealing the upper curves of her breasts. "Better... one thing's for certain, if Hoffman sees you, he'll want to fuck you."

"Nothing is certain," the girl said.

I looked at her. She was expressionless.

"All right, Aaron, you've got the beer hall, Gabriel, the bar. Call if he shows, yeah." They both nodded and started to put on their jackets.

"What about us?" said the girl.

"Us? We do the same as we always do, sit and wait for the wolf."

An hour later the call came. It was Gabriel. Hoffman had just walked into the bar.

"All right," I said, hanging up the phone. "We're in luck, he went to the bar across the street from his apartment."

"Why's that lucky?" said the girl.

"Beer halls are crowded and noisy. He'll notice you at the bar. Just get him drunk and lead him back here, yes?"

"Yes," she said.

"You want a shot of schnapps before you go? Always

165

helps me," I said, offering her the bottle on the kitchen table.

"No, I'm fine."

"Good, good."

Redlich took her aside, spoke to her in the corner. I couldn't hear their conversation. I stayed by the window, smoking.

I heard the door close. I turned around and the girl was gone. From the window, I watched her walk down the sidewalk. I don't know why, but watching her move, she reminded me of the grey wolves, as though each step she took was precisely measured.

All we could do now was wait. "Schnapps?" I offered to Redlich.

"Not during an operation, Zoya," he sighed.

"Yeah, yeah..."

Hours passed. Every fifteen minutes Gabriel would call from a pay phone across the street from the bar and check in.

"She's made contact... getting drinks... still talking... still talking..."

"What do you think?" I turned to Redlich, who was slouched down in a chair, glass of schnapps in his hand. "Can she, do it?"

"I don't know," he said, taking another drink.

"What did you mean earlier, when you said she wasn't in the right frame of mind?" He drank again.

"We brought her here to see something from her past, today. Something terrible..."

"What was it?"

The phone rang, startling me. I picked it up. "Yeah, still talking?"

"No," said Gabriel in a tense voice. "They left the bar and

went up to his place."

"What?"

"She was led by him up there, boss… what do you want me to do?"

"What is it? What's going on?" said Redlich, putting down his drink and leaning forward.

"Boss, what do you want me to do?" demanded Gabriel.

"Go in, get her. Understand? Get her. We're coming," I said and hung up the phone.

Aaron ran ahead. Redlich and I followed, two middle-aged Jews running through the streets of West Berlin. Hoffman's apartment was only three streets away, but when we arrived, I could hardly breathe.

"Fucking cigarettes," I said looking up at Hoffman's apartment building.

Redlich ran past me. "What number is it?"

"Forty-eight," I huffed and ran after him.

Redlich opened the front door to the apartment building and went in. I followed. Pulling open the glass door, I went inside and looked around. The elevator doors were taped shut with a sign, "Maintenance Required".

"Fuck!" I ran to the stairs.

Entering the stairwell, I heard Redlich's footsteps echoing a floor or two above me. "Why forty-eight… fucking stairs," I said, beginning to ascend.

I reached the fourth floor and entered into the hallway. Aaron was stood outside apartment forty-eight. He looked at me and shook his head.

"Boss…" he said.

"What… what is it?" I said, out of breath.

I stumbled down the hall and through the doorway, my

hands gliding along the walls. "A fucking mess, boss..." Aaron said as I went in.

I saw Redlich first, standing in the living room looking down at the floor. Gabriel was in the kitchen, sat on the floor holding Eliana in his arms, a blanket wrapped around her naked body; her hands covered in blood. I came up alongside Redlich. The thick carpet was soaked with blood. Hoffman was naked, dead, a broken beer bottle stuck in his throat.

"Well..." I said, "one less Nazi, at least."

17
Tristan

We ran as far from the war as we could, to Cornwall, to Land's End, where the English isle's rocky shores disappeared into the blue waters of the Celtic Sea. Sighting the coast, Evelyn said it was a like a dream. The rugged shoreline had been shaped by millennia of crashing waves and surf; islets, separated from the mainland by the ceaseless tides, dotted the foaming breakwaters of hidden beaches. We drove straight from London to the coast, crossing the River Tamar, then sped along the narrow country roads, cutting through pastures and meadowlands apportioned by stone walls dating back to the Normans.

My father's old roadster still handled well, and Evelyn loved the summer wind in her hair. Our only companions on the roads were the flocks of sheep being herded from one pasture to the next, and farmers bouncing along on tractors, pulling flat beds laden with summer crops. There were a few near misses on the narrow roads as we zipped toward the coast, but each time Evelyn would look at me and laugh. She felt safe in my hands. The war couldn't touch us, here we need only worry about stubborn farm animals blocking the roads or which secluded beach to make ours for the day, and how long to bathe in the sun...

She didn't ask about it. How it was up there. Not because she didn't care or wasn't always sick with worry; she didn't want the dream to end. I could see in her eyes, in the way she stayed close me, pulling my arms around her, that she wanted to stay here forever, in this place by the sea. There was no death or suffering here, at least on the surface, but if one examined the land closer, they would find a different war being waged: one where varieties of grasses and wildflowers pushed up against encroaching thickets of bracken; where beleaguered farmers worked tirelessly to feed a nation on the brink of starvation, where the land's rocky shoals were tirelessly assaulted by the unforgiving sea...

We stayed in a secluded cottage perched on a hill overlooking a rocky inlet where the tides and afternoon sunlight were as clear and sharp and fresh snowmelt. Even in summer, the nighttime temperature in Cornwall was cold enough for a fire.

"Do you see the hearth's back plate?" said Evelyn, laying on the floor in front of the fire.

"No, what is it?" I said, coming over with another bottle of wine, one I'd snatched from the officers' lounge before leaving this morning.

I poured more wine into Evelyn's glass.

"A solid iron plate, dated 1588, the year of the Spanish Armada... the last time England was under threat of invasion."

I studied the dark grey plate through the crackling fire. Inlaid were designs of seafaring life: anchors, fish, and sails, along with a royal crown, below which stood a proud lion.

"I'm sorry, darling," said Evelyn. "I didn't mean to say that," referring to a possible German invasion. "I know we said we'd forget about all that this week."

"It's all right," I said, laying down on the floor next to her.

She lifted my head and placed it in her lap, running her

fingers through my hair.

"Do you think it will ever end?" she said, her voice denoting a seriousness and dread she'd contained within herself all day, all week, all month… since the war started, perhaps.

"All things must end," I said, staring at the fire, which was consuming the last of the wood and turning it to ash, "especially war."

In the morning, I journeyed up the road to a local farm and purchased some eggs and bread. It was only upon my return that I could smell last night's fire lingering in the cottage, the earthy scent of burnt chestnut. We fried the eggs and toasted the bread on the stove. Evelyn had found some wild orange and lemon trees in the grove adjacent the cottage. She cut them in half and squeezed the juice into a bowl, seeds and flesh included. The meal was as simple as any but tasted far better than most. After breakfast, we drove along the coast in search of a quiet beach. The drive was a constant interplay of light and shadow as we sped beneath tree canopies, beneath parading white clouds obscuring the sun. The beach, when we found it, had been hidden away, like a place long forgotten by geographers. It was surrounded on one side, like an ancient amphitheater, by towering pillars of stone, in whose crags and cracks, grasses, wildflowers, and saplings grew. The rockfaces fronting the sea were covered in a soft green moss, fed by the surf's spray and the dew from the morning's fog. The beach itself was both sand and stone. It was only us and the sea; the sound of waves breaking along the shore and then receding.

Evelyn tiptoed into the water. "It's so cold," she laughed.

I came running up behind her, gathered her into my arms and carried her into the crashing waves. She screamed from the sudden cold, but I held her tightly against me, laughing.

"I knew you were going to do that." She smiled.

I tasted the salt on my lips.

"It's always best to just dive right in, darling."

We laid out a blanket on the beach. Ate more bread. Drank wine. Evelyn read, *I, Claudius*, by Robert Graves as I tried to skip flat stones across shallow tide pools. Later, we made love, then wrapped the blanket over our heads so that it was only the two of us, and the sound of the waves.

"What are you thinking?" she said.

"What am I thinking..." I said. "That we're already out of wine." I smiled. Evelyn smiled. She had sand on her nose and chin. I cleaned it off.

"I'm thinking about what we will do when this is all over," she said.

"Our trip?"

"The war," she said.

I didn't know how to answer.

"Will you go back to teaching?" she asked.

"I suppose. I haven't given it much thought. The others, they always say it's bad luck to think about the future."

"Is that what you think?" she said.

"That luck and fate are simply two sides of the same coin?"

"Always so profound, Master Epping," Evelyn teased.

"If I were, I would be more than a schoolteacher perhaps."

"Elite bomber pilot not prestigious enough for you? Need to be like Monty, general of the whole show?"

"God, no, I can't think of anything worse... only generals receive accolades for cowardice, and awards for inaction. Honestly, I despise being an officer. The only time things make

172

any sense at all is when it's just me and the crew, up there, no radio… in all that black with only the sound of the engines to let us know we're still alive."

Under the blanket, with the waves lapping upon the shore, Evelyn was quiet. "Do you ever think about me when you're up there?" she said.

"Yes, but not until I make the turn for home."

Driving back to the cottage, the western sky was on fire as the sun began to set; below it, the sea's mirrored surface shimmered and rippled.

"It's like champagne," smiled Evelyn.

I looked out at the sea. Yes, it was like champagne in a way, warm yellows and golds, effervescent and sparkling. It was the opposite of what I knew the war to be; cold and black, the only light being the incendiary phosphorus, which we dropped atop targets for the trailing bombers. How could anything be more beautiful than the sun on the water, and her, Evelyn…

"Tristan!"

We slammed into a tractor stopped in the road because of a fallen tree branch. I was dazed, and half blind from the blood pouring into my eyes.

"Evelyn," I said, reaching out for her. "Are you all right?" The sweet smell of petrol filled the air.

"Tristan…" said Evelyn, though her voice was weak.

Flames began to grow and swirl around us. I reached out for her but was snatched away by the farmer and his son who dragged me clear of the flames.

"Evelyn!"

"Tristan!"

"Save her!" I begged of them.

"Tristan!

"Evelyn!"

"She's gone, boy'o!" said the farmer, trying smother the fire eating at my clothes.

Evelyn was trapped beneath the tractor, and now engulfed in flames, but I could still hear her crying out for me...

"Is this correct, Mr Epping?" said Eliana.

I stared out the window, having lost myself in Charlie Parker's saxophone.

"Tristan?"

I turned around. "What's that, Eliana?"

She held up the page of English composition. I took the page from her and reviewed it.

"Yes, very good, Eliana. Just be careful about splitting infinitives when doing your entrance exam. Most readers at Oxford and Cambridge detest modern usages of language or parlance in the written form."

"Why?"

"Anything that breaks with tradition is distasteful to them. The same as it is for many others in this country. The same for my parents."

"Your parents detest split infinitives?" said Eliana in a coy tone.

I laughed.

During the last two months, Eliana had slowly begun to change. Zelda said she no longer slept on the floor and had taken to her bed. She was still inherently shy, but exuberant in other ways; for example, after I taught her a new compositional phrase in English — *I think, therefore I am* — she would translate it into five or six other languages, as a sort of game, though she was the only participant. I had never witnessed anything like it. Certainly, I had read accounts of vast intelligence — Einstein, Darwin, Newton, Dickens — but had never personally witnessed such a thing at work, seen its magnificence. Her understandings of language and mathematics, in particularly, were vastly superior to mine. Even more astounding was the fact she was entirely self-taught, so she claimed. What she was missing, however, was a classical education, that of history, philosophy, and art; subjects that instill a nobler sense of life, so say college entrance exams. We listened to Chopin and Charlie Parker, Mozart and Louie Armstrong. She aggressively studied philosophy, specifically arguments concerning divinity and humanism. After watching her read Plato's *Allegory of the Cave*, I concluded she no longer believed in God, though I am unsure if she ever did.

Often, after one of our lessons, she would sit quietly at my kitchen table reading. Her eyes were never far from me; studying the scars on my neck and face when she thought I wouldn't notice her gaze. What she was searching for in my flesh, I didn't know… solace, maybe. I had tried to reconcile what had happened to her, to all of them, with what religion and philosophy said. The entire expanse of human thought and logic was laid out before us, and not a single treatise or teaching capable of translating the holocaust into something, anything, tangible. It was as black as the night sky I had flown through, and as bright as the flames I still see surrounding Evelyn in my dreams. It was pure annihilation of our collective human soul, and I did not know if Eliana, to borrow from Plato, would ever escape from the darkness of that cave her young life had been cast into.

As part of Eliana's reintroduction to life, as Zelda and Efrayim put it, she was encouraged more and more to venture out on her own, down the street to the bakery or butcher shop, to the bookstore or the post office. Eliana was even kind enough to visit the local apothecary for me and retrieve the medications meant to help with my pain.

One afternoon, after Eliana returned from the apothecary, she asked me about my scars.

"How did you get them?" she asked suddenly while in the midst of studying a painting by Goya, *Saturn Devouring his Son.*

Only a handful had ever been brave, or indifferent, enough to inquire. *From the war*, I had told them all; it was simpler that way. Most, I believe, just assumed my injuries were the result of wounds sustained in combat. Only my family, and the War Ministry, knew the truth: I was pulled from the wreckage of a burning car. I don't know why I decided to tell Eliana the truth. In a strange way, it seemed simpler.

"A car accident," I said, unraveling the apothecary's package. I knew her eyes were studying me.

"Does the medication ease the pain?"

"Partly, but never entirely," I said, dividing the medications up, crushing two pills and adding them to my tea which I drank immediately.

I took the remaining pills and separated them out, taking another two and placing them aside in a small chest on my desk.

Something for a rainy day...

"Did it hurt?" she said.

"The crash?"

"Being on fire."

I looked up at her; I studied her pale face the same as she studied my scars.

"No… not at the time. I don't remember feeling anything. But memory is malleable." I looked away.

"Yes…" she said.

I could feel the burning now, crawling up my spine.

"I try not to think of it, I suppose, same with any bad memory."

"What if you're whole life is a bad memory?" she said.

I looked at her. A breeze filled the sheer white curtain covering the window, giving it a bulging form for a moment; Louis Armstrong drifted through the air.

"Then we must learn to forget entirely, and begin again," I said.

I wrote to a fellow officer in Pathfinders, Charles Monroe, whose father held a chair at Oxford in Mathematics. I described Eliana to him, her past, and current situation, and whether he would be willing to approach his father about allowing her to sit for an entrance exam. Weeks later, Charles wrote back that he was not unsympathetic to Eliana's circumstances, and that he would forward my recommendation onto his father, but that we should not inflate our hopes. A month later, Eliana returned from an errand to the post office, and handed me an envelope with an Oxford Christ Church College insignia on it, post marked from Professor Howard Monroe, Charles' father.

Howard Monroe provided many courtesies, but concluded with, "We cannot take on each and every war refugee that happens to come our way…"

I folded the letter up and put it in my pocket. I looked over at Eliana. "How would you like to take a trip up to Oxford?" I smiled.

It had been well over a year since I had left my flat's building. I wore a hat, scarf, and sunglasses to hide my disfigurements. But many eyes still fell upon me. Eliana helped me through the train station. It was a great journey for both of us, one that took much convincing of Zelda, who had come to care for Eliana like her own child. Efrayim was very pleased, but I could see the worry in his eyes when we departed Lambeth. Eliana was the only link he had left to his family and did not wish to see her harmed in any way.

Though it was early autumn, and the light was still sharp as the train neared Oxford, the meadowlands, stitched together by tree groves and dense bramble thickets, reminded me of Cornwall, of Evelyn. Eliana quietly studied the changing landscape as well. Only once did she sit up and peer out intently, pressing her nose and cheeks against the window as the train churned past expansive fields of strawberries, picked clean from the summer harvest.

Oxford was as I remembered it; the colleges' high white stones walls encasing private gardens and dormitories; the clattering of hurried feet and bicycle tires over cobblestones; the chiming of bells denoting the start of a new hour, a new class.

"Let's see if I still remember my way around this old place," I said to Eliana. "Looking to find our way over to Christ Church College, tell me dear, what does that street sign say, my eyes have trouble at distances."

"High street," she said.

"High street, all right, and what about that one over there." I pointed to an intersection.

"Catherine street."

"Ah, good. High and Catherine, follow me then. I may have the eyes of an old man, but my ears still work, and I can hear Tom's chiming as clear as ever."

"Tom?" said Eliana.

"Great Tom, the name of the bell in Tom Tower, designed by Sir Christopher Wren. The tower and surrounding quad area encompass Christ Church College."

"Do all the colleges have their own bells?" said Eliana, as we began walking.

"Yes, many do, but old Tom is distinct to me. I attended Christ Church before I became a teacher, long before the war."

"Do you miss it?"

"Teaching?"

"Yes."

"I'm helping to instruct you, my girl," I said, patting her on the arm.

I felt Eliana clench my arm a little tighter as she helped guide my steps.

"Though we both know your abilities far exceed mine. All I hope to do is progress you on to greater minds that can help you flourish."

"I know my father was talented at mathematics," said Eliana. "I remember very little of him. Almost nothing, in truth."

"Brilliance passed down from one generation to the next, it seems."

"Did you lose your family in the war, Mr Epping?"

She'd referred to me as Mr Epping, formalizing the question, trying to take the sting out of it.

"No... my parents are alive and well, living in Sussex.

179

You will be wondering then, why it is they never come to visit me?"

Eliana stayed quiet, indicating I need not answer my own question.

"During the war, I was in love with a woman," I began. "My parents didn't approve of it, of her. Her name was Evelyn. I was with her in the car when the accident occurred. She didn't survive. And now I find myself having trouble thinking of anything else save her."

"Why did your parents not approve of her? Was she a Jew?"

"No, worse…" I looked over at Eliana and smiled. "She was black."

"There were blacks in the camp. I remember them," she said.

"Come, let us think of the future now, of better things."

We entered Christ Church College. The quad was largely empty; the central grass plaza had a smooth velvet look to it. I went into the old mathematics department spaces and began wandering back toward the Professors' offices. A secretary sat at a desk asked if we needed assistance.

"We're looking for Professor Monroe; his son is an old friend of mine from the war," I said, taking off my hat, scarf, and glasses, revealing the full extent of my injuries.

"Oh… yes, well, you've only just missed Professor Monroe," she said in a sweet voice. "He's teaching this hour."

I inquired as to which classroom, telling the young secretary that Eliana and I would happily wait outside the room for the Professor, who I again promised her was a dear friend.

We walked down the stone hallway and then up steps.

180

Light seeped through stained glass windows at the top of the steps.

"Warmer than regular windows, don't you think?"

Eliana looked up. "Light is still light, whatever its color."

"But made all the more beautiful."

Professor Monroe was teaching in one of the college's small amphitheater classrooms. There were perhaps twenty students. Eliana and I, after strong insistence from myself, entered the classroom mid-lecture and sat quietly in one of the high echelon seats. The blackboards were covered in equations, graphs, and geometric designs. I could make little sense of it, as though Monroe was speaking and writing in a foreign language, something pertaining to the algebraic geometry of projective spaces is all I could grasp. I could see in Eliana's eyes, however, that this was another language in which she was already fluent.

Professor Monroe hadn't noticed us enter; his back turned as he scribbled an equation on the blackboard.

"Anyone want to take a guess at this... so many young minds," said Professor Monroe, turning and addressing his class.

"Come now," he continued. "Homogeneous polynomials..." None of the students, all young men, dared posit an answer.

Eliana raised her hand.

18
Isaac

I drained the pool after Yitzak's death. It's a strange thing to look at now. It has no purpose, like a dull blade, or an old soldier. The pool is slowly being filled by nature's waste: dust, dry leaves, wildflower seeds, pillowy-white bird feathers; when the winds swirl, this detritus forms a brief whirlwind, and that which was ugly and meaningless is made beautiful for an instant. But then the wind dissipates.

Most days Miriam keeps to herself. We hardly speak. Grief permeates the house like mist, creeping into every grain of wood and stitch of fabric, reminding us all of Yitzak. Every other day we visit Chaya and Peter. It has been two weeks since the burial and Chaya is still inconsolable. She has the same look as soldiers stricken with shellshock, her eyes, disentangled, are unable to focus on anything, so they wander. Neither Miriam, Peter, nor I know how to pull Chaya out of her grief, so instead, we have all waded into its shallows with her. Miriam cooks food; Peter focuses on work; I do the only thing a soldier can, stand watch.

One afternoon, sitting in the living room, I pulled a book from one of Peter's shelves and began reading it. It was a Polish explorer's account of his travels in Africa during the late 1800's. I know next to nothing about sub-Saharan Africa, its nations, peoples, tribes, languages... even its geography is a mystery to me. In one of the later chapters, the explorer describes his encounter with a group of men, known as Bushmen, who live in a desert called the Kalahari. He accompanied them on a hunt, which was unlike any the explorer had ever witnessed. The Kalahari is so dry and bereft of water, few trees grew there, and those that do don't produce wood suitable for crafting throwing spears and bows. Moreover, the open desert makes stalking prey nearly impossible. Without missile weapons, and an inability to close distance with the prey, the Bushmen developed an entirely new form of hunting, as described by the Pole. A hunting party, generally three to five men, sets out in the early morning before the sun has risen, tracking fresh prints of large beasts. Once a herd is found, usually near one of the few watering holes, the Bushmen would sit and search, not for the weakest and smallest beast on the plain like all other predators, but for the strongest and most robust. Once the beast is selected, the Bushmen, who each carry only a short spear and gourd filled with water slung across their chest, spread out and surround the beast. They dare not approach the animal for fear of being trampled or gored by its long twisting horns. Instead, they keep a safe distance, only going near the beast when it is headed toward water. The Bushmen scare the animal away simply by walking toward it. This continues all day, and into the next, until finally, the beast, sick with thirst, is felled by its own massive weight and strength. At that point, a Bushman walks over and put his spear through the exhausted animal's throat.

The phone rang.

Peter was closest, but Miriam rushed over and answered it. She wanted to feel as though she were doing something.

"Hello," she said.

"Oh, Jacob, is that you?" she continued. "How are you…

what? Yes, he's here... I'll get him..." Miriam moved the phone away from her mouth.

"Isaac, it's Jacob, he needs to speak with you."

I closed the book and laid it on the sofa. "Coming," I said.

"He's coming right over," said Miriam. Miriam held the phone against her chest.

"Something's wrong, I can hear it in his voice," she told me. I nodded and took the phone.

"Jacob, what's going on?" I said.

After getting off the phone with Jacob, I drove south to Tel Aviv. Miriam asked where I was going. I said Jacob needed help with some administrative things that he was unable to see to himself at the moment.

"What things?" she asked.

"I'll be back as soon as I can," I said, and kissed her on the forehead.

Jacob told me Eliana had been arrested and was being held at Kele Arba, a military prison and detainment facility located in Camp Tzrifin just north of Tel Aviv. Thankfully, the camp commander was an old friend of mine, Colonel Ganit Yadin. Arriving at the camp, I informed the watchmen on duty that General Isaac Nazarian was here to see Colonel Yadin. The watchmen looked at my civilian clothes and my car.

"Do you have an appointment, sir?" said the guard. I looked the young man up and down.

"General Isaac Nazarian to see Colonel Yadin, Corporal. Make the call."

Ganit met me in his office twenty minutes later.

"General Nazarian," Yadin smiled, looking up from his desk, as his adjutant showed me in.

"Ganit, my friend, how are you?"

"It is good to see you, if so unexpected."

"I apologize for the unannounced visit, Ganit, but I urgently need your help."

"What is the matter, General?"

"I received an urgent call from my son, an army Captain in the commandos. He's been informed that his wife is being detained here."

"Your son's wife is here, at Tzrifin?"

"So, he says. I am here to see and speak to her."

"I'll see what I can do. What is her name?" said Yadin, picking up his telephone.

"Eliana Nazarian…"

"Eliana?" said Yadin, the telephone slightly dropping from his ear. "General, what is your daughter-in-law's maiden name?"

"Wasserman, Eliana Wasserman."

Yadin hung up the phone.

"The special package," he said, as though talking to himself.

"What are you talking about? Is she here, do you know of her?"

"She arrived three days ago in the custody of State Security and the Justice Ministry. I have orders to hold her until she is transferred to Jerusalem."

"I want to see her immediately."

"I'm sorry, Isaac, I have orders that she is to see no one, only her husband or blood relatives. I am only to keep her well, and alive."

"Alive? What the hell is going on?"

"She's on suicide watch. I don't know any of the details of why she's been arrested. I'm merely the gatekeeper in this

185

instance."

"I must see her."

"Only her husband or blood relatives are permitted," said Yadin again.

"My son is away, and Eliana has no family left. They all perished in the war."

"I'm sorry, my friend. There's nothing I can do."

"Do you have contact information? Who from the Justice Ministry arrived here? I want to talk to them."

"It's no use, Isaac, this comes from the prime minister's office... it has something to do with diplomatic relations with West Germany."

"West Germany? What are you talking about?"

"Like I said, I don't know the details... the only thing I can tell you... do you remember Sagiv Redlich?"

"The Major whose body we recovered from the olive grove?"

"Yes, I know the family. His younger brother, Elon, he works for State Security now."

"And he might be able to get me some information about what's going on?"

"He knows what's going on... he accompanied your daughter-in-law all the way to her cell when she arrived."

I drove to Tokhnit Lamed, a neighborhood in northwest Tel Aviv where Yadin said he last knew Sagiv's parents were living. I parked my car and began walking around, asking passersby whether they knew the Redlich residence, Abel and Rachel. After an hour it was already night. I stopped at a corner cafe and asked around.

"Excuse me, do you happen to know an Abel and Rachel Redlich?" Each person shook their heads, no.

I continue on, stopping a street down in front of a synagogue. If anyone would know the locals, it would be the Rabbi. The synagogue was dim, its cavernous space illuminated by a single oil lamp flame, the eternal light set before the ark where the Torah scrolls were kept. I let my eyes adjust. The temple was empty save a single man sat in a chair near the altar. He was rocking back and forth, praying. I approached him.

"Excuse me, Rabbi?"

He was a large man; his dour eyes reflected the wavering eternal light. "I'm not the Rabbi, sir."

"Pardon me for disturbing you."

"It's all right," he said.

"Do you know if the Rabbi is in? I am looking for a couple that live in this area but am unfamiliar with it."

"I have not seen him. Who is it you are looking for?"

"Abel and Rachel Redlich, but more importantly, their son, Elon."

"Then we have both witnessed a small miracle. Abel and Rachel are my parents, and I am Elon. What is it you are looking for?"

"I am Brigadier Isaac Nazarian, retired. You should know that name, Nazarian, and therefore know why I have sought you out."

"I have seen the name in her file, but at the Office she goes by Wasserman. I take it you are Eliana's father-in-law."

"Yes."

"I don't know how you found me, but you should not have come looking, General."

"Israel is a small place, and I come for my son, and for Eliana. I love her as though she were my own blood."

"You know I can't tell you anything, General."

"What has happened to her? You can at least provide that. I have come all the way from Haifa. I left my daughter and wife, who are in the midst of mourning the loss of our only grandchild, not two weeks ago."

Elon turned away and looked at the flame.

"I'm sorry, sir. I can't say anything, that is the oath we take."

"Can you tell me when she will be transferred to Jerusalem?"

"No, that decision is far above me."

I sat down in a chair. Pain from my hip shot up my side. I let out a sharp breath.

"Are you all right, General?"

"Yes... I'll be fine."

The pain began to subside, though my hip still tingled.

"I came to this synagogue looking for you. Why is it you're here so late?" I said.

"My mother is dying. I am asking God's forgiveness and mercy."

"For her, or for you?"

"Both," he said in truth.

"You will not know this, but I was one of the men that recovered your brother, Sagiv's, body from the olive grove in 1948 when the Palestinians took him."

"You found him in the grove?"

"Yes."

"And you saw him?"

"Yes."

"How did he look? The army would never say."

"It was a kindness they didn't."

"Is that what you think?"

I held my tongue a moment.

"They had soaked him in petrol and lit him on fire just as we got there. I shot your brother in the head so he wouldn't have to feel what it was like to burn to death. We carried what was left of him back with us, so your parents had something more than ash to bury the next day."

"And for this... kindness you afforded my family, you wish the favor returned?"

"All I ask is to know what happened to Eliana," I said.

The eternal flame burned between us. Redlich bowed his head.

"Eliana was in West Berlin," he began. "There to identify a Nazi war criminal..."

"How would she know anything about Nazi war criminals? Her parents sent her to England before the war."

"Is that what she's told you?"

"Yes. Her father, Askel, sent her to live with his brother, Efrayim, in London a few years before the war started, before things got too bad and the rest of them couldn't escape."

A sad half-smile crept across Redlich chin.

"Eliana Wasserman wasn't sent to England. In 1937, Eliana, along with the rest of her family, was rounded up by the Gestapo and taken to Buchenwald concentration camp just outside Weimar. Sometime in 1943, she was transferred to Mittlebau-Dora, where she worked as slave labor constructing V-2 rockets. Eliana survived eight years in the camps before being liberated. From a displaced persons camp, she requested asylum in England based on her uncle's status there, arriving in London in the summer of 1945."

"My god..." I said. "All this time, and never a word..."

"In West Berlin, she was tasked with identifying a Nazi war criminal, a doctor named Sascha Ziegler, who spent the war experimenting on Jews, Roma, and Russian POWs at Buchenwald. Once Eliana completed the identification, her presence was requested in support of a covert operation."

"Covert operation? She's only a secretary at State Security," I said.

Elon looked at me and I suddenly realized my own ignorance.

"During the course of the operation, Eliana killed a man. Not the worst thing; he was a former Nazi, from what we know now, but unbeknownst to us, he was also an agent for the West German Federal Intelligence Service, who had surveillance on his apartment."

"What does that mean for Eliana?"

"It means the West Germans have a recording of her killing the target."

"All this for a fucking dead Nazi?"

"I haven't heard the recording... but Eliana is under investigation from the Justice Minister... apparently before she killed the target, he identified her as Dr Ziegler's assistant, the Jewish girl notorious amongst Buchenwald survivors, known as the *Angel of Death*."

I walked to my car and started the long drive home to Haifa. It was past midnight when I pulled over to the side of the road, shaking. I got out of the car and walked out into the darkness beside the roadway, and for a moment I thought I saw a group of African Bushmen in the distance, slowly walking towards me.

19
Fenna

When, in the summer of 1954, I learned I'd conceived the child that would become my son, Matthijs, I was filled with utter joy. Maarten, my husband, also a survivor of the camps, held me tightly and kissed my cheek.

"My loves," he said, placing his hand on my belly.

That afternoon, we celebrated by having a picnic on the banks of a river by our home in Dokkum, a small farming community in northern Holland near the sea. Maarten wanted to invite family and friends, but I told him I just wanted it to be us, at least for a day... just the three of us.

"Of course, my love," he smiled. "I'm just going to head to the market, pick up a few more things."

I started to fill our basket: dried fish, crackers, cheese, a bottle of sparkling wine. When Maarten returned, we rode our bicycles down to the river, then walked along its southern bank until we found a beautiful spot beneath the shade of a large beech tree that caught the cool breezes coming off the river. I laid out the blanket while Maarten unpacked the basket.

"I got some fresh fruit at the market," he said, laying raspberries, oranges, and strawberries out next to the cheese, fish, and bread.

We made dried fish and cheese sandwiches, after which Maarten opened the bottle of sparkling white wine, pouring us each a glass. He dined on the fruit, eating raspberries one by one. I meticulously peeled an orange, casting the bits of rind into the river. The orange was warm and juicy, though having just ripened I could still taste a slight bitterness. Maarten picked up a strawberry and dropped it into his glass of wine; bubbles fizzed around the dark red fruit. He did the same for me.

Maarten raised his glass. "To our family," he toasted.

"To our family." I smiled.

"And to all those we lost," he said.

We drank. Through the sharpness of the wine, I could taste the strawberry's delicate sweetness. It was a taste I had not known for many years, I thought. I reached down into my glass, picked the strawberry out, put it between my lips and bit down.

"How many hours of direct X-ray radiation do you estimate you were subjected to?" said Lieberman, the prosecutor. He was a short man, shorter than most, and was missing his left eye, a fact he did not try to conceal with a patch or glass eye. Instead, he seemed proud that the entire courtroom was privy to his scarring.

"I'm not sure," I answered into the microphone.

"More than one hour?"

"Yes," I said.

"More than… six hours, perhaps?"

"Yes, definitely," I said.

"Definitely… In your written statement you noted that Dr Ziegler would subject you to what seemed to be at least an hour of radiation every time you visited his medical compound."

"Yes, I think so."

"For what reason would you be brought to Dr Ziegler's

compound?"

"He would perform abortions on women and girls, the ones used for sex by the SS."

"And did you ever witness Dr Ziegler take part in this, see him rape any of the women in the camp?"

"Yes, he would always rape the same one, every week on the sabbath. She was my friend."

"How many times were you made pregnant after being raped by one of the SS at Buchenwald?"

"Seven," I whispered.

"At least seven," Mr Lieberman reiterated in a thunderous voice.

"Seven, exactly," I said with more confidence. "A woman knows how many children she has lost."

"Seven abortions... seven hours of X-ray radiation... and where did Dr Ziegler aim the X-rays?"

"At my pelvis... my uterus," I said, looking down for an instant.

"Why there?"

"Ziegler said he was trying to devise methods to sterilize Jews."

"He said this to you?"

"Yes," I said. "I remember he told us we should thank him."

"Thank him?" said Lieberman.

"Yes, he said, with sterilization... there would no longer be a need for the gas chambers, the Jewish race would instead go extinct on its own."

"Were all the women irradiated, the same as you, for an hour, after an abortion had been performed?"

"No... I was one of the lucky ones in that way, I suppose."

"You consider yourself lucky?" said Lieberman, rocking onto his back heels and then forward again.

"Yes... as strange as it might sound... I was one of the luckier ones."

"How so?"

"Some of the other girls, their sessions would last hours at a time... and multiple areas would be targeted. There were men and boys there as well sometimes, the X-ray machine directed at their... genitals. Ziegler had a particular interest in young boys, those who had not gone through puberty. I heard him discussing the young boys with another doctor once, debating whether a high dose of X-rays at a young age would sterilize a boy for life. This, they thought, would be the most effective method for mass sterilization of Jews."

"What were the physical side-effects you experienced after each session?"

"My skin was badly burned, like being in the sun too long on a summer's day... bloody discharge... blood in my urine and feces... weakness, loss of appetite... then the skin would blister. Sometimes I would vomit for days."

"And the others, those who weren't so lucky as you, as you put it?"

"Most died... their skin would turn yellow, then black, and finally semi-translucent... they were terribly sick for days, vomiting, diarrhea, blood leaking out from every orifice. They were in terrible pain. When the pain was too great many asked us to kill them, out of mercy..."

"When you were finally liberated from the camp, you returned to Holland?"

"Yes."

"You were married in 1949?"

"Yes."

"Did you and your husband try to have children?"

"Yes."

"Did you succeed?"

My contractions started the same night as the winter's first ice storm. The power went out around eight o'clock. Maarten ran outside and tried to bring in as much dry firewood as he could.

"I don't know how long the storm will last," he said, his arms full of wood as he shuffled past me, dumping the split logs next to the fireplace before heading outside again.

"The phones aren't working either… I tried calling the hospital, Dr Vissar… we may be on our own tonight, my love," he said, trying to sound reassuring. "After I get more wood in, I can try to get over to the De Vries down the road, see if their phone is working."

"No, Maarten, don't leave me here alone," I pleaded.

My heart raced.

Matthijs for a boy, Mila for a girl…

"It will be all right, my love, it will be all right," said Maarten, as he dashed back out into the storm. Another contraction started.

"Please, God, help us," I said, trying to breathe.

"Yes, I conceived a child, a boy, Matthijs. He was born in the winter of 1955."

Lieberman turned toward the three judges sitting behind raised desks on a platform. "How was the health of the child?" he said softly.

By morning the storm had passed, but thick ice coated everything. Maarten had managed to keep the fire going through the night. He tried the phone again, still nothing. The contractions were coming very quickly now. Despite seeing my lungs' vapor each time I exhaled, my entire body was dripping with sweat.

"Maarten…" I said, tears running down my cheeks, filling the corners of my mouth.

"I'm here, my love," he said, cradling my head.

"I'm scared… I don't know what to do."

He pressed his forehead against mine. "You're strong, my love."

I took a breath and pushed. I could feel my child leaving my body. I pushed again. "I see it, my love, our child," celebrated Maarten.

But after the child left my body, I looked into Maarten's eyes. There was no joy in them; they had become stone.

"My son…" tears began to well in my eyes; I fought to keep them there. "Matthijs had many deformities."

"I know it is extremely difficult, madame, but could you detail the deformities for the court?" said Lieberman.

"Matthijs… was missing his right arm… he had no ears or nose… part of his spine was exposed… and his heart had grown on the outside of his chest." I felt a single tear fall down my left cheek.

"How long did your son live after he was born?"

"We couldn't get to the hospital. There had been a terrible ice storm the night before…" I shook my head. More tears fell.

"When did he pass?"

"I held him in my arms for three hours that morning… then he slipped away. It was my fault. The doctors had warned me that conceiving a child after what had happened would be extremely difficult, but when I became pregnant, I thought

God had given me a miracle... after so much torment, he'd given Maarten and I the gift of new life."

"I only have one more question for you, madame," said Mr Lieberman. "Is the man you knew as Dr Sascha Ziegler, the man who raped, tortured, and murdered thousands of Jews, is that man present in this courtroom?"

I looked up and over at the man sat on the opposite side of the courtroom. He was in a glass booth, wearing headphones to hear the translation of my words.

"Yes, he is."

"Can you point him out?"

I raised my hand and pointed to the man in the booth, who smiled and happily waved back at me as though he were an endearing grandfather.

Mr Lieberman excused me from the testimonial stand. I straightened my dress after standing, stepped down, and was guided out of the courtroom into an adjacent antechamber where other witnesses waited to testify against Ziegler. When I entered, the others all looked at me, not with sorrow, as many of them had suffered far worse than I; instead, they acknowledged me, and I them; we'd survived and now had to find a way to live with our grief. My left thumb grazed against my ring finger, reflexively searching for my wedding band; it had been gone for many years now.

I walked down the hallway of the courthouse, threading through those who had gathered to be close to the trial: journalists, family members of the deceased, curious on-lookers. An older man exited the courtroom's main entrance just as I was passing. He made eye contact with me and smiled. I half smiled in return, then put my head down and continued walking.

"Ms Meijers," said the man, walking toward me. "Ms Meijers, may I have a moment of your time?"

I stopped. "Yes?" I said.

"I'm very sorry to bother you, Ms Meijers. My name is Uzi Willner. I want you to know I thought your testimony was very brave. You stood before a monster and did not cower."

"Thank you, Mr Willner," I said, looking down.

"I do not mean to distress you further, but might I ask you to look at something for me, a photograph taken in the camp, in Buchenwald?"

"I... I'm not sure what you mean," I said.

Mr Willner quickly took a black and grey photograph out of a folder he was holding and held it in front of me.

The picture was of four men in the lab where Ziegler conducted his experiments. Ziegler was stood centrally in the photo; two of the others were young SS doctors, Goetz and Lanker, if I remember correctly; the fourth was a tired-looking man, an assistant to all three men, I couldn't recall his name.

Mr Willner pointed to the photo, not to the four men, but to a figure in the background, a young woman with pale skin and dark hair. Partially turned, and blurred, I could only see a ghostly resemblance of her face, a single dark eye, staring at Ziegler and the others. She was dressed in the clothes of a Jew, a prisoner.

"Do you remember this woman, Ms Meijers? Do you remember anything about her?"

20

Stanislav

I was sleeping in the wooden tiered bunks when Sergei shook me awake. I'd been dreaming about fishing in the Volga with my brother and father. We'd caught a long sturgeon. Father cut it open, and we ate its eggs right there on the riverbank. Mother could use the rest of the fish to make a thick stew with celery, potatoes, leeks, and carrots.

"Hey, Stani, wake up," said Sergei, pulling at my ear lobe.

"What is it?" I said, half awake.

"Here, take it," said Sergei pushing something into my hands.

It was dark but I could still see Sergei's big black-and-yellow-toothed smile.

"A present," he said. "I snatched a few when we were in the woods today cutting trees."

Sergei scrambled away like a rat, crawling over dozens of sleeping bodies. The bunks overflowed with men. Even after a storm of typhoid traveled through the camp, winnowing our numbers, there was still hardly any room to sleep. Fleas and lice feasted on us during the nights. Men suffered from fevers, persistent coughs, diarrhea, others were simply losing their minds, seeing and hearing things that weren't there. Nikola, a fair-haired middle-aged man who'd been a field surgeon before capture, said the crazy men were suffering from something called pellagra, a particular vitamin deficiency.

I brought my hands up to my face and smelt strawberries.

There were three of them, small, only just ripe, but with a sharp scent that cut through the barrack's diseased air. I picked one out and brought it right under my nose and inhaled. I felt its distinct texture with my tongue, a delicate skin woven with rough seeds, like an armor of chain mail. I set it on my lips and could feel the seeds even more acutely.

After first arriving at the camp, the SS put us to work building new rail lines connecting the nearby munitions factories to the wider German rail network. We worked under the hot summer sun, then slogged through mud during autumn rains, and finally suffered frostbite in winter. We dug trenches, laid rails, cleared forests, leveled earth; the new rail lines now extended outward like a vast system of veins and arteries, all leading back to the munitions factories full of Jews pumping out thousands of bullets, bombs, and artillery shells every day to feed the German war machine.

I most enjoyed working in the forest. There was shade, and sometimes you were lucky enough to come by food: wild mushrooms, nuts, berries, a dead squirrel if you were lucky. Whenever the SS thought our work rate was too slow, or they simply needed to amuse themselves, they would select a number of us to be dangled from the trees. Those selected had their hands tied behind their backs. Another rope, slung over a high tree branch, was tied to the bindings and the man was hoisted into the air. The SS cackled with laughter. We worked as our comrades hung above us, screaming until exhausting themselves.

"They can't kill all of us," opined Sergei as we worked together to notch the teeth of a two-man saw blade into the trunk of a tree.

"They can if they want." I shrugged my shoulders. "They can always capture more Russians, healthier ones."

"Yes, but if they kill all of us, and bring in fresh stock, think of all the time they'd lose having to teach the new prisoners how to properly lay rail lines or cut down trees," he said with optimism.

"So, they just kill most of us, and keep a few around to train the newly arrived," I said.

"Like foremen?"

"I suppose."

"I always wanted to be a foreman at a big factory. I think I would be good at this."

"Telling others what to do?"

"Yes, I have the natural instincts for it, don't you think?"

After the ground thawed in the spring, the Germans made us into moles. We started digging deep into the earth, excavating rocks, sand, and dirt. Just when we thought we could go no farther, the Germans ordered us to continue digging. And so, we dug deeper into the earth with only lanterns for light. We dug caves and networks of tunnels; we laid rail lines. It was an underground production facility; what the Germans intended to build; however, I didn't know. Many of us died during the construction, most from exhaustion and disease, others from cave-ins or accidents. Through all this, God kept me healthy and strong. Yes, my body withered, but God fed my soul and so, day after day, Sergei and I, along with all the others still alive, went to work, descending into the darkness with shovels and buckets.

He tried not to show it, keeping up the same optimistic talk, but Sergei was getting weaker each day. I was helping him back to the barrack one evening when an SS officer ordered every prisoner from barracks 5-7 to muster in the central courtyard where roll call was taken each morning. Sergei put much of his weight onto me as we hobbled to the courtyard.

"Maybe they're having a lottery to see who among us will be set free," he said.

"I doubt it," I said.

"Always the pessimist, Stani... maybe it will be links of sausage, or a week of no work... which would you prefer, sausage or no work, hmm?"

"No, work... then I wouldn't have to listen to you talk all day."

"I would have the sausages, I think. Germans really know how to cook them, fat and juicy."

Once gathered in the courtyard, the SS officers walked around inspecting us. There was one man in particular, a Sturmbannfuhrer, who took his time examining us, as though we were crops and he a farmer looking for signs of rot and decay

"What do you think he's looking for?" I said to Sergei. "Let's hope it's who he thinks can eat the most sausages."

After the Sturmbannfuhrer reviewed us, probably five hundred or so in total, he went around again selecting men one by one. He would point and an SS guard would pull the man out of our ranks. He came to our section and pointed at both Sergei and I. The SS snatched us and pushed us into the center of the courtyard with the others, nearly fifty in all by the end. There was no common trait among us, none that I could discern. Maybe the selection had been completely random, but I didn't believe this, not with the way the Sturmbannfuhrer had looked at us, taking his time. Whatever we were, we were important to him.

The rest of the prisoners were dismissed back to their barracks. We were marched deeper into the camp to the area where the Jews and political dissidents were housed.

"Why are they moving us in with the Jews?" said Sergei.

"Maybe we're some kind of new work detail, since most of the Jews work in the munitions factories," I said.

I looked at the hollow-faced Jews stood in the doorways of their barracks, curiously staring at us trudging past. One man was sat outside on the ground in a mess of his own filth; he smiled at us.

"Brothers," he said in Polish, pointing to the sky, "do not fear, God is looking over you."

The SS yelled at us to walk quicker, beating one man with a truncheon. We arrived at a large cantonment. The SS opened a gate, and we were driven inside the building like sheep or oxen being herded. Once inside, it was chaos, the SS screaming at us as we were placed in cells; six or seven men to a single cell. Sergei and I, along with four other men, were placed together, the iron bar door slammed shut and locked.

"What is this place?" I said.

Many of the other prisoners were yelling. An SS guard took out his pistol and shot an uncompliant prisoner in the temple. He dropped to the floor. The other guards got angry at the one who had shot the prisoner, probably because they had to dispose of the body now. After we were all locked in, food was delivered to us, large bricks of bread and cheese. We were ravenous and ate as quickly and as much as we could. Men ate so much they became sick, throwing up on the floor. Not wanting anything to go to waste other men dived down and ate the vomit, licking the floor clean.

The next day, at least what seemed like the next day, I have no idea how long we were in our cells, a guard in rubber boots and a smock suddenly appeared, flicking on bright white lights that stung my eyes. He had a clipboard and was reviewing it as he walked down the row of cells. He came to our cell and muttered something to himself in German. As he opened the cell door, we all tried to scramble away, pushing to the back of the cell, climbing atop one another like rats. He pointed at Sergei.

"Raus," he ordered. Sergei didn't move.

"Raus," he said again, but still Sergei, a look of horror upon his face, refused to move.

The guard sighed and shook his head. He called out, waving his hands. Two more guards showed up and physically dragged Sergei out of the cell. He fought back, twisting and squirming like a sturgeon pulled from the Volga.

One of the guards hit him with a truncheon on the back of the head. "Stani!" said Sergei. "Help me!"

"Sergei! It will be all right."

"Stani!" Sergei cried as he was dragged into the next room.

A little while later, the guards returned, depositing Sergei back into the cell. They'd tattooed a large number on his stomach: 1301. They took me next. Once in the adjacent room, I was strapped down on a table and a Jew began tattooing my stomach, finishing a crooked 1302 fifteen minutes later. And so, it was for the rest of the prisoners, 1300-1349. That day, the first day, that is all that was done to us.

Soon thereafter, the horrors began. Prisoners were exposed to X-ray radiation for hours. The smell of burnt hair and flesh filled our cells. We were instructed to ejaculate into glass specimen cups after our genitals had been subjected to varying amounts of radiation. Prisoners unable to manually do so were induced; the guards rammed truncheons into their anal cavities, causing a sort of knee-jerk reaction to fill the glass cup. There was a Jew girl there too, the one I'd seen on the commandant's terrace the first day I'd arrived at the camp, exposing her breasts to the men filling the glasses with semen. She never spoke, instead she walked around, floating from one cell to the next like a ghost.

Our numbers slowly began to dwindle as men died because of radiation sickness, or infection. In time it was only Sergei and I left in our cell. One day, the girl stood in front of our cell. I looked up at her. Though young, she was beautiful, not in a sexual way, beautiful as in a work of art, a painting. Something to be cherished in a place so sterile.

"Hello," I said. "What's your name?"

"Eliana," she said.

"Eliana." I smiled. "I am Stanislav."

"The doctor told me to choose one of you to die."

I turned and looked at Sergei who was asleep in the corner of the cell, curled in a tight ball. "Why must you choose?"

"He wants me to, and if I do not, then he will," she said.

"You don't have to choose," I said.

"I must choose, or he will," she repeated.

"Then choose me… and let my friend sleep a little longer. Perhaps he is dreaming of a place far from here."

She turned and looked back down the hallway. Two SS guards walked over. Eliana raised her hand and pointed at Sergei.

"That one," she said.

"No, take me, please," I said, as the guards opened the cell and pushed me aside. Sergei was still half asleep as they dragged him away.

"I told you to choose me!"

"We must do what we can to survive," she said. "Your friend is weak and will die no matter what. A simple equation with only one answer."

21
Illa

Mother was wrong. The Witch was real. Her name was Margarete Ilse Koch. She was married to the camp commandant, Karl-Otto Koch; middle-aged and red faced, he enjoyed drinking and eating too much, torturing Jews, and raping young women. Little Ilse, as Karl referred to her, didn't seem to mind her husband's many affairs. One morning, while I was scrubbing the bathroom floor, he came in drunk and still wearing the same clothes from the dinner party he and Ilse had hosted the night before; he urinated in the toilet as I stood in the corner, head bent down; he turned around, half-surprised to see me standing there. He let his pants drop to the floor, approached, spun me around, lifted up my dress and began to rape me. Almost as soon as he inserted himself, did he begin to go soft. Angry, he spat into his palm and tried to manually excite himself, but it didn't work. He grabbed me by the neck and threw me down to the floor.

"Fucking Jew bitch," he said.

I started to scrub the floor again. The commandant stumbled back into his bedroom and collapsed faced-down onto the mattress, snoring almost instantly.

Unlike her husband, Ilse was always full of energy. She rose early in the mornings. Eliana and I helped her bathe. Eliana would ensure the bath water was kept warm. I would scrub the Witch's back, armpits, breasts, and genitals with a soapy sponge. Most important to the Witch was her fiery red hair. She put curlers in it before bed each night, and never allowed water to touch it. One morning, Eliana accidentally spilled some hot water on the Witch's hair while filling the tub. The Witch had Eliana tied to a chair and boiling water poured over her feet and hands to teach her to be more careful in the future.

Once out of the bath, and her curlers removed, I would gently brush out the Witch's hair while she stared into her beauty mirror putting on her makeup.

"Turn your wrist as you brush, you stupid Jew," she said to me. "Otherwise, the curls will begin to straighten."

"Yes, Madame," I answered promptly.

After bathing, applying makeup, and dressing, the Witch would eat an early breakfast, usually a steaming hot plate of eggs and sausage, garnished always by her favorite treat, ripe strawberries. She would dine on them throughout the day; strawberries were included in every meal, especially the evening's dessert. So indulgent was her appetite for the sweet fruit that she ordered Eliana and I to build a large, raised garden near the commandant's house specifically to grow hundreds of strawberry plants. Part of our daily duties included caring for the strawberry garden: watering, weeding, planting, sowing, and harvesting when ripe.

After breakfast, the Witch often enjoyed riding through the camp on her black horse named Odin. The camp's prisoners were expected to drop to their knees and bow their heads whenever she rode past. To please his wife, or just to keep her occupied, the commandant had a fully enclosed ring constructed for his young wife so she could ride Odin during the winter months. In the afternoons, the Witch pursued various interests, one being tanning flesh flayed from prisoners' bodies. She particularly liked tattoos, for their uniqueness. She liked having the tanned tattooed flesh made into lamp shades or other pieces of furniture to decorate the house. She was intensely involved when it came to selecting which flesh would adorn her home. She enjoyed sitting on the terrace and reviewing all incoming prisoners.

Eliana would often have to attend to the Witch while she was on the terrace, standing beside her holding a bowl of freshly picked strawberries. The Witch could get very upset if she was hungry and her favorite treat was not at hand.

At night, Eliana and I would set the dining room table for dinner, serve food, and wash up. After dinner, the Witch would usually take another bath, his time with various scented perfumes. I would heat the curlers and help put them in her hair, then dress her in a night gown. She didn't seem to mind that her husband preferred not to share a bed.

"Terrible snoring," she laughed. "Best he has his own bed."

It continued like this for many months. The commandant raped me several more times, usually when he was drunk. Each night, after Eliana and I had put the Witch to bed and cleaned the kitchen and pantry, we would return to the barracks. The only women in the camp, we'd curl up together for warmth, and I would tell Eliana a story before she fell asleep.

"Where's Papa?" said Eliana one night, shivering in my arms.

"I don't know," I said, holding her more tightly.

"We have to find him," she said.

"We will."

The next morning, after seeing to the Witch's demands, we went to the garden and picked strawberries. I was bent over, basket in one hand, carefully selecting the ripest ones. Eliana was working in the next row. I saw her pick a large bulbous strawberry, almost the size of an apple, and start eating it.

"What are you doing? Stop!" I said immediately. She didn't listen and took another bite.

"Eliana, stop it! Stop! What if someone sees us?" I hissed. Eliana didn't stop eating the strawberry.

I dropped my basket, stepped over the row of plants and snatched the strawberry out of Eliana's hand and threw it to the ground. She looked down at it.

"What if the witch saw you?" I said, taking her chin in my hand and lifting her face up so that I was looking directly into her eyes.

"We cannot eat them. Do you understand?"

"I'm so hungry," she said.

She pushed me back and then reached down and plucked another strawberry and began eating it. I slapped it out of her hand, and then slapped her across the face.

"Spit it out! Right now! Do you hear me? Spit it out." She swallowed, her lips, stained red.

"Look at your lips, Eliana, how are we going to explain them?" I tried to rub the color away.

"It's not coming off," I said.

I picked up a handful of dirt and smeared it across Eliana's mouth. She spat, kicked at me and pushed me away.

"Stop it!" she said, spitting the dirt out of her mouth.

"Eliana, you can't go back into the house with lips so red, she will know... she will know you ate her fruit. Remember the last time you made her angry?"

Eliana looked down at her feet.

"Next time, I won't scream," she said.

"Next time? What do you mean next time?"

"When the Witch tries to cook me in boiling water…"

The next spring, I started to feel unwell. I was tired all the time. My bones ached. I woke one morning with a terrible red rash covering nearly my entire body. Thankfully, it had not progressed up my neck or to my hands, so I was still able to work, my dress concealing much of it. The rash was painful and itchy. Strange bumps and blisters began to appear on my lower half.

I was standing in the food line one afternoon, my body burning with a fever, and I became dizzy. "Illa…," said Eliana. "Are you all right? Shall I get you some water?"

Everything went black.

When next I woke, I was in the barracks. Our family's old doctor, Gershom Hofstein, was standing over me, patting my forehead with a wet rag.

"Hello, Illa," he said. "How are you feeling?"

"Doctor Hofstein?"

"Yes…" he said. "I was put into the camp two days ago. Eliana saw me and brought me here to look after you."

"Where is she?" I said, trying to sit up.

"Working at the commandant's house. Lay back down, Illa, please," said Gershom, dabbing my forehead.

I was weak. Just talking was tiring. "What's going on?" I asked.

Gershom put the rag back into the bowl of water beside the bed.

"You've been in a fevered state for the last twenty-four hours or so… I hope you don't mind that I examined you." His eyes darted down to my midsection.

"Illa, I believe you have something called syphilis. It's a disease transmitted from one person to another during sexual intercourse."

Warm tears began to fill my eyes. I could feel a heavy sadness welling in my heart. "This is difficult to ask, but who here have you had sex with, Illa?"

I began to cry. Gershom tried to comfort me, but I pushed him away. "Illa, you must let me help you."

"The commandant..." I said.

"You had sex with the commandant... did he force himself on you?"

I nodded my head.

"And he's the only one?"

I nodded again.

"And Eliana, do you know if he's... touched Eliana?"

"No..." I said. "I keep her away from him, from his bedroom... I always clean it."

"You're a very brave young woman, Illa. Your mother and father would be proud."

"My mother is dead... and we... can't find papa."

"Rest now, sweet child. Rest."

The fevers abated but I continued to deteriorate despite Doctor Hofstein's efforts.

"All she needs is a course of antibiotics," I heard Doctor Hofstein tell Eliana during a hushed conversation. "There's nothing else I can do..."

"I can steal some from the medical ward...," said Eliana. "The witch sends me there sometimes to fetch the doctor when she's feeling unwell... she's sick with something called gout... that's what the doctor says."

"You must be careful, Eliana... if they were to catch you..."

"Is she going to die?" said Eliana.

"No, not immediately, anyways. Patients with untreated syphilis can live for years, decades even... she will just have to deal with potential effects of the disease."

"What do you mean?"

"In some patients, syphilis can cause dementia... that is, it damages their brain, or causes them to go blind."

"Blind?" gasped Eliana. "I will get the medicine... how will I know it?"

Doctor Hofstein's shoulders drooped.

"I will steal the medicines," snapped Eliana. "All of them if you don't tell me what to look for."

"I just need penicillin, that's all."

I turned toward my sister. "Eliana," I wheezed. "Eliana..." She looked at me and came over.

"I'm going to get you the medicine, Illa. You'll be all right."

"Don't... don't do it... don't give them a chance to catch you," I pleaded.

"Doctor Hofstein says you could go blind if I don't. It will be all right, Illa. I will be careful. I promise."

"Don't, Eliana, please... don't risk your life for me... don't go."

Eliana leaned over and kissed me on the forehead. I looked at her. My vision was blurred, watery, as though I were submerged in the tub our mother bathed us in, staring up at Eliana standing over me.

"It will be all right, sister. I'll be careful."

22
Eliana

He looked an old and fragile man and smelled strongly of vodka and vomit. He introduced himself as Uzi Willner, a former prosecutor of Kapos turned traffic lawyer. I asked about the ring on his finger, and he told me he'd swallowed it for three years, over and over. He took off his jacket, rolled up his sleeve and show me a large scar on his arm, the place where his tattooed registration number had been, that he'd heated a pocketknife over a stove on the anniversary of his marriage many years ago and sliced the corrupted flesh from his body.

"I threw it in a fire," he said.

"Why do you want to help me?" I asked him. "Years spent prosecuting Kapos, and now you're sitting with someone accused of crimes against Jews."

"I don't know if I will... my friend, he asked me to sit with you, listen to what you have to say."

"Say about what?"

"Your story... what happened to you in the camps," he said, a bead of sweat rolled down the side of his face.

"Would you be surprised or think me a liar if I told you I don't remember?"

"No... many survivors block out what happened to them, it's called compartmentalization... it's a defense mechanism... the different parts of our mind construct walls to protect themselves from our own memories."

"And this is what I've done?" I said.

"I don't know… I'm not a doctor… can you tell me what you do remember?"

"Funny…" I thought. "Not long ago, my husband asked me a similar question… *what do I remember most about my childhood*… he wants us to have children," I said.

"Children are a beautiful thing," said Uzi.

The sweet taste of strawberries filled my mouth. I could smell them too. I raised my hand; my fingers brushed my cheek where Illa had struck me while in the Witch's Garden.

"I remember the taste of strawberries," I said. I rubbed my tongue against my front teeth.

"Others have told me we were a happy family," I said. "Before the war, we were happy. My mother was kind and beautiful, my father bright and endearing, my sister feminine and obedient. I have trouble remembering their faces…" I stopped a moment.

"That is not uncommon," said Uzi.

"No? Can you not remember your wife's face? Because as much as I try, I don't remember my mother… her voice, though, sometimes it becomes my inner voice, as though she and I have become the same person, and she speaks through me."

"I'm getting to be an old man… I have trouble remembering most things, but never my wife… I sense her everywhere."

"You're one of the lucky ones… those lost are never really gone for you."

"Or it is a curse…" he said.

"Remembering loved ones is never a curse… I have only a single photograph of my father. It's from when he was a young man... that is the face I remember now, not the one he wore when I was growing up... we would go on picnics in the summer, and he would put me on his shoulders and run around making sounds like a horse." I smiled. "I remember feeling safe with him then..."

"What happened to your father? Did he die in the camps?"

"I don't know... my mother..." I heard the sound of the pistol shot that killed her...

"My mother was shot as soon as we got to the camp, to Buchenwald... they sent my father away, we never saw him again."

"Both you and your sister?" said Uzi.

"Yes... surely, he perished... but sometimes I find myself dreaming he survived, he's somewhere safe, the sun upon his face..."

"What about your sister?"

"She is gone..."

Uzi was quiet at moment, then abruptly asked, "Are you guilty of what you are accused?"

I knew he was studying me, the same as I was him. There was a tremor in his hand, which he tried to hide.

"Of crimes against humanity?"

"Yes," he said in a stern voice.

"As guilty as any who survived," I said.

"That is not an answer."

"Isn't it? Why did you not resist? Instead of loading thousands of us into the ovens, why didn't you fight back, throw yourself on the first German you saw and try to kill him? You were a grown man, why didn't you fight back? I was only a girl, ten years old when I was sent to Buchenwald. I fought back the only way I knew how."

"How was that?" he said, leaning back in his chair uncomfortably.

"I survived..." I whispered.

"We all did terrible things to survive," admitted Uzi. "Some killed, some became Kapos and beat other Jews, some stole food from children, some worked with the SS..."

"My sister and I worked for the Witch of Buchenwald, Ilse Koch... after that... Doctor Ziegler..."

"The Nazi currently on trial?"

"Ziegler... he selected me to work in his lab, where he experimented on Jews... Russians... anyone, cut them to pieces, irradiated them..."

"Then you were sent to Mittlebau-Dora?"

"Yes, constructing V-2 rockets; rockets that killed thousands... I'm guilty of that, the same as any Jew who worked in a munitions factory assembling bombs and bullets..."

"What was your work with Ziegler like?"

"Do you know about Ziegler? What they say he did?" I asked.

"Only what I have read in the papers about the trial."

"What do they say in the papers? I'm not allowed to read in here."

"That he experimented on thousands... trying to determine effective methods for mass sterilization."

"I've never seen anyone enjoy their work as much as Ziegler... to him, everything was an experiment... we were all lab rats... I'm not sure he even cared much for the National Socialist cause, being a Nazi was just a means to an end for him, a way to conduct his research as he saw fit."

"Why did he choose you? Of everyone in the camp, why

a young girl?"

"I don't know... he took a liking to me," I said.

"What did he ask you to do for him?"

"He never asked me to do anything," I said.

"What do you mean?"

"I was his pet... later, when I'd matured, I believe he'd fallen in love with me."

"So, these things you are accused of... working with Ziegler, helping him experiment on prisoners, performing abortions on women in the camp..."

"I tried to save as many as I could..." I said.

"How?"

"Those who entered Zeigler's labs might as well have been walking into a gas chamber, only death at the hands of Ziegler was far lengthier and crueler... I chose for him... I chose those who would die."

"In the file they have on you, it says you were called the *Angel of Death* by survivors of Buchenwald?"

"I don't know what they called me... there were many who were going to die no matter what... I tried to save those who had a chance, those who could survive."

"You sacrificed some to save many, like pawns in a game of chess."

"I was only a young girl..."

"And yet you were smart enough to stay alive for eight years in the camps... did you not take to Ziegler and his work because it offered you sanctuary and protection from labor, from execution? This is what the prosecutors will say, I know, I used to be one of them."

"Then I am guilty," I said pushing back to the wall, resting against it. "I'm so very tired."

"What else did you do, to try and help the others? Bring them food or medicine?"

"Yes, when I could... for those I could get nothing to, I tried to comfort them as best I could in their last moments."

"Where are those people you gave food and medicine to? What are their names? We will want them to testify on your behalf."

"Recently someone told me, *memory is Israel's most powerful weapon*, not missiles, or tanks, or guns, but memory... I don't remember their names; I don't want to... I don't want to remember any of it... Ziegler knew... he knew I was giving food and medicine to them, comforting the dying... the things we do to survive..."

"You wish to have Ziegler testify on your behalf?" said Uzi, nearly laughing at the proposition.

"He's the only one who knows the truth... that I was one of his experiments too."

"He experimented on you?"

"Yes, but not in the same way he did with the others. It doesn't matter anyways, no one can get to Ziegler any more."

"He's on trial, being held in this same building as you, I can request to interview him."

"Whoever that man is, the one on trial, he isn't Ziegler."

"He's not?" said Uzi.

"You know I work for State Security... I was part of the team sent to identify Ziegler in West Berlin. I told them he was Ziegler."

"And now you are saying he's not Ziegler, I don't understand," said Uzi, both hands now beginning to tremble.

"Memory is our most powerful weapon, he said, give Israel Eichmann, give them Ziegler, let the people have their vengeance. The false Ziegler, he will be the lamb laid upon an altar for our people…"

"If he is not Ziegler, you must say so. The real one is still out there," said Uzi.

"No, he's not," I said, lying down on the bed and closing my eyes. "I killed him in 1943."

23
Chaya

I kept having the same dream. I'm lying at the bottom of the grave dug for Yitzak. All I can see is a framed view of the sky. It is clear and blue, like summer; then white clouds begin to drift by, only to turn grey and black; there is a boom of thunder and a sudden downpour of rain. Floodwaters spill quickly. I'm unable to escape and begin to drown...

This is when I wake up.

There is a moment, every time after I wake, a terrible moment, when I think it has all been a dream; Yitzak is safe and sleeping soundly in his crib...

Then the memory of his death washes over me. Each time I wake, he dies again. I have lost my son a hundred times...

Peter came into the bedroom and pulled the curtain back to let the light in. I lift the blanket over my face.

"Chaya, you must get up," he says, standing at the side of the bed. "You must eat something."

"Let me sleep," I said.

I hear my mother in the kitchen, humming while she cooks; the smell of it, of any food, makes me nauseous. I get out of bed and scramble into the bathroom. Slamming the door behind me, I throw up into the sink.

"Chaya..." said Peter, standing right outside the door. "Please..."

"Just let me sleep... please."

I heard him sigh.

"I'll bring you some tea… to help calm your stomach." I heard him walk away.

I turned on the shower and undressed. I studied my wasting body in the mirror: my skin is colorless, almost translucent, I can see the blue webbing of veins just below the surface; I've lost weight, all my bones are defined; my breasts are smaller and will no longer produce milk; my menstrual cycle has stopped. I'm incapable of producing life.

I stepped into the shower, closed the drain, and slowly lowered myself down, lying flat. I let the water strike me. The bath began to fill…

Yitzak…

Grief, like love, is not bounded by time, so when I entered the living room and kitchen, I didn't know what day, week, or month it was. The house was dark. In the library there was a single lamp on. I walked over. My father was sat in a chair beneath the lamp, asleep, an open book lying on his lap. I didn't know where Peter or Mother were. I went into the living room and fetched a blanket from the sofa and used it to cover my father. I removed the book from his lap: *The Dark Continent — The Adventures of Ryszard Zajac.* I smiled because it was the kind of book my father was so unlikely to read. Growing up, I only recall our house being littered with military books: manuals, theories of war, memoirs, Sun Tzu and Clausewitz. I placed a bookmark in the pages, closed it and laid the book on the side table.

I left the library and went to Peter's office to see if he was working there. I knocked before opening the door. He wasn't there. He must be at work. His office was a mess. Boxes full of files were stacked along the wall, his desk and even the floor were covered in stacks of papers and photographs. I wandered through, eyeing the photographs, terrible scenes from the camps. All the boxes were labeled: *Buchenwald*. On his desk were cut out newspaper stories, all with similar titles: *The Butcher of Buchenwald Stands Trial; Buchenwald Butcher Found Guilty of Atrocities; Doctor Sascha Ziegler, the Butcher of Buchenwald, Sentenced to Death.*

Underneath the newspaper clippings were numerous notepads scrolled with notes, annotating dates and persons related to the photographs stacked on the floor. Peter must have been doing work for Yad Vashem. I read one of the newspaper clippings. It detailed the testimonies of numerous survivors, along with evidence submitted to the court: documents seized by the Americans when the camp was liberated.

I put the clipping down and noticed a large folder on the table, tightly bound with string. Written in heavy ink on the folder: *Eliana.*

Why would Peter have a folder titled Eliana? *Our Eliana?* I wondered.

I sat down, picked up the folder, and unbound it. The contents were a series of photographs and Nazi registration logs from Buchenwald concentration camp. Peter had used a red ink pen to circle information in the logs from August 1937: *Askel Wasserman, Weimar, No. 0197; Illa Wasserman, Weimar, No. 0198; Eliana Wasserman, Weimar, No. 0199.*

The logs continued; almost one for every month from 1937 through to August 1943, when *Eliana Wasserman, Weimar, No. 0199* stopped appearing. Next, there were pages of prisoner transcripts, testimonies about life in Buchenwald. In each transcript, Peter had circled: *Angel of Death.* A name apparently given to a young Jewish girl who worked with Doctor Sascha Ziegler, the Butcher of Buchenwald. The prisoners' accounts were heart-breaking... unimaginable torture using X-rays, the surgical removal of male and female reproductive organs...

Finally, I looked at the photographs, black and grey, depicting the horrors of Buchenwald. Men and women as thin as coat rakes, their shrunken bodies absurdly dressed in oversized striped uniforms like wind-filled sails tied to narrow masts. Peter had circled an individual in each of the first few pictures and written an annotation next to them: *Ziegler.* Then in the next set of photographs, he'd circled the same man: *Ziegler.* But he'd also circled a young girl in the photographs' backgrounds, often hidden or half-turned; he'd annotated it: *Eliana?* The next series of photographs all continued to identify the young girl, often obscured or in the background, but always the same marking: *Eliana?* As the photographs progressed, so too did the girl's maturity, growing into a young woman. More and more, with each photograph I examined, my eyes searching the grains of black and grey, the woman circled in red began to look more like Eliana as she aged: dark hair, dark eyes, high smooth cheek bones... was it our Eliana, my brother's wife?

"Darling, what are you doing in here?" said Peter, standing in the doorway. "Are you all right?"

"Peter, what is this?" I demanded.

"Darling, that's my work," he said, rushing over and taking the photos from me. "You shouldn't be looking at such awful things."

"What is that? Why is Eliana in those photos?"

"Darling, please..." he said, trying to grab my arms.

"No! Why do you have those? Why is Eliana in those photos with that Nazi doctor?"

"Please, calm down," said Peter more sternly.

"Calm down? What have you been doing all this time? Have you even grieved for your son?"

"Why do you think I'm doing this! It's for Yitzak," he said.

"What? How is any of this for Yitzak?"

"Chaya, listen to me, please. The doctor, the Nazi monster, Ziegler, he was put on trial. Yad Vashem asked me to look through all the files they'd recently received pertaining to Buchenwald to see if I could find anything to support the trial. Going through it, this is what I found..."

"Found? Found what? Eliana? How can she have been in the camps? Her family sent her to England before the war."

"That's what she told Jacob... told us... but what if it's a lie?" said Peter, backing away from me. "What if everything she's told us about her life, her family, is a lie?"

"Why would she do that? Why lie about not being in the camps?"

"I didn't know... until I started to read these..."

"What?" I said, my eyes shaking as they followed Peter to his desk where he picked up some of the survivors' testimonies I'd read.

"Survivors of Buchenwald. Many of them describe a young Jewish girl who worked with Ziegler; they called her the *Angel of Death* for the part she played in selecting which Jews would be taken to Ziegler for his experiments."

"So... you think, Eliana is what, insane? A Nazi? What?"

"Look at what she was a part of," said Peter, turning and looking at everything laid out on the table. "The horror of it all... and she was left alone with Yitzak..."

"What do you mean she was left alone with Yitzak?"

"What would being in a place like that do to a person... what if Yitzak's death wasn't an accident?"

I began to tremble.

"Are you telling me Eliana killed our son? Is that what you're saying... Peter? Are you saying she murdered Yitzak?"

I dropped to the floor, my heart racing, and unable to breathe; the world collapsed around me.

24
Askel

I, along with three other educated Jews, weren't sent to the forest to cut down trees, or to the rail lines to lay new tracks, or the munitions factory to build bombs; we were tasked with overseeing planning and logistics of camp life; Buchenwald grew quickly with hundreds of new prisoners arriving daily.

The SS officer in charge of camp logistics, Hegelmann, had no education beyond primary school; his only previous training for the position was managing a hotel in Munich owned by his father. I suppose the SS thought if Hegelmann could manage a hotel he was qualified to oversee a labor camp. While the four of us worked, Hegelmann spent his days napping, eating, reading Kiebitz comic books, or just wandering around the camp, hands clasped behind his back as though strolling through a park.

Our team worked diligently, partially because we thought if we were good workers, Hegelmann would keep us alive. It was also in our natures. Each man had distinguished himself in his previous career: Gregor, an engineer, Josef, a senior accountant, and Elijah, a brilliant young physicist. We all got on fairly well. Gregor could be hot-tempered at times, Josef was the most practical, and Elijah often daydreamed, but always completed his work. Being the eldest, Hegelmann saw fit to put me in charge. I reported to Hegelmann, and Hegelmann presented our work to the camp commandant.

We worked in a converted barracks. I positioned my desk facing the window looking out at the commandant's residence hoping to catch a glimpse of Illa and Eliana. I had no idea if they were still alive. My section of the camp was completely isolated from other sections, and so getting information across camp lines was difficult, and no other Jews but my daughters, as far as I knew, had access to the commandant's residence. Barbwire fences separated us, but it just as well could've been an ocean; my girls, stranded on an island in a vast ocean of death, with only each other for protection.

Buchenwald continued to expand. Soon there were two munitions' factories, and a vast new encampment for Russian prisoners of war. Buchenwald spawned several sub-camps. Word of Hegelmann's fine work, *our work*, became known throughout SS High Command; Hegelmann became giddy when the commandant informed him that his name had been mentioned to Hitler. Soon thereafter, Hegelmann's expertise was being requested throughout the Reich as dozens of new labor camps were being established each year. Our group became a traveling carnival of sorts, going from one camp to the next, helping to establish efficient operations. Hegelmann took to his new status like a fish to water; always welcomed by the next camp commandant with a dinner party in his honor; praises were heaped upon him; he even received an Iron Cross for services rendered to the Fatherland.

In the autumn of 1942, Hegelmann was ordered to survey Natzweiler-Struthof concentration camp in the Gau-Baden Alsace region, a territory formally part of eastern France. We, Gregor, Josef, Elijah, and I, were loaded into a tarp-covered truck, along with a single SS guard, and the driver.

Hegelmann, with his personal driver, drove just ahead of

our truck in a small Volkswagen Kommandeurswagen. I didn't know how long the drive from Buchenwald to Natzweiler-Struthof would take, a day or more, most likely. Poor Elijah was suffering from a terrible case of dysentery. He was weak and feverish. Josef tried to comfort him, using his hat to wipe away the sweat on Elijah's forehead and cheeks.

"How much longer, you think?" said Gregor in Yiddish so the young guard sitting in the back of the truck couldn't understand us.

"I don't know," I said, looking out the back of the truck at the tree-covered mountains.

"Ever been to Alsace?"

"Yeah, spent time here fighting during the first war," I said.

"You fought in the first war?" laughed Gregor. "And they've thrown you in a camp now..."

I laughed as well at the irony of it.

"Captain Askel Wasserman, at your service." I saluted Gregor.

"I was born in 1905," said Gregor, "too young..."

"That's good, it was a terrible thing..." I said. "I was drafted just as I was preparing to teach at university."

"Where did you fight?"

"The Low Countries, Belgium mostly. You think the mud at Buchenwald is bad... I watched men drown in it... the earth simply swallowed them up."

"Doesn't sound like a bad way to die..." Gregor shrugged his shoulders. "Better than the gas chamber or getting sent to Ziegler's lab for experiments."

"I was in artillery..." I said, looking back out of the truck again. "I was good at it too... I always thought, if I were going to die, that would be how it would happen... not a sniper's bullet, machine gun, or gas, but a bomb hurtled through the air, following a perfect elliptical trajectory right on to the top of my head," I said, whistling and making a motion with my finger, tracing the trajectory of a shell through the air, and landing on top of my head.

Gregor smiled.

"No pain that way," I said. "It's over... you don't even know what happened, gone, just like that." I snapped my fingers.

Gregor looked down at Elijah.

"Yeah," he said, "there are worse ways to die."

"Josef," I said. "How's he doing?"

Josef looked at me and shook his head. "If the fever doesn't break soon, I don't know if he'll live."

Because he was the youngest, Elijah reminded me of Illa and Eliana. His face was still young, not requiring a razor. I didn't know if Illa and Eliana were alive. It had been almost five years since I last saw them. There were always rumors of the two young girls working in the commandant's house, and that one of them had been sent to work with Ziegler, the insane doctor performing experiments on Russian prisoners. All I could do was ask God to protect them and stay alive myself in the hope one day we would be reunited.

The truck began to rattle and vibrate. Suddenly, it bounced up into the air; we swerved to the right, throwing us all onto the truck bed, including the guard, who quickly righted himself after the truck came to a stop. One of the back tires had completely disintegrated, leaving a scattered trail of rubber bits along the road.

"Damn it!" said the guard, who ordered us all out of the

truck. He hopped out, then pointed his rifle at us.

"Raus!" he said.

Gregor jumped out first, then me, followed by Josef and Elijah. We all helped Josef carry Elijah to the side of the road. The driver and the guard argued with one another. Hegelmann's Volkswagen came circling back around. Hegelmann got out and berated the driver.

"You fucking idiot, now we're going to be late for dinner! Well, what are you standing around for? Fix the damn thing! Put the Jews to work, quickly!"

The guard marched over, struck me in the back with his rifle's butt and ordered us to begin working on the truck. There was no jack, so Gregor devised an effective lever so that we were able to raise the truck for a moment and place stones under the other back wheel to keep the truck's end raised while we fastened the spare tire.

"We could all just as easily fit in the Volkswagen... I don't understand why Hegelmann doesn't invite us to ride with him?" joked Gregor.

"It's because you stink so bad," smiled Josef.

Hegelmann was napping under a tree on the side of the road. His driver was cleaning splattered bugs off the Volkswagen's windshield. The SS guard and truck driver were standing around, smoking cigarettes.

"Hey!" said the guard. "Shut up, Jews. Work faster and maybe I won't kill your friend, ja?"

The guard walked over to Elijah, who was still pale and burning with fever, and prodded him with the muzzle of his rifle, testing whether Elijah was still alive. Elijah groaned, squirming a little.

The guard laughed, half-turned to look at us and said,

"Not looking good for this Jew. Better work faster, and maybe we get him to a doctor…"

Before the guard could turn back around, Elijah suddenly snatched the rifle out of the unexpecting guard's hands, spun it around and shot the guard through the mouth, popping his metal helmet off like a champagne cork.

"Fuck," said the driver, trying to reach for his pistol.

Gregor grabbed the tire iron and lunged at the driver, landing a heavy blow across his back which caused the driver to crumple to the ground. Gregor went on beating him with the iron until the driver was dead. Hegelmann's driver took off running into the woods. Elijah, after pulling the bolt back on the rifle to reload it, fired at him, but missed. Josef grabbed the truck driver's pistol and ran over to Hegelmann, who'd taken off his boots to nap. Hegelmann raised his hands, surrendering.

"What do you think you're doing, you fucking Jews… I gave you everything, kept you safe from the gas chambers, the work details, kept you fed… you'd all be dead without me!"

Josef pressed the pistol against Hegelmann's heart and pulled the trigger, but nothing happened, a dull click.

"Josef…" I said, motioning with my finger. "The safety is on… and shoot him in the head, my friend; we'll need his uniform."

Hegelmann looked over at me, his fat round face bristling with fear.

"Fucking Jews…" he said, as Josef clicked off the safety and shot him in the head.

"Get the bodies cleared off the road, quickly, before any vehicles come!"

Josef and I dragged Hegelmann behind a tree then helped Gregor with the SS guard and truck driver. We undressed them and put on their uniforms.

"What about the other driver?" said Josef. "Shouldn't we go after him?"

"In the forest and mountains? It's too big; we'd never find him," I said.

Gregor handed me Hegelmann's uniform.

"Captain," he smiled.

"Where do we go?" said Gregor. "It will be dusk soon."

"That's good," I said. "Less chance of being seen."

"What about the checkpoints?" said Josef. "We have their papers, but if anyone looks at the pictures…"

"I'm a captain now. How many captains will be manning checkpoints during the night? I'll order them to let us through."

"Through to where?"

"Back to Buchenwald," I said.

"Are you crazy, Askel, you want to go back to Buchenwald?" said Gregor.

"I have to get my daughters," I said. "I can't just leave them there."

"Askel, we can't go back that way. The border with France is only a little farther up the road. We get into France, we keep driving south, maybe we find a quiet place to hide out, maybe we find the resistance," argued Josef.

"I don't have a choice. I can't leave my daughters," I said.

"Askel…" said Elijah, who was sat up against a tree, while we all changed into the German uniforms. "Going back into Germany… that way leads only to death… getting to them is impossible. The only choice is France… the only path back to your daughters is France, where you might have a chance to live long enough to see them again."

"I can't abandon them," I shook my head.

I turned around and walked into the middle of the road and stared back into Germany, at the vast mountains and forests stretching to the horizon.

"Askel," said Elijah. "There is no choice... they're in God's hands now, all you can do is survive."

"Illa... Eliana, my loves," I said, raising my hand toward the sky, their faces appearing in the light and shadows of the fading day.

"Askel," said Elijah, "Do you hear me? There is no choice..."

25
Sascha

The Israelis served awful food. Whether this was because all Jewish food is dry and tasteless or merely just the food in jail, I'm unsure; I have no way to compare. For breakfast I'm given bread, no butter, jam, or honey... just measly bread. My first morning in the jail I complained to the guard, quite vociferously; however, the next morning, instead of rectifying the situation, I was given bread, still no butter, jam, or honey, but now the bread was stale and moldy. The midday meal was none better, fried potato cakes, no butter, or salt, served with boiled carrots, and more stale bread. The evening meal was by far the worst, however; a cold fish stew, accompanied by raw white onions and more boiled carrots. I believe the carrots were just leftovers from the midday meal and the kitchen staff didn't want them to go to waste.

The same three meals, day after day; I brought it to the judges' attention on the first day of my trial. After Mr Lieberman, the prosecuting lawyer, finally sat down, red-faced from his impassioned opening statement accusing me of a litany of crimes, including mass torture, terror, murder and so on, I spoke from inside the glass detainment box in which I would reside throughout the trial. I removed the translation headphones I was wearing...

"Yes, thank you, judges..." I began in German, standing up in my box, reading my prepared statement. "I would like to begin by informing you, and the Israeli people, as to the grave and inhuman conditions in which I'm being detained. For the past thirty-seven days, I have been served the same three meals every day. The first meal, breakfast, I am served bread, just bread, unaccompanied by either honey, jam, or butter; and more recently, my morning bread is served stale, and often covered in mold. The midday meal is terrible as well: potato cakes, which I know Jews are fond of, however, again there is neither butter nor salt; the potato cakes come with boiled, flavorless carrots, and more stale bread. The final evening meal is the most atrocious, a stew of cold fish; its pungency befouls my cell long after it has been removed. The fish is paired with raw onions, and more carrots; my strong belief is that the dinner carrots are merely leftovers from the midday meal and haven't been prepared anew."

I shifted my weight and continued my opening statement.

"I hope you will reflect on the cruelty I have endured these last thirty-seven days and will advise jail leadership and staff to amend their food menus. I speak not only for myself but also on behalf of all those persons detained in the same jail house as I. And having not yet been found guilty of a single crime, I can't imagine why I have been subjected to such inhuman treatment... even street dogs eat better than I..."

I sat back down, feeling rather pleased with my statement. Hopefully, it would lead to some changes. The courtroom was silent. The lead judge leaned over and spoke into his microphone.

"Mr Ziegler, do you not wish to address any of the charges that have been levied against you?" said the Judge in Hebrew.

The guard stationed in my glass box tapped me on the shoulder and motioned that I should put my headphones back on.

"Oh, ja, ja..." I said, putting the headphones on.

The translated voice came through, a woman's voice, "Mr Ziegler, do you not wish to address any of the charges that have been levied against you?"

I stood.

"Charges? What charges?"

The judges looked dumbstruck.

"Of War Crimes, Crimes against Humanity, the torture and murder of thousands of Jews, Roma, and prisoners of war?" he said.

I waited for the translation.

"Oh, ja... tell the people of Israel, I did none of those things..." I smiled at the judges and everyone in the courtroom.

I couldn't believe how long the trial was taking. Day after day, except for the Jewish Sabbath, Lieberman questioned an endless string of Jews. Each day, I reiterated the inedible state of my meals, but nothing changed.

After Lieberman questioned each witness, the judges would ask if I would like to rebut, and ask the witness anything; I only ever asked one question, the same question: "You remember me from the camp, this face?"

Their answers, though varied, were always a resounding, "Yes."

One Dutch woman, her eyes full of tears, said, "I will never forget the face of true evil, especially when the light of justice has finally been shined upon it." After which, she spat in my general direction.

Shortly after she departed, I was overtaken by a terrible fit of coughing. I felt as though I were drowning. The guard on duty tried to assist me, helping me to my feet; I suddenly ejected a stream of black blood onto the glass pane in front of me. The courtroom gasped in horror. The judges adjourned the remainder of the day's session, and I was taken to the jail's medical ward and examined. Given the limited equipment on site, I was soon transported under heavy guard to a local hospital. Doctors and nurses carried out a number of tests, including taking blood samples and X-ray images of my chest.

Later that day, a cheerless doctor informed me my lungs were riddled with cancer. I smiled and thanked him, then asked when they would be serving me food. Earlier, while walking to the X-ray room, I'd noticed another hospital patient eating ice cream, vanilla, I think. The doctor informed me I would not be receiving any food, instead I was being discharged and sent back to the jail. Hearing this, I became very sad. I was taken back to the jail in a wheelchair and almost immediately after I arrived, I was served the evening meal of cold fish stew, sliced raw onions, and leftover boiled carrots. That night, I didn't eat anything. I pushed the food as far away from me as I could to try and keep the smell away; I pulled my blanket over my head and tried to sleep.

The trial continued the next morning. I felt weak. Gnawing on bits of the stale bread that morning didn't help. The endless string of witnesses... survivors, whatever you wish to call them, continued. My fits of coughing grew worse throughout the week. Finally, on the Jewish Sabbath, I was allowed to rest in my cell. Just after the midday meal, one of the guards tapped on my cell's bars with his truncheon.

"Ziegler, you have a visitor," he said in a sharp voice.

"I don't understand Hebrew, you know," I said in German, slowly sitting up in my bed.

237

"Then we will speak in German," said a gentleman in a tired suit, about my age.

"Good afternoon, sir." I smiled, finally able to converse in my native tongue.

"Good afternoon, Herr Ziegler, my name is Uzi Willner. I'm a lawyer."

"A lawyer... well, I'm sorry to tell you, but I'll continue to be representing myself during the trial... I think I'm doing quite well."

"Herr Ziegler, I'm not here to offer you representation... I'm here on behalf of Eliana Wasserman."

Petite Princesse... how long it's taken you...

Herr Willner continued, "She informs me you are not Doctor Sascha Ziegler."

I smiled; it was almost a relief.

"None were more surprised than me to see her in Berlin... of all the people to come, it was her... the world is a funny place, no? And then for her to still say I was Ziegler, well... it was an interesting day to say the least. You'll have to ask her why she did so, for me."

"What is your name?" he abruptly asked.

"I am Doctor Sascha Ziegler, Herr Willner, born 22 May 1913, in Leipzig, Germany." I smiled.

"Eliana told me she killed Ziegler in 1943."

"Yes," I said.

"And still, you call yourself Ziegler, and stand trial for his crimes?"

"Yes... to be honest, I was hoping for better food here. The food at the British embassy in Berlin was wonderful... and people always speak so poorly of English food. Have you ever had an English scone with butter and strawberry jam?"

"I don't understand, why would a man impersonate a Nazi war criminal and stand trial for war crimes he didn't commit?"

"I'm German...that is crime enough for the Jews. Have you been watching the trial? Forgive me for not noticing if you've been in the audience. But I've asked every witness if they remember me, and every single one has said, yes, identifying me as Ziegler. To them, to Israel, I'm Ziegler."

"Sir, when I say I am here representing Ms Wasserman, it is because of your sudden appearance and trial that she is now incarcerated, indicted of crimes against humanity... that while in the camp, Eliana worked closely with Ziegler during his experiments, that she was known as the *Angel of Death*."

"They have put Eliana in prison?" I laughed.

"She is awaiting trial. I will be defending her."

"You Jews... you are a strange people. You didn't deserve what happened to you, I say that truthfully, but now you put Eliana on trial... what a strange people... wolves eating their young."

"You can save her," he said.

"Me? How can I do such a thing?"

"Tell the court who you really are... tell them you're not Ziegler, that Eliana didn't do the things of which she is accused..."

"I've already told you, Herr Willner, to Israel, I am Ziegler, every witness has said so, even Eliana... soon I will be found guilty, and Israel will rejoice..."

"You can testify as Ziegler that she had nothing to do with the experiments, the murders..."

"We were all guilty, Herr Willner, Eliana too; she chose her life over theirs, day after day, selecting the weakest... but even if I did testify, who would believe me, a convicted Nazi war criminal, the insane *Butcher of Buchenwald*? Not a very credible witness, yes?"

"Then I will prove you are not Ziegler..."

"I will tell you who I am right now, Herr Willner, but I don't see how it will help poor Eliana... why would anyone believe me? Do you have any idea what that girl endured? It is beyond all reason that she is even alive... a miracle, really; that she is alive is a sign God surely exists, for only God's grace has protected her, and now her own people, not us, will finally slay her."

"What is your name?" he demanded. I smiled.

"My name is Tomas Ziegler, born 22 May 1913, Leipzig, Germany, the brother, and fraternal twin, of Sascha Ernst Ziegler..."

"Why are you doing this?"

"Herr Willner, is there any way you could perhaps get me some better food while you're here?" I smiled.

26
Jacob

The High Plateau of the southern Negev desert looks out to the wastelands of eastern Sinai where hundreds of destroyed and abandoned tank chassis loom in the sands and dry wadi beds like ancient caravans frozen in time. It's been four years since the Arabs' failed invasion; we remain, watching and waiting for the next attack; it will surely come. At night, the High Plateau's terraced mountains of exposed limestone glow like lighthouses when struck by moonlight, pointing the way through the darkness. Our encampment is surrounded by hills littered with ruins, ghostly clay stone pillars and arches of burnt bricks; the remnants of Greek and Roman towns that once gave shelter to spice traders coming from the Red Sea, bound for Jerusalem and Petra. This desert is a desolate, lifeless place now, home only to men stood guard, and brittle groves of acacia trees growing in the shadowed foothills of the mountains.

Each night I inspect the perimeter, checking to make sure gun and mortar emplacements are well kept, and the men assigned to night watch are still awake. Every so often the mortar team sends up a flare, illuminating the desert. Night becomes day; the flare sweeps across the land like a curtain of light, revealing the once dark stage. During the day, the Plateau's temperatures turn our camp into a furnace, but at night the desert releases its heat, and the wind grows cold;

where else can men die of heat exhaustion during the day and hypothermia at night...

A private, Aarons, found me lying against a merlon of sandbags watching the latest flare disappear beyond a sand dune.

"Captain Nazarian," he said. "Command staff is on the radio for you, sir."

"Thanks," I said, pushing myself upright.

I returned to the command hut and picked up the radio receiver and held it against my ear. "Dagger 4/9 to Actual, over," I said.

The radio buzzed a moment.

"Dagger 4/9 this is Actual, please hold, over." A fizz of static...

"Dagger 4/9 this is Major Bercow... Jacob... you're returning to Jerusalem immediately..."

Four days later, I was walking through the entrance of the jail where Eliana was being held. I went to the reception guard on duty.

"Good morning," I said. "I'm here to visit my wife."

He looked up at me. I'd worn my Captain's uniform. "What's her name, sir?" he said.

"Nazarian."

The guard flipped through the registration log.

"I'm sorry, sir, there's no one here by that name."

"I was told this is where she's being held... Nazarian, Eliana." The guard checked again.

"I'm sorry, sir, there's no Nazarian listed. The log is updated every morning."

"What about Wasserman? Eliana Wasserman, it's her

maiden name."

The guard checked again.

"Yes, sir, Eliana Wasserman... can you please fill out this form and return it to me. Afterwards, you'll be shown to the reception area and a guard will have your wife brought to you."

"Thank you," I said.

I sat down to fill out the form. I was the only visitor.

I was alone in the reception area as well, a blank room, empty tables and chairs, and a single clock on the wall. All I could do was wait. A thousand questions were on the tip of my tongue, but all I really wanted was to make Eliana safe, to take her away from here.

The door opened and Eliana entered, followed by a guard. She was wearing a dark blue uniform. She looked tired, large dark half-moons under her eyes; she'd lost weight as well, I could tell just from her face and delicate wrists. I stood as she approached. It was only then I noticed the chains on her hands.

"No physical contact," said the guard, as he pulled a chair out for Eliana to sit in.

I nodded.

"Hello, darling," I said, sitting down and looking into her eyes, but her face was downcast, hidden.

"Why are you here?" she said.

"Darling?" I was surprised. "I was notified and came as soon as I could. What's going on?"

"They didn't tell you?"

"Everyone's told me a lot of different things... the Ministry of Justice, Father, Peter... I wanted to hear it from you."

"Why would Isaac or Peter have anything to say?" she

said, finally looking up at me... such dark eyes.

"I called my father when I first reached the regional headquarters, so that he could see you. They wouldn't let him in... only the husband or blood relatives."

"Of which I have none..."

"Darling, I must tell you, Peter sent his findings to the Justice ministry... he's why you're in here; he thinks... after everything he's found, he thinks you drowned Yitzak..."

"What?" she exclaimed, tears filling her eyes. "Why would I do that, to such a beautiful child... does Chaya think that? I don't understand... found? What did Peter find?"

"Chaya doesn't know, she hardly comes out of her bedroom. Why did you lie to me about your past, about the camps? Why did you say your family sent you to England before the war? Darling, I don't understand..."

"What's there to understand... I don't remember anything from my childhood... just darkness, the end of all things... why would I bring that here with me? When I left Oxford and came to Israel, it was to have a new life..."

"Why are they saying you helped murder and torture Jews and prisoners of war? Why would they say those things?"

"Is that what Peter told you? What he believes? What did he find?"

"I don't know... photographs of you with some Nazi doctor... witness statements from prisoners after the camp was liberated by the Americans..."

"He finds some photographs and thinks he understands what happened, what it was like in the camp? That every day was a decision not just between life and death, but all the decisions you had to make in order to stay alive. None of you were in the camps. How can Peter judge... how can you?"

"I'm not judging you, my love, I just want to understand, I want to know what happened to you."

Eliana began rocking back and forth like a metronome.

"You wouldn't understand... you weren't there."

"I grew up under Nazi occupation," I said.

She became incensed.

"You think because your father was in the resistance, and some Nazi soldiers patrolled the streets where you lived, you can understand what it was to be in the camps?"

"Eliana, I want to understand. I don't know where the lies end, and my wife begins; you have to start telling me the truth."

"About what? About how I watched my mother be shot in the head, or my sister slowly die in a filthy barracks, or how loudly men scream when their genitals are cut off without anesthetic? Do you want to know how many times I was beaten and raped... or the number of abortions I witnessed, the number of abortions I endured... how I had to crawl inside the fuel tanks of rockets and scrub them clean, rockets that were being hurled at civilians across Europe?"

I didn't know what to say... the guard stood in the corner looking down at the ground.

"Those who are dead and those who are living..." Eliana continued, tears slipping down her cheeks, wavering for a moment on her jawline before falling... "we are the same... the living... they didn't just destroy our bodies, they annihilated our souls... no, you don't want to know the truth, neither does Peter, or your father or mother. None of you were in the camps..."

She fell silent, rocking back and forth. I hardly recognized her.

"Darling, I love you," I said in reaction, as though it would repair the void between us.

"Don't say that, not any more... I have an attorney... he'll take care of things for me... tell your family, I'm sorry about Yitzak. I loved him, I would never hurt him... but his *death is my fault*, tell them it was my fault... and that I don't ask their forgiveness. You should contact the rabbinical courts and request a divorce... goodbye, Jacob."

She stood and walked toward the exit.

"I want to leave now," she told the guard.

"Eliana..." I said. "Stop. Eliana. Talk to me, please."

The guard opened the door and Eliana disappeared into the dark hallway as though descending into a catacomb.

27
Uzi

I was delirious after my first encounter with Eliana Wasserman. I no longer had control of my body, instead, it was a sinking vessel, every inch of skin bailing out sweat. I was unmoored, drifting... stumbling into the nearest bathroom, I threw myself into a stall. I could barely steady my fingers enough to unlatch my briefcase's brass lock. I took out a bottle of Newport; the briefcase fell to the floor, and I twisted the cap off with my trembling hand. I was drowning...

I drank half the bottle before coming back up for air.

Come back to me, my love...

I was barely conscious on the bus ride home to Tel Aviv. An hour into the trip, I wondered if I had gotten on the correct bus. The passengers' voices were echoes, the faded semblance of words. I pressed my forehead against the window and watched the daylight begin to fade; soon it was dusk. In the distance, I saw the glowing lights of Tel Aviv, and beyond those, the shimmering waters of the Mediterranean reflecting the light of the setting sun. Once in the city, the bus drove through crowded streets: merchants hawking food and goods; children returning from school, running through the streets in their white and navy uniforms; wealthy women pushing their children in carriages through parks, talking with friends while enjoying vanilla and strawberry ice cream cones.

We'd chosen names, remember, my love... Aaron or

Amira... the night before they took us, I dreamt it was a girl, Amira... how old would she have been now, nearly eighteen, a woman... how dearly we would have loved her...

Walking home from the bus station, the air whined with the agony of the summer's lingering heat, like a lame beast calling out to the migrating herd. I removed my jacket, threw it over my shoulder, and cleaned the sweat from my face. The local market street was abuzz with music; men sat outside cafes in short-sleeve shirts, drinking and smoking, playing chess or backgammon; cars and motorcycles zipped down alleyways, honking at slow moving pedestrians; shopkeepers and restauranteurs invited passersby to become customers; children skipped ahead of their parents... it was nearly night, but the city's lights only grew brighter in the darkness.

Had we dreamt of this too, my love... would this world exist without the camps? Is that what it was all for... so these children would know peace...

The bleating sound of gunfire rippled through the market. Fear swept the crowds as people ran every which way; parents scooped up their children, holding them tightly against their chests; tears streamed down the children's cherry-red faces. Some of the men stood and went toward the gun fire, helping people escape as they went; lifting up the fallen, encouraging those hiding under tables and market stalls to stand and run away. I don't know why, but I walked toward the gunfire as well. I saw dead bodies lying on the street stones, surrounded by blood; there were others, wounded, trying to crawl away.

Across the market square, three Arab men with automatic rifles were shooting indiscriminately. I continued walking toward them; when they passed a body, they would spit on it or kick it. I thought it strange they didn't notice me. I was so close to them now; I could smell burnt gunpowder in the air. The nearest Arab had his back turned to me. I was standing an arm's length from him when suddenly he turned around; his dark eyes full of fear; a face flush with sweat, the veins in his neck beating madly; he was only a child, younger than Amira...

He raised his rifle to my chest and pulled the trigger. "It's all right." I smiled.

Snap.

The rifle jammed. Panicked, the boy stepped backward, pulling the bolt back to clear the chamber. I took a step forward.

Snap.

The boy pulled the bolt back again and again, but the rifle wouldn't fire. He looked up at me, eyes wide and luminescent, as though gazing at the night sky. He was shot in the chest and fell to the ground. The other two attackers were shot as well as dozens of police stormed the plaza. The boy was not dead though. He lay on the ground gasping for air, blood streaming from the corners of his mouth. I knelt down next to him; his eyes were filled with hatred, the same that had burned in the eyes of every Jew at Auschwitz, day after day, like eternal flames...

None of the police noticed me, their care and attention going to the dead and wounded. I walked away from the massacre, back to my apartment; it was only there, when putting my key into the door lock that I noticed my hands were covered in blood. I went inside and tried to wash them in the sink; I even tried using the other bottle of vodka in my briefcase. I looked in the mirror; my face was old, and a ghostly white. Speckles of blood painted my cheeks and forehead, my shirt too. I began to shake uncontrollably; I vomited into the sink. I picked up the bottle of vodka, brought it to my lips, but didn't drink. The smell sickened me; I vomited again. I threw the bottle into the bath, shattering it against the tiled wall. I tore off my clothes and threw them in the bath as well. Staggering into the kitchen, I took an armful of vodka bottles back into the bathroom and began smashing them one and two at a time against the tiled wall. When I was done, the bath was filled with a pile of glass shards, like the jagged pieces of scoria ejected from a furnace.

For a time, I don't know how long, I was on the bathroom floor watching an endless parade of Jews pass through my living room on their way to the gas chambers... then the crematorium where I would be waiting for them... each set of eyes looked at me as they passed, and each time I called out, "Forgive me!"

The faces of those I burned: wives, mothers, sisters, daughters; the old, the young, infants, women with pregnant bellies; each one, I committed to the flames. Afterwards, we would scrap and brush and rake their ashes into great heaps which were loaded onto trucks, driven away to be dumped in the wilderness of Poland.

Why did I do nothing, my love... why did I not take you away from that place...

"Uzi," said Mrs Fishkin, the elderly woman who lived next door. "Time to wake up and eat something, dear..."

I opened my eyes. Mrs Fishkin was sitting on a chair next to the bed, a tray of food on her lap.

"Mrs Fishkin..." I said in a weak voice.

"Ah... and so he's alive," she said. "God works miracles

every day."

"Mrs Fishkin, what are you doing here?" I said, looking around, realizing I wasn't in my bed, or my apartment.

"So much racket you were making... moaning day and night. I finally got the building owner, Mr Fitzgerald, to open your door... and there you were, naked on the floor, crying like a little child..."

She placed the tray on my chest: a steaming bowl of bone broth soup and slices of rye bread. "Eat," she ordered.

"I'm sorry, Mrs Fishkin," I said.

"Just call me Vera, Uzi... no more standing on pretense after what we've been through..."

"What happened?"

"Four days of you sweating through my sheets and promptly expelling everything I tried to feed you... let's try to keep it down this time. I had to hire some of the young boys down the hall to pick you up every day so I could clean you... what a mess you were, Uzi... all that drinking... we found what you did in the bathroom... you could have just poured it down the sink, you know; no need to destroy a perfectly good bathroom. Mr Fitzgerald was not happy."

"Why didn't you just send me to the hospital?" I said.

"In the midst of all that chaos... ha!" Vera said. "The doctors had more important things to do than clean up a drunk."

"The massacre..."

"Terrible... thirteen dead, including two children, and so many more injured... I have seen too much," she sighed.

"I was there..." I said, "walking home through the market when the shooting started."

"Oh, Uzi...," said Vera.

"One of the men... a boy, really... he pointed his rifle right at me. He was as far from me as you are now when he pulled the trigger, but the rifle malfunctioned..."

"What?"

"The police shot him right in front of me."

"Come, Uzi, you must eat. Please, try and eat something, and forget about all that," said Vera, lifting the spoonful of broth and bringing it to my lips. I studied the faded registration tattoo number on her forearm.

I swallowed the warm broth. It felt like mercury running over my dry tongue. We remained silent as Vera fed me the soup.

"Why did you do this, Mrs Fishkin... I am filled with such shame that I will never be able to repay your kindness."

"I suppose it's been a long time since I cared for anyone... and what else could I do? Leave you there? No, an old woman can still be good for something..."

"Which camp were you in?" I said.

Vera put the soup bowl down and lifted the tray away.

"From the ghetto, they sent me to Majdanek... I survived because I could sew, can you imagine? My husband and boys went straight to Treblinka... to the gas chambers. It wasn't until August of '43 that I was finally sent there too. But can you believe, the day after I arrived, the 2nd of August, the camp prisoners revolted, storming the main entry gate to the camp. In all the chaos, some of us were able to escape... I ran into the forest with a few others. We ran all day under the August sun... we hid... we survived... God's miracle."

She smiled.

"We survived..." I said. "I'm sorry for your husband, for your sons..."

"We are too old now to be sorry, Uzi... your wife, my husband and boys, none of those who perished would want to see you like this... being so selfish with the life God gave you... he spared you for a reason, Uzi, same as he spared me, that we could make something of life... that we could find joy again. The dead... they are waiting for us, and we will be with them soon enough, but not yet," she said.

Wait a little longer for me, my love... there is someone I must help...

28
Miriam

I woke in the middle of the night. I thought I heard a baby crying. I left Isaac in bed and wandered through the dark house. Having only just moved in, the furniture was still in odd places, so I kept my arms out in front of me, feeling my way forward. I couldn't remember where on the wall the light switches were.

A wail...

Yitzak...

I stood still in the living room, listening. I could hear Isaac's snoring, and Chaya's deep breathing in the other bedroom. She was staying with us while Peter was away traveling.

Another cry...

I snapped my head around, orientating myself toward the sounds. They were coming from the back garden. I unlocked the glass door and slowly drew it open. It was nearly autumn, and the nights were becoming cooler. The denser air retained the smells of our new garden: the pungent citrus of the pomelo trees, the roses' deep fragrance, and the warmth of the lavender beds.

Another yelping cry...

I stepped out into the garden, my silver night dress catching the moonlight. Threading through the roses and lavender beds, I was soon among the pomelo trees, their bulbous fruits dangling from bowed branches. I heard scraping, then the trickling sound of rocks and dirt skittering across the earth. Walking beyond the pomelo trees, I came to a small clearing where the garden gave way to the wildness of the northern desert. Just in front of me was a golden jackal caught in a snare, the wire pulled taut around its neck, crushing the windpipe. The jackal was losing strength, though it still kicked out sporadically, yelping in pain. Blood dripped from its mouth. I approached, kneeling next to it. Its eyes, golden and reflective in the darkness, followed me.

I carefully reached down and tried to undo the snare. The wire was old and rusted, something left by the previous owners. I felt along the wire, locating the rod to which it was anchored. I tried to pull the rod out of the ground, but it wouldn't move. I rocked it back and forth, cracking the dry soil around it. I pulled again, and then again with all my strength. It suddenly came free, like a rotted tooth; the wire now loosened, the jackal freed itself, lunged and bit my hand, tearing away a piece of flesh, then bolted into the desert, disappearing into the low brush. I held my hand up in the moonlight. The blood looked black running down my hand and wrist. The jackal's attack was instinct, it didn't know what else to do.

Some days later, Jacob arrived from Jerusalem. He looked tired. Eliana's trial would begin soon.

And for once I agreed with her...

"You should go to the rabbinical court in Tel Aviv, Jacob," I said. "She told you to do so... only someone guilty would do such a thing... you must learn to forget her, we all must..."

"How can you say that? She's my wife," he said.

"A wife that refuses to speak to her husband. What kind

of marriage is that? A wife that will spend the rest of her life in prison… a murderess and war criminal…"

"Miriam!" said Isaac, using a voice once reserved for insubordinate soldiers.

"Should we remain blind to the truth? To what she is? She took Yitzak from us," I said. Chaya walked in, having just woken up.

"What's going on?" she said.

"Nothing, darling," I relented. Walking over to Chaya, I took her hand. "I'll make you something to eat."

The doorbell chimed.

Isaac grumbled as he went to the door and opened it. I couldn't see who was there. They had a long and hushed conversation. "Isaac, who is it?" I said.

He didn't answer.

The door closed and I heard two sets of footsteps on the tile floor. Isaac and a gentleman with a briefcase stood at the edge of the foyer. We all looked at them.

"This is Mr Uzi Willner," said Isaac. "Eliana's lawyer."

Mr Willner smiled.

"Good morning to you all. I'm sorry to have come so early. I hope I'm not disturbing you."

"Why have you come, Mr Willner?" said Jacob. "Did Eliana send you?"

"You must be, Jacob… no, Eliana hasn't sent me, I'm here on my own volition. Jacob, I was hoping to speak with you… all of you, really, if you'll permit me. Again, I'm sorry for the sudden appearance. I contacted army staff headquarters in Jerusalem; they told me you were on leave in Haifa… I must have only just missed you at your other house. The new family there gave me this address…"

256

"We couldn't stay in that house, not after what she did," I said.

"Mother…," said Chaya. "Please sit down, Mr Willner… can we get you any coffee or tea… something to eat, maybe?"

"That's very kind of you, but no thank you."

Isaac led Mr Willner into the living room, offering him a seat. "Thank you," he said, putting down his briefcase.

His suit was old, frayed at the edges; the rest of him looked old too, save the eyes, bright little things he used to study our new home for a moment before speaking.

"I do not wish to make this time any more difficult for you than it already is. But I think you all deserve to hear the truth before it all comes out during the trial… of what happened to Eliana."

"She's told you what happened to her?" said Jacob.

"Yes… at least, more than she has imparted to anyone else, I believe. I understand she told you to petition for divorce, Jacob…"

"Yes, she refuses to see me at all now, but I keep going to Jerusalem, trying to see her."

"I think she is only trying to protect you, all of you, in her own way… keep you away from the trial, and the journalists."

"We already know what happened to her," I said. "Peter, my daughter's husband, already showed us all the files, and photos, and transcripts of the survivors from that camp…"

"Buchenwald…" said Mr Willner, turning his attention to me.

"I have seen all those too, Mrs Nazarian," he said. "And yes, taken together, those images and accounts tell a certain story about Eliana and Dr Ziegler, the German that was just tried in Jerusalem."

"I read all about the trial," I said. "Everything that Ziegler did... that Eliana helped him do... killing innocent Jews, and prisoners, killing children... babies."

"The war was a time of collective madness," he said. "I worked in the crematorium at Auschwitz... burning thousands of Jews. When I came to Israel, I spent years going after Kapos, rooting out the traitors among us, so I thought. But now I look back at it, the camps... what were any of us trying to do, but survive? And now we live, I live, with such regret in my heart."

"We weren't in the camps, Mr Willner, but that doesn't mean we didn't endure the Nazi as well..." I said. "My husband fought them, and I kept the children safe the only way I could... there is always a choice, Mr Willner, always..."

"Mama, what are you talking about?" said Chaya.

"Your father was gone, fighting in the mountains... why do you think the Nazis left us alone, out of the kindness of their hearts? No, I kept them at bay by taking them into my bed."

"Miriam, please..." said Isaac, his voice full of sadness.

"No, Isaac, no... we all survived however we could, but that didn't mean we betrayed our people, that we killed them like Eliana did, just to survive..."

"You're absolutely right, Mrs Nazarian. We all had a choice, to fight back or not. Many did. I'm not here to assuage your anger, or to place on the scales the choices we each had to make... the judges of Israel are already going to do that for Eliana soon. I am only here to tell you what she has told me... these will be her worlds, not mine. After, I suppose it is for you, each of you, to decide what to do with those words."

"Then begin, Mr Willner. Tell us Eliana's story," said Jacob.

Mr Willner eased back into his seat, one hand reaching for the other, his fingers slowly rotating his wedding band.

"From what Eliana has told me, and I believe her... she was trying to save lives while in the camp. Mrs Nazarian, you may have been following the trial of Dr Ziegler, the man they call *the Butcher of Buchenwald*, but I need you all to understand, the man standing trial, that wasn't Dr Ziegler..."

"What do you mean he wasn't Ziegler?" said Jacob. "Who was he?"

"The man claiming to be SS Sturmbannfuhrer Dr Sascha Ziegler, was actually his brother, Tomas Ziegler... they were fraternal twins."

"This is ridiculous," I said. "This is just more of Eliana's lies. She's been lying to us since the beginning. She never said anything about the camps, not even to Jacob."

"Perhaps, some things are better left unsaid," Mr Willner looked at me. "Tomas revealed his impersonation to me. During the war, Tomas Ziegler was just a typist in the Wehrmacht. Sascha, *the Butcher*, requested his brother's transfer to Buchenwald just before Tomas's division was to invade Russia. Sascha wanted to keep his brother safe. Tomas was in the camp, working alongside his brother... alongside Eliana."

"Why would Ziegler's brother replace him?" said Chaya.

"A sort of misguided guilt, I suppose," said Mr Willner, a fog of confusion descending down his face. "Honestly, he was dying of cancer, and I think he just wanted some attention before his death... he went on and on about trying to get better food. A good meal seemed to mean more to him than anything else, really."

"And the courts went along with this? Convicting Tomas

259

instead of the real *Butcher*?" said Jacob.

"I'm working on sharing the information with the appropriate officials…"

"And the real Ziegler?" said Isaac. "He's still hiding someplace?"

Mr Willner turned to my husband, then looked at all of us.

"No… in fact, Eliana's story begins where Dr Sascha Ziegler's ends… in 1943, Eliana, just sixteen years old, killed Sascha Ziegler."

"And you believe her?" I asked.

"Yes," answered Mr Willner.

"Why?" I said.

I didn't want to believe any of it. In some terrible way, I wanted there to be an explanation for Yitzak's death, not for it to be simply a random accident.

"Because," said Mr Willner, twisting his wedding band faster. "No one would do what she did to kill Ziegler… my only conclusion, after hearing it, is that such a story must be true, because even the most accomplished liar would never dare tell such a thing and expect to be believed."

29
Elon

After returning from Berlin, I was debriefed several times over the course of a week. After a sabbatical to tend to my mother, I was summoned to Director Harel's office. I knocked on the director's door before entering.

"Come," I heard.

I went in. Harel was sitting behind his desk. Another gentleman, dressed in a well-tailored suit and smoking a cigarette, was already sat across from him.

"Good afternoon, sir," I said, approaching both men.

"Have a seat, Elon," said Harel. "This is an advocate from the Prime Minister's office... but as far as anyone else is concerned, only you and I are having this conversation, understood?"

"Perfectly, sir," I said. I did not turn to look at the unnamed party's face, though I could still see he was slouched down a bit, his right leg crossed over the left, while delicately holding his cigarette with thumb and forefinger.

"I've read the full report," said Harel, making a point to pick up and then drop the heavy folder on his desk, "including the transcript of the West Germans' audio tape of Wasserman killing Linz."

Harel reached into folder and pulled out the bound transcript and tossed it across his desk at me. "Have a read," he said.

I picked up the transcript and flipped through it, skimming the dialogue:

(Subject 1: Male; speaking German) I call it my hide away...

(Subject 2: Female; speaking German) Who are you hiding from... your wife? Kids?

(Subject 1) *Laughs* My wife and I have an understanding... she has her (static unintelligible) ... right along with everyone else... and my kids are grown now...

(Subject 2) You're very good at justifying affairs...

(Subject 1) *Heard opening bottles of beer* Is that what we're doing... having an affair...

(Subject 2) (static unintelligible) I haven't decided yet...

(Subject 1) What if I can help you decide...?

Sounds of Subject 1 approaching Subject 2, followed by kissing and undressing

(Subject 1) I haven't smelled a cunt as lovely as yours in years...

(Subject 2) I remember you telling me the same thing in the camp... right before you raped me for the first time...

Unintelligible sounds

(Subject 1) What the fuck are you talking about...

Sound of apparent beer bottle being broken

Subject 1 cries out in pain

(Subject 1) Crazy fucking bitch...

Sounds of struggling

(Subject 2) Don't you remember me, Wolfgang? The little whore you liked to play with at Mittelbau?

(Subject 1) Ziegler's bitch...

Sounds of struggling

I'd read enough and put the transcript back down on the

table. The Prime Minister's man puffed on his cigarette.

"Are we going to continue to hold Eliana at Camp Tzrifin?" I said.

"She's being transferred to Jerusalem as we speak," said Harel.

"For what reason, killing a Nazi?"

"Suspicion of collaboration with the enemy... and crimes against the Jewish people," said Harel, lifting up another file on his desk.

"This was recently sent to the Justice Ministry from Yad Vashem...," said the nameless man. "A researcher of theirs came across them while studying recently obtained records from Buchenwald concentration camp."

I looked through the file: photographs, in each a young woman was stood to the side or in the background; she was circled and identified as Eliana Wasserman; in the forefront of each photo was the man Eliana had identified as Dr Sascha Ziegler; after the photographs were survivor transcripts recounting how a young Jewish girl assisted Ziegler during his experiments, even preforming some herself; finally, registration records — *Eliana Wasserman, Weimar, 0199.*

"She's going to be charged as a war criminal?" I said.

"It'll be kept quiet," said Harel. "The Office's involvement... must remain opaque. That she was ever one of ours is already a significant failure."

"Israel's attention will be turned to Ziegler," said the unknown man. "The Prime Minister is looking to make a public show of it, the same as Eichmann... to spur the nation's confidence, and to show the world, Israel doesn't forget."

There was nothing I could do to help Eliana. One man cannot turn the tide of a nation. I went home in the evening and took care of my dying mother.

I cursed God for not taking her sooner.

The slow-moving cancer had been eating away at her for years, diminishing her physical state one piece at a time like the cutting of a puppet's strings. The pain was so great she could no longer walk or feed herself. God even took her ability to speak. All she could do was look at me, her eyes expressing her agony. Each night, I carried her into the bathroom and bathed her, cleaning the sores that had developed on her legs and back. Tonight, while bathing her, silent tears rolled down her cheeks.

"Do you want to go now, Mama?" I said.

She blinked, pushing more tears welling in her eyes down her cheeks. "Okay, Mama…"

I dried her and carried her back to bed, fitting a heavy blanket around her so she was warm. I went to the record player and put on her favorite music, the pianist *Claudio Arrau* playing *Beethoven*. Her lips made the slightest gesture, a smile. I opened the window so she could smell the night air. Rain was coming.

I waited, holding her hand, until the record was nearly done. I slipped open the drawer next to her bed and took out the doses of liquid morphine I'd been saving. I broke the glass cap on the first dose. She smiled again. I carefully rolled back the blanket and injected the first dose into her abdomen. Her eyes quickly became glassy. I broke the cap on the second dose and injected it. Her breathing slowed, and eyes shut. She had always been a slight woman, but the cancer had left nothing; she was a skeleton. I pressed the needle of the third dose into what muscle tissue remained and held it there until the clear liquid morphine was gone.

That was enough… her breathing became slower, then she simply drifted away.

"Goodbye, Mama," I said, kissing her on the cheek.

I pulled the blanket over her like a shroud.

It was only the rabbi and I at the funeral. Her husband, my father, had died when I was a child.

My brother was gone. The rest of her family perished in the camps. I buried her on a mount outside of Tel Aviv beneath an ancient olive tree; a tree so old, freed Jews returning from Babylon or Egypt could have taken refuge in its shade.

That night, I was sitting at home listening to Claudio Arrau when the doorbell chimed. I opened the door.

"General Nazarian… what are you doing here?" I said.

Isaac Nazarian looked a tired man, dark spots beneath his eyes from a lack of sleep. I can't say I looked much better. Standing with him was a man of similar age holding a briefcase.

"Mr Redlich, we're sorry to bother you so late at night. We drove down from Haifa this afternoon to speak with you," said Isaac. "This is Mr Uzi Willner, my daughter's… Eliana's lawyer."

Mr Willner nodded his head. "Good evening, sir," he said.

"Good evening," I replied. "Isaac, you should not be here, and neither should you Mr Willner… I've tried to help Eliana, I promise you, but it's out of my hands. The Prime Minister's office is involved now."

"With all respect, Mr Redlich," said Mr Willner, "you don't have all the information, neither does the Prime Minister's office…"

"What are you talking about?" I said.

"It's the wrong Ziegler," said Isaac.

I invited them in. We sat in the living room. Arrau continued to play in the background, and although my mother couldn't speak the last few months of her illness, the house felt silent without her.

"Anything to drink?" I said, walking over to the bar.

"No, thank you," said Isaac.

I turned, half looking at the lawyer. "And you?" I said.

"I'm fine," he said.

"Suit yourselves," I said, pouring myself a glass of whisky.

I returned to the living room and took a seat and lit a cigarette.

"Now... what do you mean, we've got the *wrong* Ziegler, eh?" I said looking at the pair. "Eliana identified him herself as *the Butcher*. A public trial and scores of witnesses identified him as such."

"The man on trial was not Dr Sascha Ziegler," said Isaac. "But his brother, Tomas Ziegler... they were fraternal twins..."

I laughed...

"Are you joking? Isaac... this is ridiculous, like something out of a bad spy novel."

"Eliana killed the real Sascha Ziegler in 1943, while she was still at Buchenwald."

"She did, did she? How'd she do that... kill the most famous Nazi doctor, and there's no record of it anywhere, eh?" I drank some whiskey. "You want to go to the Prime Minister with this, Isaac? And it doesn't change what she's accused of."

"Tomas was at Buchenwald as well, working with his brother as an assistant. Sascha Ziegler had his brother transferred to Buchenwald just before Tomas's division was

266

about to invade Russia. Sascha was keeping him safe... Tomas saw Eliana there, saw what she did... that she didn't do what they said..."

"Just so I understand, you want to tell Ben-Gurion that the Nazi butcher we just tried, publicly, isn't the man we said he is, not the man Eliana said he is, instead, it's his twin brother, also a fucking Nazi, who can testify that Eliana is in fact innocent. This is what you want?"

"I know how it sounds, Elon," said Isaac.

"It's fucking insane, Isaac," I said. "Why did Eliana even say it was Ziegler... the real fucking Ziegler?"

The lawyer leaned forward. "Eliana said Director Harel made it clear to her... Ziegler was to be identified and returned to Israel."

I laughed, thinking back on the meeting Harel and I had with Eliana before departing for Berlin.

"Harel wanted Ziegler more than anyone..."

I took a drink. "Israel's most powerful weapon is its memory... its divine right for vengeance... he says that shit all the time. Living in the glow of capturing Eichmann in Argentina... glory can become an obsession..."

"And what about Eliana... she spent eight years in German concentration camps... somehow managed to survive... then her own people cast her into the flames?" said the lawyer.

"I'm sure by now you've read the Justice Ministry's file on Eliana, Mr Willner. I have as well... scores of survivor statements denoting Ziegler's little helper, the Jewess, the *Angel of Death,* they called her... that Eliana would stroll through the barracks with SS guards selecting which Jews Ziegler would conduct his experiments on... as if she were walking through a market selecting pieces of fruit... that she cut open Jews herself... how does Tomas Ziegler, or whoever the fuck he is, explain away all of that?"

"You have to talk to Tomas... and to Eliana...," said the lawyer. "She was trying to save lives..."

"Save lives?" I said. "How was she doing that exactly by cutting Jews open?"

"Death can be a form of salvation...," said Isaac.

I turned sharply toward him.

"What the fuck are you talking about?" I said.

"I've done it myself... your brother. I killed him instead of letting him suffer an even worse fate..."

The lawyer spoke up "When Eliana went through the barracks and medical cells, she chose the weakest, those who would die no matter what...so that perhaps others would survive."

"And that exonerates her? Playing God... how did she know who was weak... who would die?"

"No," Isaac shook his head. "But it is an understanding."

"And cutting Jews open, how was that a kindness?"

"She would sever arteries... they would bleed out in minutes. It was that or let them suffer at the hands of Ziegler for days or weeks, after which they were disposed of like farm animals," said the lawyer.

"She was saving them from more suffering... from an even worse agony," said Isaac.

An even worse agony...

Arrau's gentle notes floated through the air, and for a moment I rejoiced that my mother no longer suffered.

30
Eliana

Illa was getting worse. Her fever wouldn't break. Gershom and I would prop her up during the morning roll call; I would acknowledge for her when the SS guard with the clipboard shouted her registration number. Every night, after returning from forced labor on the rail line or in the forest, Gershom would tend to her as best he could, getting her to sip water or swallow mouthfuls of broth; he would stay up with her at night when the fever was at its worst, then in the morning, exhausted, head out with all the others scheduled for endless labor.

I was working twice as hard in the commandant's villa, hoping neither the commandant nor the Witch would notice Illa's absence. I scurried through the house each morning, cleaning, dusting, seeing to the laundry, scrubbing the toilets, raking the ashes from the fireplace; thankfully it was Otto's birthday soon, and his Witch was busying herself with preparations which didn't allow much time for her to pursue other dalliances, torturing Jews and Russian prisoners. From what I overheard, the commandant's birthday was going to be a grand affair; high ranking SS officers and other commandants from nearby camps were all traveling to Buchenwald for the celebration. There would be festivities of some kind, followed by dinner and dancing. Large quantities of food and drink were imported, which I helped store in the kitchen. I accidentally dropped a bottle of schnapps. When the Witch saw this, she flew into a fury, beating me; she placed a metal spoon on the stove, heating it up until it began to blacken. She picked up the scalding hot spoon with a mitted hand and lifted up my dress.

"Scream and I'll burn you again, you dirty little Jewess," she said, and held the spoon down on my pubic hair just above my genitals.

The air filled with the smell of burnt hair. I bit my lower lip, which bled into my mouth. "Now clean that up, you little rat," she demanded.

I hurried over to the broken bottle and picked up the sharp pieces of glass one at a time. The Witch came over and stepped on my hand with her sharp black heel, pressing it into the shards.

"Faster!"

The alcohol seeped into the cuts on my hand — a thousand bee stings all at once, far worse than the burning between my legs. Still, I didn't cry out.

At last, the Witch, her shoulder-length red hair catching the light glittering through the windows I'd cleaned that morning, grew bored and relented. She stomped away, her gait unsteady, her fatty ankles and feet stuffed into petit, stylish shoes... ones all the women in Berlin were wearing, I'd heard her say the day they'd arrived.

The Witch wanted a band for the party. She ordered the SS guards to scour the camp for Jews or Russians able to play instruments. Once collected, the musical prisoners were brought before the Witch for her ears' inspection. The first violinist misplayed a handful of notes. To address the prisoner's failings, the Witch ordered me to retrieve her gardening shears; she snipped his fingers off as though pruning a rose bush.

The morning of the commandant's birthday, the August sun already sweltering, the Witch made vigorous love to him; her embellished wails could be heard all throughout the house. After they were done, I was called into the bedroom to clean up. The Witch lounged on the bed naked, smoking a cigarette, the lamp light casting oblong shadows across her lumpy body.

"Jewess, tell the kitchen I'm hungry… and bring me a wet towel."

I fetched the towel from the bathroom and soaked it under the sink faucet. The Witch used it to clean the commandant's diseased semen out of her genitals. When done, she threw the towel at me.

"Now, get my breakfast, you stupid girl, and make sure there are strawberries…" she said.

Dashing down the stairs, I could hardly breathe; the towel's rank smell, the commandant's semen and the Witch's drippings, spoiled the air like rotted fish. I threw the towel into the laundry and rushed past the kitchen. I had snatched a small basket from the kitchen and hurried outside to the strawberry garden. Up and down the rows of plants I went, searching for large, ripe strawberries… her favorite. Many of the plants were struggling because of the summer heat, their leaves curling brown, stems bowing like listless passengers on a night train. I could only fill the basket a quarter of the way with strawberries that would be *acceptable* to the Witch. The garden needed more water, much more water.

Back in the kitchen, the strawberries were cleaned, topped, and cut, then laid out in a pattern, just the way the Witch enjoyed. Served with two sausages and a steaming bowl of oats, topped which a cube of solidified goose fat left to melt, I carried the tray back up to the bedroom. The Witch asked for her silken robe. I put the tray on the table and fetched her robe. The Witch stared at her naked body in a full-length mirror, grabbing, lifting, prodding at her lumps, the crinkling fat deposits. She was proud of her roundness, like the landed aristocrats of old, those who had the time and pleasure to eat and grow plump from sugary treats.

"Brush and curl my hair, Jew," she ordered, sitting down at the table and eating her breakfast.

I fetched the brush from the Witch's bathroom and tended to her fiery locks. I could still smell the commandant's rotted odor corrupting the air. My stomach began to turn. I clenched my teeth and continued brushing, long… slow… soft strokes.

Later that evening, when the first party guests began arriving, I was made to stand at the villa's entrance holding a tray of champagne flutes.

"The finest… imported from Paris!" the Witch made sure to inform each guest.

It wasn't long before most of the guests were drunk and infatuated, dancing and eating and carousing in corners as though the commandant's villa was a Roman palace, a festival of bodily delights. The Witch made a show of torturing Jews and Russian prisoners for the guests' pleasure. I couldn't bear to watch. I hid in the kitchens all night listening to their laughter and raucous shouts… all mixed with the dying cries of Jews and Russians… what were they be doing to them…

In the morning, before the sun had risen, I began cleaning the villa. The dining room's wood floor was smeared with dried blood, prints of hands and feet. I filled a bucket with warm water and soap, knelt down and began scrubbing the floor; the water, soap, and blood all mixing into a dark froth. Stale alcohol and sweat lingered in the air, even with the windows open. I cleaned all morning. Later, there was crying from upstairs; the Witch was in pain.

"Jewess!" she said. "Jewess, where are you? Jewess!"

I scrambled up the stairs to the Witch's bedroom. "Yes, Madame?" I said.

The Witch lay in bed, her face disfigured by pain. The gout was coiling itself around her joints, tightening like a serpent.

"Get the doctor, you stupid girl! Get Ziegler," she moaned.

I immediately thought of Illa as I hurried downstairs and out the villa.

I must be brave for her...

I made my way across the camp, my eyes searching for my father as they were always wont to do. I was having trouble remembering his face now, Mother's too, but I could still hear her words to me... sifting through each of my thoughts...

Do what you must, my darling...

The Singing Forest was already being tuned as I reached Ziegler's medical barracks. Penicillin, Gershom had said. He'd explained to me where Ziegler would likely keep it, that it would look like a brown powder, almost like clumped beach sand. I steadied myself and opened the door to the medical barracks. Inside, the sharp antiseptic air stung my nose. I could hear Ziegler's test subjects in their cells, snoring, weeping, crying out in muffled moans. I walked down the hallway, quietly. Many of the lights were still off. I froze when I heard shuffling feet... feet in rubber boots... it must be Ziegler's assistant, the one who's always about, but whom I have never

273

heard speak, only merrily whistle as he goes about his duties. I edged farther down the hall, careful to keep my steps hidden amongst the moans and snores. I was passing by the cells, the naked, ragged subjects lying on the floor like heaps of dirty laundry, their skin burned and blistered by X-rays. Stepping along, a wood plank bowed and creaked, panicking one of the prisoners who must have thought I was Ziegler approaching... he looked up at me, eyes yellowed with jaundice, and screamed in terror. I tried to calm him, but it was too late, Ziegler's man in the rubber boots stomped into the hallway and flicked on the lights.

"What are you doing here?" he said.

The prisoner continued to scream in terror.

The man, wearing a rubber gloves and smock, both covered in blood, kicked out at the cell door. "Be quiet in there," he said.

"The Madame," my voice trembled. "Madame Koch sent me to fetch Dr Ziegler. She is ill, very ill and requests him."

The man sighed. "All right..." he said. "I'll go rouse him... but I warn you, he's probably still hungover from the party last night."

The man turned round and walked through the lab, his rubber boots squishing.

"Sascha..." I heard him calling, which I thought was strange, a private addressing an officer in such a manner.

"Sascha, wake up," he said.

I heard grumbling.

"Stop shaking me... what is it?"

"The commandant's wife requests you," I heard the man say.

"What does that bitch want now?" said Ziegler.

"The girl, her little Jewess, says she's ill."

While they spoke, I carefully crept into the lab, suddenly discovering why Ziegler's assistant was covered in blood; a cart full of bodies was in the middle of the lab, expired test subjects... I looked away, my cheeks tingling with a rush of fear.

My eyes frantically searched the lab. I recalled Gershom's words, *look for glass jars... powder the color of beach sand... Penicillin... take a handful, hide it wherever you can, even your shoes if you must...*

There were so many things in the lab: files, bottles, jars, mason jars, instruments, supplies, knives, scalpels, saws, needles, bandages... I rushed over to the glass jars. There seemed to be nearly a hundred or more of them, varying in size... white, black, blue, grey powders filling them... I searched for beach sand...

I heard the rubber boots squishing toward the lab.

My heart nearly seized as my eyes came upon a medium-sized jar, filled nearly halfway with what looked to be beach sand... it was labeled: *Penicillin.*

Squish... squish... squish...

I didn't know what to do. Before I could think, I turned myself around and faced the hallway.

Ziegler's assistant entered.

"He's coming," he said, lifting one of the dead prisoner's dangling arms and tossing it into the cart.

"Off to the crematorium for me," he sighed, pushing the cart with all his strength out of the lab and down the hallway. Suddenly he stopped, turned around and poked his head back into the lab. My body felt as stone; if I moved, I should crumble into a thousand pieces.

"Little Jewess, next time you come, could you bring some strawberries from the garden?" He smiled. "How I would love to have some."

"Yes," I nodded.

"Wonderful!" he said, turning back down the hallway.

I heard the back door open. Ziegler's assistant wrestled with the cart before the door slammed shut again.

I turned back toward the jars, hesitating a moment, listening, my ears straining in the silence to hear the slightest sound.

Nothing.

I reached up for the penicillin jar, grasped it tightly and brought it down. I removed the lid and a strange, musky odor wafted around me. I reached into the jar and took a handful, clenching it tightly in my fist... where to hide it?

A snapping creak of wood...

I panicked... Ziegler was near. How quiet he'd been... I opened my mouth and shoveled the sandy penicillin in, and held it there...

I put the lid back on and returned the jar to its place. I stopped myself from gagging, turned and began scurrying out of the lab when in stepped Dr Ziegler, half undressed... I could see the drunkenness in his weary red eyes. His lower half was exposed, engorged.

He looked down at me.

"It's the commandant's little princess," he said, moving toward me. I tilted my head down, staring at the floor.

Ziegler lurched forward, stopping just in front of me. His long fingers wrapped themselves around my chin and tilted my face up. I didn't move, nor speak, holding the penicillin as still as possible, lest I suddenly cough it out.

"Such a beautiful thing," he said, caressing my cheeks.

He lifted up my dress and inspected me. "A woman now too," he said.

Before I knew it, he had thrust me against the wall, injecting himself inside me... he started to rape me. I dare not speak... not a word... not a sound... nothing. I did not move a muscle.

Do what you must, my darling... save Illa...

Ziegler's violence ended abruptly, his wiry, insect-like body contorting around me like a spider webbing its prey. He was sweating and panting for air.

"How beautiful you are... my *petite princesse*," he said.

He let my dress fall back down to my knees, then spun me around, kissing me on the cheeks. He was close enough now that I could smell the alcohol and his hot breath.

Ziegler tilted my chin up once more, his vein-ridden eyes looking into mine, unblinking. "You must understand... I am not like the others... I'm trying to help the Jews... save you from yourselves... that's what all this is, I'm saving you."

After Ziegler released me, I went outside and coughed the sandy penicillin into my hands. I staggered back to the barracks, my lungs burning in a fit of coughing. I tore away a bit of my dress and wrapped the penicillin in it. Once in the barracks, I hid the pouch of penicillin between slats of wood where I slept. I covered it with some hay I took from my sleeping mattress.

I checked on Illa. Her face was pale. She was still burning with fever. "Illa..." I said, stroking her cheek. "Illa, can you hear me?"

She didn't open her eyes, continuing to shake and draw sharp breaths of air.

"I have the medicine... it will make you better. Gershom will be back tonight... he will make you better... I promise."

I returned to the commandant's villa, hoping my presence wasn't missed. As soon as I entered, I heard the Witch summoning me to her bedroom. Upstairs, she was writhing in pain.

"Where's the doctor?" she demanded.

"Coming, Madame."

"Coming! Where is he? I need him now! I need morphine... he must bring morphine..."

A little while later, Ziegler arrived, looking not at all as he did before. Like a ruffled animal that had licked itself clean, Ziegler's eyes were clear, his hair combed and slicked back with heavy pomade; he was dressed smartly, and did not stink of alcohol, rather a sweetness floated about him like summer flowers.

"Ziegler! Is that you? Hurry, damn it! Morphine," demanded the Witch.

"I've told you, Ilse," said Ziegler, putting down his medical bag, and standing beside the bed, hands on his hips. "Too much schnapps and sausage... and the gout flares up, terribly so..."

"Just give me morphine, damn you! I'm suffering with only this stupid Jew here..."

"A clean, healthy diet, and exercise is the cure, Ilse..."

"I'll tell Otto you denied me morphine, kept me in agony..."

Ziegler sighed, opened his medical bag and took out a clear vile of liquid morphine and a syringe.

The Witch slept blissfully the rest of the day. I continued to clean the villa, all the while thinking of Illa. It was all I could do to stop myself from trembling at the memory, the coarseness, of Ziegler inside me.

Illa will be better soon, safe. Do what you must, my darling...

It was night by the time I returned to the barracks to find Gershom tending to Illa, dabbing her forehead with a wet cloth.

"Gershom," I rejoiced. "I got the penicillin."

I went to my bunk, pushed away the hay, and retrieved the pouch. I brought it to Gershom and unwrapped it, revealing the sandy medicine.

Gershom's eyes lit up like circus wheels.

"Eliana!" he said. "Praise God for this miracle... he has surely anointed you." Gershom carefully took the pouch from me.

"It must be dissolved in warm water," he said.

He filled a metal cup with water and held it over a candle as the flame danced about. When the slightest bit of steam began to rise, Gershom pulled the cup away and carefully poured in nearly a quarter of the penicillin, stirring it with his finger until it dissolved.

"Good..." he said. "Will you help me, Eliana... keep Illa's head up, while I help her drink."

I came around behind Illa, who was restless.

"It will be all right, sister," I told her.

I gently tilted her head up as Gershom pried open her mouth, and carefully poured in a small amount of the liquid penicillin. Careful not to spill any, Gershom only poured a little at a time, as much as would have filled mother's sewing thimble.

"Very good, Eliana..." Gershom smiled.

I smiled too.

Exhausted, I climbed into the sleeping rack beside Illa, wrapping my arm around her, and holding her close to me. I began drifting to sleep when Illa began to softly wheeze, as though she were trying to cough. She rustled around, then fell quiet. I closed my eyes again. The wheezing returned, stronger now. It continued to get worse. I sat up.

"Illa?" I said.

Illa squirmed in her bunk, trying to breathe, grabbing at her throat. "Illa! Gershom!"

Gershom climbed down from his bunk and examined Illa. "Oh my God…" he said.

"What? What's wrong, what's happening to her? Is the medicine not working?" Gershom tried to force his fingers into Illa mouth.

"It's an allergic reaction, anaphylaxis! Her airway is closing…"

"What? Illa!" I cried.

Everyone around us was roused from sleep, nearly five-hundred sets of eyes watching Illa struggle for air.

"Do something! What does she need?" I said.

"I can't stop it… I don't have what I need to stop it!" said Gershom, the strength draining from his voice.

Illa was drowning.

"I've never seen a reaction this bad…," said Gershom.

Illa's head jerked violently to one side, she began to seize, shaking uncontrollably. Her face and lips turned blue; her eyes welled with blood. And then she was gone, still at last…

Gershom wept. I crawled atop her, shaking her lifeless body. "Illa!"

That which should have saved her, destroyed her…

31
Mira

His name was Askel: a soldier-physicist, if ever there were a more unlikely pair. He spent much of our first conversation explaining the theories of Albert Einstein to me. I smiled politely as he spoke. He noticed the smile, something most other men would miss as they prattled on about this and that, but Askel stopped talking, and returned the smile.

"I'm sorry," he said. "I often get taken away when it comes to physics... I don't mean to bore you."

He was thin, underfed, and I could see the lines of grief around his eyes. So many of the returning soldiers wouldn't dare speak of what life was like at the front. All the Jewish families in Weimar knew about Askel Wasserman, the decorated war hero with a brilliant mind. After Temple, after everyone had gathered outside in the plaza, my mother practically threw me at Askel as he walked past our family.

"Good morning," I smiled.

He stepped back at first, momentarily stunned by the sudden interruption; he seemed to have been lost in thought.

"Oh, good morning," he smiled.

"I'm Mira..." I said.

"Asbert... I mean, Askel."

His smile grew.

"Sorry..."

"Asbert?" I laughed slightly.

"It's what my comrades during the war affectionately nicknamed me…"

"Oh? There must be an interesting story there…"

"Yes," he said. "More silly than interesting…"

"Good," I piped. "I like silly things."

He was handsome, still young in his face, with a wiry frame like a sapling; as he spoke excitedly about Einstein and the universe, I recognized, although young, he was in fact an old soul, an ancient tree with deep roots, that had seen more seasons than most, freely offering its many fruits of knowledge and purpose without judgement or inhibition.

Askel didn't know it, still to this day, that I named Illa after him… Illa is Hebrew for *tree*. And so, two became three; Illa, a precious new life, which Askel and I would have to shield from the world until her roots were strong and deep enough to stand alone. Askel had been so worried during her birth. I heard his whispered conversations in the hallway with our doctor, a pleasant gentleman named Gershom.

"A miracle if she survives…" I remember Gershom saying.

I had no fear of death. It is something necessary for life, new life. My fear was for the child, and for Askel, who seemed concerned only with comforting me. After Illa's birth, Gershom again said it would be a miracle if Askel and I were able to conceive another child. That night, holding Illa in my arms, I didn't ask God for another child, I asked that my family be kept safe, and that if he deemed Askel and I well-suited to protect another life while its roots took hold in the earth, then that gift, that miracle, would be granted to us.

In Hebrew, Eliana means *God has answered,* and so this became her name. From her very first days, Eliana was a rambunctious little thing, so full of life and energy. She hardly took to my nipple and yet had endless amounts of energy. We had trouble keeping track of her when she began to crawl; we were always craning our necks and backs, looking under tables, beds, and sofas, all places that she would scurry underneath. Illa, on the other hand, a sweet child, was quiet and always kept close to Askel and I... ensuring she was shielded from the elements.

I noticed Eliana's intelligence early on. She spoke full sentences when other children her age were still grappling with single words. Askel took pride in both his daughters, but Eliana especially. I would not say he loved Eliana more than Illa, only that their minds were kindred, and he found a sort of warmth and grace in that connection. At night, Eliana would sit on his lap in his study while Askel worked, formulating equations I would never understand, but Eliana's large brown eyes followed every stroke of his ink pen.

As the girls matured, Germany grew a dark and troubling place. Askel kept saying it would pass. Once the economy recovered and the wounds of war healed, people would return to their senses. But all I sensed was a deepening fear and hatred in the eyes of those who stared at me in the marketplace. Public denouncements became commonplace. I was spat at and pushed, little children would tug at my dress and call me a *dirty Jew* as I tried to buy sundries. I no longer went to the marketplace, instead I shopped only at Jewish-owned stores.

"Why don't we leave Germany?" I asked Askel one night after an old woman had spat in my face as I walked down the Temple's steps. "She called me a foreigner, a diseased rat..."

I hushed my voice to keep its worried tone from the girls who were playing in the corner of the living room.

"My work is here, darling, we simply can't pick up and leave... where would we go?"

"Anywhere... we could follow your brother to England... now that Hitler is in power, things are only getting worse."

"Hitler..." griped Askel. "He was a corporal... what a charlatan... why do people listen to him? He is nothing but lies and hot air."

"They listen because lies sound better than truth. Does it really matter? All that matters is that they're listening... he fills them with fear and hatred, they mistake it for pride and nationalism; this is how he makes it patriotic to treat us like animals."

"Things will get better, Mira... the country will wake up one day soon and realize what's going on."

"When? When will they wake up?" I bit my lip to stop myself from yelling. I went over to the children.

"Come, my little darlings, it's time for your baths." Eliana pouted; she was never one to enjoy a bath.

My dear Askel understood the workings of the universe but not the evil inhabiting men's minds. Germany descended into darkness. By the time he realized we needed to escape, we no longer had the means to do so. Without money or a job, Askel began selling our furniture and art. He even sold the Iron Cross awarded to him for bravery. A fat little man bought it and proudly notched it on his coat next to a swastika pin. With the money he got from the Iron Cross, Askel bought a cheap bottle of alcohol and spent the rest of the day alone in his office.

It was all too much for him, I think. Even from the beginning. He couldn't face the truth. He'd already been through one war, and now he was being asked to fight another, and with no weapons; he retreated, and I hated him for it. I did what I could to keep some money coming in, sewing and repairing dresses for some of the ladies and young girls in the neighborhood. But it wasn't nearly enough.

"He just drinks and sleeps all day?" whispered Golda, as we sat at the dinner table sewing.

"Some days are worse than others... and his nightmares have returned, the ones he had when we were first married, before Illa... the one about the bomb the English put in the mine... he'll wake up screaming, covered in sweat."

"Mira... I'm sorry," said Golda, patting Eliana on the head as she ran past the table.

"I fear he's lost in the past... to the war... to the decision not to leave Germany when we still had the chance."

"No one could foresee it becoming like this... who could have imagined such a thing?" said Golda, defending Askel, and in a way, also her own decision not to flee.

"I only care about keeping the girls safe now," I said. "Nothing else matters."

I looked over at Illa. She was sitting by the window in a beam of sunlight playing with one of her dolls.

"We have no idea what's coming," I said. "But it's only going to get worse... we have to keep them safe, no matter what."

The night the SS came for us, I was bathing the girls, signing a lullaby as I used a glass pitcher to pour water on their soapy heads. I hardly had time to wrap them in towels and dry them off before we were dragged out of the house. The SS beat Askel unconscious. I didn't scream, just held the girls close as we were loaded into a canvas-covered truck with a dozen or so other Jews. Illa wouldn't stop crying; her cheeks turned red as hot tears rolled down them. I held her close to me, whispering to her that everything would be all right. She kept telling me that she wanted to go home, that she didn't want to go to the *Witch's house in the forest.*

Eliana didn't make a sound. Her eyes studied their new surroundings, the faces of others in the truck with us. I could tell she knew we wouldn't be returning home; she was adapting, already, I could see it in the way she held herself; no longer the eyes of a child.

The truck came into a clearing in the forest where all the trees had been cut down, leaving hundreds of barren stumps. We stopped. The SS ordered us out of the truck. Askel took Illa. I carried Eliana against my shoulder. I whispered in her ear...

"You're going to have to be strong, my darling... protect your father... protect your sister, she's not strong like you..."

The SS guards began to argue.

Suddenly, I understood what Askel had been talking about all these years. *Time is relative.* It slowed down as the young SS guard raised his pistol and pointed it at my head.

"Eliana," I said.

She turned and looked at me. "Yes, Mama?" she said.

"You have to be a brave girl now... Mama won't be around any more, understand?"

"Yes, Mama." She nodded.

I kissed her on the forehead.

"Do what you must to survive, my sweet, darling girl... if one of us survives, we all survive... because we are all in each other's hearts and memories, do you understand?"

"Yes, Mama..."

The last sound I heard was not the crack of the guard's pistol, but my daughter, Eliana, saying she loved me.

32
Tomas

My brother Sascha was dead.

All my life, Sascha had been the sun and I the moon; that two children, borne of the same womb could be so different. As a child, I read the Bible, day and night. It was the only book I read. I struggled with the words and letters, always mixed up, as though each time I read Genesis, I was reading it anew. My mother would beat me when I misspoke a verse, or when she caught me staring up at the stained-glass during church service. They hid me away in the basement during dinners with family and friends. When all the other children went away to summer camps, I remained home, alone. In time, I learned to read and write; I'd memorized how the words appeared in my mind compared to how they looked to everyone else. But by this time Sascha was already gone, away at university, one of the youngest students ever to attend.

After Sascha left, my parents kept me in the basement more and more, always serving me the same food. Punishment, my father said, for my sins, stale bread and crushed apples in the morning, a midday meal of oats, and a supper of fried chicken livers and boiled cabbage. How I detested the food. According to my parents, God purposefully struck me down, tainted my mind, and should they concede and care for me, even love me, this would go against God's will. I had sinned even before my birth, and only a life of redemption could see God's grace toward me restored.

In the basement was my father's old typewriter. It no longer worked. There was no ribbon, and some of the keys were missing. I started typing the words of the Bible as I read; this made them clearer in my mind, no longer jumbled as much. In time, my fingers were tapping away at the keys like bolts of lightning forking across the sky. This talent of mine saw me trained as an orderly by the Wehrmacht after war broke out and I was drafted into service. It was during training that I was able to read my first book, something other than the Bible, that is. One of my comrades gave me a copy of Hitler's, *Mein Kampf.* To be honest, it was very boring. Nothing exciting happened. Hitler just complained the entire time. It had none of the Bible's wonderful stories, the great journeys and epic battles. When I tried to return it to my comrade, he told me to keep it as he had an extra copy.

"Thank you," I sighed, not knowing what to do with it.

After my training was complete, I was assigned to the 132nd Infantry Division's command staff. Even the general was impressed by my flawless typing. He could dictate letters to me, and I would type them verbatim, without a single error.

It was a hot summer morning, and the Division was preparing to move out. Rumors were circulating that we were invading Russia in the coming weeks; however, a clerk arrived with orders from SS High Command. I was being transferred to a labor camp near Weimar called Buchenwald. The general made inquiries as to how the SS could issue such an order pertaining to a member of the Wehrmacht, but in the end, I was placed on a train heading south to Weimar the next day.

When I arrived at Buchenwald, to my great surprise, I was met by Sascha. We'd been apart since his departure for university. He was an officer in the SS, the silver skull and cross bones emblem glinting on his collar.

"Tomas, my brother." He embraced me.

"Sascha, what are you doing here?" I said.

"This is my camp!" he said.

"You're the commandant?"

"No, no, I would never do anything so menial. I am the doctor. I'm doing exciting work here, Tomas, critical work that can't be done anywhere else... and I wanted you to help me."

"Me? How on earth could I be of assistance?"

"Come, let me show you... it is the culmination of my studies and research... plus, I didn't want you going off to Russia; I hear they have nasty winters."

"I'm a typist, Sascha, I barely know how to use a rifle. I would be far from any of the fighting."

"Come, come, there is much to show you..."

The camp smelled awful, rotten, like brimstone. The ground was still saturated with the previous night's rain; as we walked, I swore I could hear the forest singing... I must have been tired from the journey.

Sascha showed me his medical lab: first, the cells where he kept his subjects, then his office and the adjacent room where a new X-ray machine had just been delivered, and finally the lab where I was to do most of my work, recording and cataloguing.

"You see why I need your help, brother," said Sascha.

"What are you doing here? What is all this for?" I said.

"We're going to change the world, Tomas... we're already working on finding cures to diseases... developing vaccines for typhus and typhoid... and I've been continuing my work on radiation therapy, how it can be used to destroy cancer cells... and other unnatural things."

"Sascha, who are your subjects?"

"Jews, of course... but soon we'll be receiving Russians and Poles, and all manner of subjects. I've put a directive out in search of twins, identical if possible."

"Twins?"

"Yes... they're perfect test subjects... can you imagine what we can do here, Tomas, given enough time?"

Sascha smiled, rising his arms in triumph.

I asked if we could have the midday meal soon.

Some months before Sascha was murdered, the camp commandant, Koch, had been removed by SS high command because of corruption, mismanagement, and black-market trading. He was sentenced to death. The SS even sentenced his wife to four years imprisonment, the crazy bitch. The new commandant, Oberführer Hermann Pister, saw no use in a Wehrmacht private after Sascha's death, and transferred me back to the army. I was sent east, where the Wehrmacht was facing relentless attacks by the Soviet Red Army; all I had was my typewriter, a black Torpedo Model 6 with an A key that would stick if not oiled.

I had no idea Russia was so flat: a sea of grass burned yellow by the late summer sun. Our train slowly jostled through towns and villages; the people, with heavy Slavic faces and bulging eyes, would look up at us, displeased for sure, like an audience after a poorly done theatre performance. The radio broadcasts in the dining barrack at Buchenwald always said how the liberated peoples of the east were joyous and welcoming of their German overseers. No matter, there would always be a few belligerents in any conquered peoples. The train ride was long, so I rested my head against my bundled jacket and tried to go to sleep.

I arrived in the city of Orsha on a Friday in the late afternoon. Stepping off the train with my clothes bag and typewriter box, holding my Torpedo Model 6, I immediately heard a string of artillery shells detonating in the distance. I dropped to the ground, covering my head. The other disembarking soldiers all laughed at me. I stood up, gathered my things, and looked around. In contrast to the other soldiers who all seemed to know where they were going and what to do, I had no idea what to do. There were another round of artillery strikes. My legs began to shake.

"What are you doing just standing there, private?" said a bullish major. I snapped to attention.

"I don't know where to go, sir," I said. He looked me up and down.

"What the hell are you? I've never seen such an oafish soldier."

"Typist, sir."

"Typist? We don't need typists here." He grabbed my typewriter box and threw it to the ground. "The Russians are that way," he said, grabbing my shoulder and spinning me around. "Now get going!"

He kicked me in the buttocks with his dirty boot. The other soldiers gaily laughed, then continued on, smoking their cigarettes, carrying panzerfausts and machine guns on their shoulders, all marching toward the Russians. I didn't even have a rifle.

I told every officer I could find that I was a typist, not a soldier. Each one yelled at me and kicked me toward the front. After a long chain of ass-kicking, I wound up in a trench alongside a squad of war-weary soldiers, their faces and lips burnt by the sun. A corporal gave me the rifle of a man shot in the head by a sniper that morning.

"Know how to use it?"

"Yes, somewhat," I said.

The corporal laughed. "Where were you before this?"

"Buchenwald."

"Buch-the-fuck? Where's that? The western front?"

"No, it's one of the labor camps run by the SS, for all the Jews and Russian prisoners."

"Must have been nice, ya? Bed, food…"

"The smell was awful, and the SS are crazy, but it was better than being at one of the death camps."

"Death camps, what the fuck are you talking about?" said the corporal, lighting a cigarette.

"The death camps… to get rid of all the Jews…"

"Get rid of Jews, what are you talking about… hey, listen to this guy, we're killing all the Jews in *death camps*," laughed the corporal; he drew smirks from the others in the trench.

"You haven't heard of the death camps… where we gas thousands of Jews every day then cremate their bodies in big ovens?"

"What the fuck are you talking about? The Jews were just sent to the camps to work or stuck in the ghettos… not death camps." The corporal turned around. "This guy's a fucking comedian," he laughed.

One of the other soldiers spoke up, a sergeant. "He's right, the SS, they're fucking crazy… how many of you were here when we first went into Poland and Russia?"

None of the soldiers spoke up. They all had young faces. Replacements, I realized.

"The SS killed every Jew they could get their hands on…

would round them up into buildings and set the building on fire… throw them in trenches and machine gun them."

Everyone was quiet, a few puffed on their cigarettes.

"Fucking SS," said the sergeant, who used a pair of binoculars hanging round his neck to peer over the trench wall.

The first thing I learned about war was how boring it was, sitting in the trench for days, doing nothing, smoking cigarettes, not even a book to read, then suddenly noise, ear-splitting noise, everywhere, all at once: bullets, bombs, rockets, artillery… everything going *pop, whiz, bang,* or *pow.* I was deaf within the first five minutes; our machine gun's *'zip… zip… zip'* rattling around in my head as I fumbled with my rifle. I had no idea what I was aiming at; I just pointed the rifle at the horizon and pulled the trigger.

Without knowing it, we'd been encircled, forced to surrender without ever seeing a single Russian soldier. It was for the best, I suppose. I wasn't cut out for soldiering; perhaps I would be a talented prisoner…

The Russians marched us east through the vast yellow-grass sea. We walked for days; hundreds of men died of thirst or exhaustion. Eventually, we were put on a train and sent farther east, arriving weeks later at a labor camp in a dense ever-green forest. The camp had no walls or electrified fences, no razor or barbed wire encircling it, only the deep forest, and the packs of wolves lurking therein, their howls echoing across the black nights. Nonetheless, many men still tried to escape, even in winter, but we were five hundred kilometers from the nearest town. There were some men who continued to peddle hope: "Those men, they've escaped, and surely lived, found a path through the snow and forest… surely there's hope." But I always thought they were escaping to their deaths. Survival meant remaining at the camp for however long the Russians wanted to keep us.

I lived and worked in the camp for six years. We ate the same thing every day. Sometimes we would get lucky and found a rat in the barracks, extra meat to put in our bowls of gruel. Gruel, as the Russians make it, is both tasteless and formless. When out in the woods, cutting down trees, sometimes I would find a grub or worm; maggots on a rotting carcass were a goldmine, but such treasure was of little comfort as months became years. The Russians didn't care how many of us died, only that the camp's quotas for coal and lumber were met. If not, we were punished, selected by random lot. One time, my torturer injected pure grain alcohol into my right eyeball with a syringe, blinding it. I suffered many other horrors: burns, beatings, coughing up coal dust, infections, and starvation. In our barracks at night, one could count the number of lice hoping from one head to the next... Sascha and his fellow doctors never did discover a vaccine for typhus or typhoid.

I never understood why God made me suffer it. *I wasn't like the others*... I never killed or maimed a Jew or prisoner, in fact, I helped them when I could... why should I have to suffer the same fate at the hands of the Russians... I never did anything wrong... I did what my mama and papa told me... what the lord instructed... what the Fatherland ordered... I was quiet and kept to myself... I was decent... I was good...

God, why am I always so hungry...

33

Stanislav

I believe I had been in that cell for over a year. Listening to the doctors talk all day in their lab, my understanding of German was improving. For the last few days, the name of the camp commandant, Otto Koch, had being repeated in conversation, along with the word, 'toten' which I knew meant *death*. Perhaps the commandant had died. I suppose it didn't matter for me. Dr Ziegler continued his experiments each week without fail, different parts of my body exposed to X-rays, sometimes for hours, charring the skin.

I was dying, slowly and painfully...

One day, a young woman showed up. I could hear the excitement in Ziegler's voice when she arrived. It was the same Jewess I had seen when I arrived at the camp. I would often peer through the bars of my cell to try and catch a glimpse of her. She was beautiful in the way wood smoke is, curling upward from a fresh fire; or how mist hovers above a field of wheat, absorbing the dawn's light. I looked at her and saw eternity.

I was surprised and joyous when she introduced herself to me in perfect Russian.

"My name is Eliana," she said, the brown of her eyes becoming amber in the medical lab's harsh white light.

"Hello." I smiled. "I'm Stanislav..."

In that instant, I forgot where I was, that we were

separated by metal bars, and war, and misery, and death... I was simply a young man talking to a beautiful young woman. Were we anywhere else, in any other time, I would have asked her if she would like to go for a walk, or have something to eat, anything to spend more time with her. Instead, we had slight glances, fleeting encounters, or hushed conversations while she was doing Ziegler's bidding.

It was always at night, when all the others had gone, that Ziegler, often drunk, would rape Eliana in the lab. I would press my face between a space in the bars, every piece of my body lurching forward, wanting to get to her. Ziegler had her on one of the examination tables, pinning her arms above her head so she couldn't fight back. She turned her head and looked at me. I reached out my hand toward her.

She never cried out. And so, neither did I. Tears rolled down my face; I wouldn't break eye contact with her. I would stay with her, no matter what. After Ziegler was done, stumbling around, buttoning up his trousers, Eliana did her best to clean him out of her. This is when she would look away, and so would I.

One morning, Ziegler's assistant, a strange bumbling man who often talked to himself, unlocked my cell door and escorted me to the X-ray room. I was strapped into the machine, worn leather bracelets tightened around my wrists and ankles, I was unable to move. Ziegler fixed the X-ray machine just above my genitals.

"No!" I cried.

The assistant stuffed a rag in my mouth, then smiled at me.

The X-ray machine hissed when Ziegler turned it on. I don't know how long I was exposed, maybe an hour or more.

After it was over, the leather bracelets were unbuckled, and I was dragged back to my cell. The assistant laid me down on the floor.

"Have a good day," I think he said in German.

I was naked. I put my clothes back on, oversized striped shirt and trousers, then curled into a ball and tried to go to sleep, wishing I would dream of Eliana and I, away from this place, walking through a meadow or swimming in a lake...

"Stanislav..." said Eliana, her voice soft and nurturing.

I turned over. She was standing at my cell door, arm pushed through the bars. In her hand was a fresh piece of rye bread.

"Take it," she said.

I reached up and took the bread. "Where did you get this?"

"Don't worry about that... you must eat to keep your strength."

"So must you," I said, tearing the bread in half and giving her the second portion.

"No... it's for you," she said.

"I will not eat unless you do," I said.

She took the bread, balled it up, and put it all in her mouth at once. I did the same. The bread was fresh. It must have been cooked that morning, I thought.

"I must go..." she said.

"Eliana... wait," I said, reaching out and grabbing her hand.

I was suddenly embarrassed that I had snatched at her, but I didn't want her to leave, not without thanking her.

"Thank you," I said.

She smiled. The first smile I had ever seen adorn her face. It was quick, like a shooting star streaking across the night sky.

She placed her first two fingers against her lips, kissed them, then put her hand back through the bars and touched her fingertips to my lips.

After she was gone, I curled back up on the floor. I smiled, and thought of nothing but her, and the feel of her kiss.

Later that week, Ziegler's assistant was going around collecting our semen. Those who could not produce the sample on demand, were forced to do so by a truncheon. Eliana went and spoke to the guards and Ziegler's assistant. She undid the buttons on her shirt, exposing her breasts to the men in the cells.

The guards had no more need of the truncheon. When she arrived at me, I felt ashamed to look upon her. "Look at me, Stanislav… please," she said.

"I will not take from your dignity," I said, tears wetting my lashes.

"I don't want them to hurt you any more, hurt anyone. Please, look at me." She reached through the bars and tilted my chin up.

"Look at me, my love," she said.

Another new set of prisoners arrived. I looked for Eliana but did not see her. I could hear her footsteps in the lab, light and measured, the barrack's wood beams hardly bowing beneath her. The new prisoners looked sick and ragged, not the fresh meat that normally came, Jews just arrived from the ghetto or Russian prisoners from the front. This batch was mostly middle-aged. The young amongst them already looked terribly ill, gaunt and coughing all the time.

Ziegler raped Eliana again that night after all the other Germans had left. Again, she did not make a sound, and so neither did I. After it was over, Eliana dressed herself. She looked over at me. I didn't know what else to do except smile. I hated myself for smiling. She looked pale and lifeless. I pressed my first two fingers against my lips and then extended them out toward her. She looked at them, then turned and left the barracks.

The next morning, I underwent my longest exposure yet, aimed directly at my chest. The burning was terrible. I was returned to my cell only to be retrieved later that day and subjected to more. It was like this every day for a week... I think. I no longer had any sense of time. My chest was terribly burnt, the skin blistered, black with necrosis. I was so weak I could hardly sit up in my cell. Any time I would eat something, I would vomit it back up.

Eliana brought me some cold water when the guards were all out eating dinner. "Thank you," I said.

I drank the water from the small metal cup. It hurt my teeth. I started to cough. "Drink it more slowly," she said, looking over her shoulder.

"Give some to the others," I said, handing the cup back to her.

"It's for you... I will not take it back," she said.

I set the cup down on the floor.

"I dreamt of home last night," she said suddenly. "I was home with my family... you were there as well."

I smiled...

"We were all having dinner together. My mother and sister were cooking. You and my father were talking... talking in the way fathers talk to the boy their daughter loves..." She smiled.

"And what were you doing?"

"I was sitting by the fire just watching everyone. Then my aunt Golda and uncle Efrayim arrived... we were all there together, eating at a table lavished with food and drink, so much we could never have finished it all… then you and I went walking through town… it was empty, an early spring sun casting golden light across the city stones… it was just you and I, walking in the day's radiance."

A trickle of blood shot out of my nose. "I'm sorry," I said, ashamed.

I balled a length of my sleeve and pressed it against my nose. "I'm going to stop him…" she said.

"Who?"

"Ziegler… I'm going to stop him…"

"You mustn't do anything, my love… we are coming. My comrades, the new prisoners, they tell of Russian victories in the east… the tide is turning, we must be patient and wait… stay alive…"

The weeks passed. I grew weaker. Eliana would bring me food when she could. But I knew I was dying. I did not know when, but I knew Eliana's dream of us together in the light could never be, not in this life.

I had difficulty breathing; anything more than a short wheeze and my lungs caught fire. I was lying on my cell floor, watching Ziegler's assistant clean the set of saws, scalpels, and knives that had been used that day. A pile of dissected bodies was stacked in a cart in the hallway, waiting to be taken to the crematorium. I would be going to the crematorium soon.

My body will burn, and I will be free…

My life's only regret was not being with Eliana. It had been stolen from us… but what hope did we have, those of us born to such madness… those would be my parting words to Eliana, that within this terrible age of humanity, we had found love, and so after everything, all the suffering… I did not bear any of it, her love had washed me clean of those things. My life was short and violent, but distilled within me is love, untouchable, even by radiation and flames... a single touch of her lips to mine that is enough for me now... I'm not scared to die. I believe I will welcome it when it comes, for I have known her, Eliana, the Jewess, I have known her love...

One afternoon, the bumbling assistant forgot a scalpel while cleaning the laboratory... he'd left it in a tray. Eliana saw it too. I looked at her, and she at me.

"No!" I mouthed silently. She turned away.

The assistant continued cleaning up. Ziegler entered the barracks, staggering into the lab, a bottle of champagne tucked under his arm.

"Ah, there you are!" said Ziegler. "Come celebrate with me; I've been awarded the Iron Cross by high command!" he told the assistant, raising the champagne bottle into the air.

"Congratulations, Sascha," said the assistant in a weary voice.

"Come, come, have a drink with me, celebrate..." said Ziegler, trying to uncork the bottle. The cork popped out, hitting the assistant's nose, bloodying it.

"Damnit!" blurted the assistant, grasping his nose.

Ziegler couldn't stop laughing. Eliana was stood in the corner, her head bent down. The cork rolled to a stop between her feet. She curved her foot around it, hiding it from view.

What are you doing, my love?

The assistant threw the barrack's keys at Ziegler. "Here, you lock up, I'm going to bed!"

"Come now, celebrate with me... Tomas!" Ziegler laughed as the assistant stormed out.

Ziegler leaned over, picked up the keys, and put them in his pocket. He turned and saw Eliana standing in the corner.

"Ah… my princess," he said, walking over to her. "Your prince has been awarded the Iron Cross…"

"Congratulations, Doctor Ziegler," said Eliana.

"You will celebrate with me, won't you, princess?" he said, kissing her on both cheeks and then her lips.

"Yes…" she said.

"Yes!" celebrated Ziegler, taking off his coat.

"Can I have a drink?" said Eliana, looking at the champagne. Ziegler looked at the sweating bottle and grinned.

"Yes, or course. Forgive me, my princess, where are my manners… I will fetch us some proper glasses for a toast!"

Ziegler looked around the lab, nothing but glass mixing bowls, and scientific equipment. He stomped off to his office to find something more suitable. I turned my attention back to Eliana. She reached down and picked up the champagne cork, then raced over and retrieved the razor scalpel left by the assistant in the cleaning tray.

"Eliana!" I hissed.

She looked over at me, her eyes wide as an owl's. She pressed her finger against her lips, telling me to be silent. She worked quickly. She cut into the base of the mushroom-shaped corked, then rammed the blunt end of the scalpel into the cork so the blade pointed outward. She undressed herself and climbed up onto the examination table, lying naked in the place where Ziegler favored raping her. She drew her legs apart and began to carefully insert the cork and blade inside her. I turned away in horror, unbelieving of what Eliana was doing. My heart raced; I forced myself to look back. When I did, Eliana was lying on the table still as a statue, her skin pale as snow... the same as it had been the first time, I saw her standing on the commandant's balcony...she had turned her body into a bear trap...hidden beneath the snow.

I heard Ziegler's uneven footsteps returning. Eliana did not move a muscle.

"I've managed to find two glasses, my..." said Ziegler, sighting Eliana lying on the table. "Princess..." he exhaled.

"A present for my prince," she said.

Ziegler hastily undressed himself, all the while staring at Eliana. Once naked, Ziegler climbed onto the table, kissing Eliana on her mouth and breasts.

"My princess... my love," he said between kisses.

Eliana grasped his head and drew him back up to her and whispered something in his ear. Ziegler smiled, shifted his weight, and then with great excitement thrust himself inside Eliana. Ziegler wailed like an animal caught in a vice. He reeled away from Eliana, hands clasping his genitals. Dark blood shot down his thighs and legs. He crumbled to the floor. Eliana reached down, and carefully removed the scalpel. Holding it in her hands, the blade glistened. She stepped down from the table, and walked over to Ziegler, who was balled on the floor. She stood over him, a single line of blood running down her inner thigh.

"For my family... for the dead..." she said.

Ziegler looked up at her, but as he did, Eliana swiped the blade across Ziegler's throat, opening it.

Ziegler died with a look of utter surprise on his face, eyes bulged, mouth ajar, tongue hanging out. Eliana dropped the blade and staggered backwards.

"My love!" I cried out. "My love!"

Eliana turned. She was in shock.

"Listen to me... get the keys from his coat... get the keys from his coat and open my cell!"

She did as I asked.

With all my strength, I stood as Eliana opened my cell. I embraced her, holding her in my arms for the first time. I felt her tears on my chest.

"Come, my love. Come..." I said, leading her away.

I set her in the hallway and retrieved her clothes. Once dressed, I brought her close to me again, then pulled back and kissed her on the lips. This brought her to life, and I felt her embrace me.

"You must run, Eliana... go back to your barracks."

"What?" she said.

"You must go... I will stay and clean this up."

"What? How?"

"I'm dying, Eliana," I said. "The SS will need someone to blame. If we don't give them someone, they'll go on a rampage... and it can't be you, my love."

"What are you saying?"

"I'm saying I'm dying, like my friend Sergei. I'm dying no matter what. A simple equation. I'm saying I love you... I'm saying, leave this place and never return..."

The realization of her own words swept over her: *a simple equation*. One life to save hundreds. "No... no... I won't let you," she wept.

"And I won't let them kill you... go, Eliana, go... and don't look back."

I pressed my fingers against my lips and then against hers. She embraced me one last time. "I love you," she said.

I opened the door for her. "Don't look back," I said.

She was gone. I returned to the lab, walking along the

hallway, opening all the cells as I went. Once in the lab, I picked up the scalpel from the floor and stood over Ziegler's contorted body. I spat on him. I turned round and sat on the floor, bringing the blade up and holding it against my throat. I could feel my heart beating for Eliana. I closed my eyes.

We were walking together in a radiance of light...

34
Eliana

After Ziegler, everything changed. Stanislav was right, the SS went mad for blood, but their fury did not extend beyond the prisoners in the medical barracks. The SS liquidated the subjects, two hundred and thirty-eight in total. Some were hung throughout the camp, left to dangle as a warning to anyone else considering revolt. The rest, about two hundred, were marched into the Singing Forest, made to dig their own mass grave, then shot. I was a member of the work detail ordered to bury them. My shovel grew heavier with each swing.

It wasn't long before I was transferred from Buchenwald to one of its sub-camps, Mittelbau-Dora, the underground camp where the Germans used slave labor to manufacture vengeance rockets, the V-2. I was chosen specifically for this task, not because I had any engineering or manufacturing skills, rather for my diminutive size. Manufacturing a V-2 rocket was a complex task, as I would come to learn; certain elements could be expedited by the right tools, in my case: slight wrists, small hands, and agile fingers capable of securing bolts or installing pieces of the rocket's internal organs where larger male hands simply couldn't fit. The SS considered using children, even experimented with the plan, however they proved incapable of the technical skills; moreover, they died too quickly... the conditions at Mittelbau-Dora were unimaginable…

We lived underground like rats in dark, dank tunnels fetid with our own stink and sewage. The air was barely breathable. The tunnels were so warm and humid, many died of dehydration and heat exhaustion. Our initial task was to finish the tunnels and facilities the Russian prisoners had begun. Each day lasted approximately fourteen hours; we cleared rocks, laid rail tracks, and installed machinery, all done in almost complete darkness as most tunnels only had a single line of light bulbs strung across the ceiling of jagged rock.

I had been transferred from Buchenwald to Mittelbau-Dora with a number of other young women, one of which knew me, and I her: Fenna, a Jew from Holland. At Buchenwald she'd been one of the girls the SS used for sex. Ziegler had performed a number of abortions on her.

"You're the one they call the *Angel of Death…*" she told me, as we both sat in the back of the canvas-covered truck delivering us to Mittelbau-Dora.

I looked down with shame, tears welling in my eyes. I didn't know they had a name for me, for what I did. But they were right. Where I went, death followed: Mama, Illa, Gershom, Stanislav, all gone now, Father too, surely. My family was gone. I couldn't remember my mother's face, but her last words still rung clear in my mind:

If one survives, we all survive…

I didn't know what to say to Fenna.

"I'm sorry," I told her, then buried my face in my hands and wept.

"We mustn't blame one another," said Fenna, reaching out and placing her hand atop my head. "They've molded us into vile things, like pieces of clay… all we can do is remember our

307

true form, the way in which God made us."

I looked up at her.

"I can't remember anything before this… I try… the faces of my family are slipping away from me, as though life before all this were a dream."

Fenna drew me close to her, holding me as I wept all the way to our new home beneath the earth.

Fenna and I grew close. We were even put on the same work detail: first clearing rocks, then laying rail lines, and then finally, in the spring of 1944, we were assigned to the assembly works for the V-2 rockets. By the time each rocket reached us it was nearly complete, a monolith of terror fourteen meters tall, and weighing twelve tons. All that remained was a final inspecting of its inner organs, for its outer paneling to be applied, and for the fuel tanks — one containing a liquid-alcohol mix, the other liquid oxygen — to be cleaned and inspected. To do this, Fenna and I had to crawl inside the tanks, scrubbing the walls with a petroleum jelly that would help stabilize the fuel from vibrating too much during the rocket's flight as argon gas pushed the fuel mixture into the engine chamber. I came to learn that the pitch and azimuth gyroscope mechanism was seated just above the alcohol-water fuel tank, near the nose of the rocket. After finishing with the fuel tanks, the rocket's outer shell had to be applied and fastened with hundreds of screws, a job suited to small agile hands and fingers.

At night, Fenna and I would huddle together in our tunnel, sleeping on rotten piles of grass and hay. Rats would bite our legs. Often, the rats knew who had passed away in the night before we did, waking to find a hoard of them feasting on the bodies, chewing the eyes, nose, ears and lips. But amongst such horror flickers of hope still burned, and only seemed to grow brighter by the day. Every night, the others would share what they'd heard or seen:

The Americans have taken Paris!

The Russians are on the outskirts of Warsaw!

I saw hundreds of planes in the sky, huge bombers flying east!

I didn't know what was true, what was rumor, what was hopeful imagination...

The Russians will be here in a matter of weeks! The Americans are three days away!

Hitler is dead, killed by a bomb!

All I knew was that we were still dying, dozens each day, and Fenna and I were getting weaker.

Curled up next to me one night, Fenna said, "Do you really think the Americans will be here soon?"

"I don't know..." I said. "Every time I think about it, I start to go crazy, so now I don't think about it."

"Eliana, you must have hope," said Fenna in a firm voice.

"Hope... my family... everyone is gone. Even if we survive, what will be left for us?" I said.

"I don't know, but the only way to know for sure is to live. I often think, all this, the camps, it is not the end, this is not God's test for us..."

"What do you mean?"

"The true test will come when it is over," she said. "When we are free. We will have to choose whether or not to go on living, whether or not to rebuild our lives, our faith, our family — be it blood or kindred. God's test was never death, it is life."

If one survives, we all survive...

"What will you do, after we are free?" I asked.

Fenna smiled. And though I could hardly see her thin face in the tunnel's darkness, I knew she was imagining a better world, one beyond all this, a world where we were safe and free of fear.

"I would like to be a mother," she said. "If God allows…"

The next morning, a new German engineer was put in charge of final inspection. His name was Wolfgang Linz. He was worse than Ziegler when it came to torture and death. He would patrol the assembly area each morning, randomly shooting a handful of Jews in the head with his Luger. I don't know how he chose who would die, perhaps he didn't either. It seemed that for Linz, killing Jews was like scratching an itch… something that had to be done. It didn't take him long to start abusing Fenna and I. Raping us when the mood struck him. He had no qualms about doing so in public, bending us over a pylon and lifting up our dresses. How I wished I could cut his throat as well…

After Linz arrived, Fenna grew quieter at night. She no longer talked of the future. She would lay on the hay-strewn floor breathing in and out. There was something mechanical to it, passive.

"Are the Americans here yet?" she would ask me each night.

"Soon… very soon," I would tell her.

One afternoon, Linz raped me in his office. As he was doing so, my eyes searched the room. They fell upon a small paperback book that had been left out. It was titled, *Partial Elliptic Differential Equations*. After Linz finished, cleaning himself up, smearing a dank towel over his flushed, sweaty face, I snatched the book, putting it under my dress, pressing it between my thighs.

"Get out...," said Linz. "Get back to work."

I was careful to walk away keeping the book pinned. That night, as Fenna slept next to me, I took the book out and began reading it in the tunnel's dim light. Suddenly, I was transported home, sitting on my father's bony knees as he bounced me up and down. I began to recall the symbols. Father always spoke aloud as he wrote...

Harmonic function...

Partial differential equation... Laplace's equation...

My mind flooded with memories. I didn't sleep at all that first night with the book, reading until the whistle sounded for our work shift to begin. The whistle startled me. I had lost all track of time. I put the book down and pushed it against the wall, burying it beneath a pile of dead grass and hay. All I could think about that day was the equations, their perfect forms... abstract and yet menacing... used to precisely calculate the trajectory of the V-2 rockets. The rockets would hurtle through the air at incredible speeds, pushed by its conical engine burning hundreds of liters of explosive fuel, following the trajectory laid out for it by mathematics and gravity, becoming an unstoppable function of the human mind.

The gyroscopes...

Without the gyroscopes, the rocket would unbalance itself, fly off course, miss its target. The gyroscopes were sealed in a metal box. I couldn't destroy them even if I wanted to. But the electrical system, running from the gyroscopes to the stabilization fins, was exposed, but only in one place: the bend to get around the fuel tanks. I could see the exposed wires behind the tank. I stepped back and looked around. SS guards were walking, observing. I could hear Fenna working in the other tank. I slowly got down on my knees, leaned forward, and reached my hand deep into the rocket, wiggling it through the maze of piping, cables, and bolts. My hand was nearly to the wires, it needed only fit through a small opening between a fuel pipe and the tank. The opening was very small. I pointed and squeezed my hand together, hoping it would be small enough to fit through.

I couldn't do it.

I pulled my hand out and checked the guards again. I dipped my hand into the petroleum jelly and tried again. The flat of my hand and thumb came up against the opening. I pushed hard; my hand slipped through. I was able to feel the delicate copper wires with my fingertips. I began scratching the wires with my nails, pulling, ripping, anything I could do to destroy them. One of the SS guards came close. Afraid, I pulled my hand out and returned to work. I didn't know if I had managed to fully destroy the wires, or whether Linz would notice them during his final inspection.

It wasn't until the next day that Linz conducted his inspection, circling the rocket with his list, checking off items one at a time. Linz would use his eyes and hands, first visually inspecting and then jostling parts to make sure they were secure. He was working his way toward the rocket's cone where the warhead and gyroscopes were located. I was working on another rocket, looking at Linz with darting glances. My heart raced.

Would he find it?

Linz stopped at the rocket's cone and bent down. I didn't know what he was looking at, or whether he'd found my attempted sabotage. Had I even done anything at all, with nothing but my fingers? Were they enough to destroy the wiring? Had I killed myself for nothing... Linz would find it and surely there would be executions.

What have I done?

Linz plucked his pencil from his ear and checked the paper he was holding, then stood and ordered the workers to begin installing the rocket's outer paneling, sealing it.

He hadn't seen it... my God, he didn't see it...

I started to breathe again, cleaning sweat from my forehead with the back of my hand. I hardly realized I'd smeared jelly across my forehead. Fenna started laughing at me. I smiled at her as I used my sleeve to rub it away.

I wasn't expecting to learn whether my sabotage had worked, but two weeks later I overheard Linz on a phone in his office having a heated conversation. From what I understood, a rocket was launched that morning, rose a few hundred meters into the sky before pitching forward and plummeting to the earth.

Had it worked?

I continued to sabotage the wiring as best I could. In the following weeks, Linz had dozens of panicked phone calls. Rockets were falling out of the sky like birds with broken wings. High command wanted answers, immediately. A team of specialists arrived to see to the matter. It was either sabotage or incompetence, I heard one of the specialists say, their leader I presumed; he was a tall man with wavy brown hair. The others referred to him as Wernher. Each missile at the final assembly point was thoroughly examined piece by piece. It wasn't long before Wernher himself discovered what I had been doing.

"The gyroscope wiring has been shredded! You idiot! How could you miss something so simple?" he cursed Linz. "Fix it!"

The SS gathered all the workers together. Three hundred were selected at random to be executed.

Linz stood before all of us, giving a speech, as each of the three hundred were shot in the head one by one.

"This is what mercy looks like..." he began. "I have selected only three hundred to die, instead of all of you... remember my mercy the next time you think about sabotaging my rockets!"

Crack... crack... crack... went the Lugers.

Every shot fired; my heart skipped a beat.

What have I done...?

At night, when we were in our tunnel, I drew Fenna close to me. "I was cutting the wires," I wept.

"What?" she whispered. "Eliana?"

"I did it once, and Linz didn't find it, so I did it again and again... they're all dead because of me." Fenna put her arms around me.

"Shhh... shhh..." she tried to sooth me.

"What have I done..."

"You fought back, Eliana... you fought back. Look at me," she held my chin up. "Don't stop destroying the wires, all right."

"I can't, not any more... I can't..."

Fenna held me as I wept. All I could see in my mind were the faces of the dead, all of them lying on the factory floor.

I stopped sabotaging the wires. I worked like a good Jew. Eventually, the end did come. The SS frantically closed down the camp as American and allied forces approached. Some of the prisoners rejoiced.

The Americans are coming!

The SS responded by liquidating the camp. All prisoners

deemed too weak to travel were shot or simply left to die. In all the chaos, I snatched Fenna.

"We must hide! The SS are killing everyone."

We raced through the factory, the sounds of screams and single-round gun shots following behind us.

"Where will we hide?" said Fenna.

I looked around the factory. I grabbed her hand and pulled her along behind me to one of the half-completed rockets.

"In the fuel tanks... come quickly, get inside."

We each climbed inside a fuel tank and remained there. The SS continued to cleanse the camp for another two days. Neither Fenna nor I moved; we did not make a sound. Then, on the third day, everything was silent. No more gunshots, no more screams.

"Fenna..." I whispered. "Are you still there?"

"Eliana..." she said in a weak voice. "I'm so thirsty..."

I pushed the fuel tank covering open slightly, peering out at the factory. It was empty. Pieces of machinery, rocket parts, tools, all scattered on the floor... bodies too. I opened the covering more, pushing it off. I climbed out and helped Fenna get out of her tank.

"I think they've all gone," I said.

Fenna looked around. She was pale and shaking. "Where is everyone? Where are the others?"

"I don't know... let's find some water and food, if we can."

There was nothing in the factory. We walked above ground. I could smell smoke. "The sun is so bright..." said Fenna, holding her hands over her eyes.

I shielded my eyes as best as I could and looked around. The camp above ground had been liquidated as well. There were only a few lonely souls alive, aimlessly walking past all the bodies covering the ground like wheat chaff. Greasy lines of smoke floated up from burnt barracks, charred bodies housed within. We struggled onward, into the camp. There was no food or water there either. I knew there was a river nearby, the *Zorge*. I spun around, looking for it, spotting it in the distance, its waters glimmering in the morning light near the edge of the beech forest.

"Fenna," I pointed at the river.

We walked together, holding one another up. Finally reaching the riverbank, we began to drink. After having our fill, we laid for hours on the bank resting, feeling the warmth of the sun and the rush of the wind on our skin.

"Is it over?" said Fenna, staring up a group of parading white clouds.

"I don't know," I said. "I think so."

"What should we do?"

I stood up. My legs had so little strength left. We had to find food.

"Come," I said. "Maybe we can find something in the forest. If not, we can hide there; we don't know if the Germans are going to come back."

Walking toward the forest's edge, I spotted what looked to be a grouping of wild roses, vibrant balls of red shining in the afternoon light, but as we drew closer, I realized what they were instead.

"Strawberries!" celebrated Fenna, who ran over to the knee-high plants growing at the forest edge.

Fenna immediately began picking and eating the strawberries, stuffing them in her mouth so quickly her cheeks swelled up like balloons as the sweet juices ran down her chin.

"It's a miracle!" Fenna managed to say with a full mouth.

I smiled and began eating as well, picking the largest strawberries I could find, some as big as apples. I took great bites out of them, their warmth and sweetness filling my mouth. We ate all afternoon. Fenna ate until she was sick and then ate some more. Night came and we huddled together for warmth. I stayed awake most of the night, listening, fearful the Germans would return. In the morning, we started walking through the forest. Patches of strawberries patterned the forest floor, and without knowing it we followed them, like a chain of islands, plucking and eating as we went. We walked all day, resting at times, but always moving on. I didn't know where the strawberries were taking us, only that they were keeping us alive. On the second day, we arrived at a clearing, thousands of cut tree stumps stood immobile in a sea of sifting strawberry plants, their bright green leave and red fruit oscillating back in forth in the wind.

"An entire sea of strawberries..." said Fenna in amazement. "How is this all here?"

On the other side of the clearing, through a thin veil of trees that had not been cut down, I saw a series of structures, surrounded by razor wire: it was Buchenwald. The strawberries had led us back to Buchenwald, to the Witch's Garden. The wild strawberries had all come from the garden Illa and I planted to feed the Witch; the seeds, spread by wind or animals, in the feces of SS guards who ate them and then shit them out in the forest as they went about their work, killing; the strawberries spread like an infection, growing healthiest in the soil where mass graves had been dug, the roots feeding off the nutrients of the bodies below and the ash-smoke spread by the crematorium.

I screamed.

The guard banged on my cell door. "You have a visitor," he said.

I woke and rubbed the sleep from my eyes. It was probably Jacob again. "I don't want to see him," I said.

"It's not your husband, it's a woman."

I sat up.

Miriam? Chaya? How did they get in?

The guard escorted me to the visitors' room. I walked inside. A single woman, dressed in a blue wool sweater and long skirt, was sitting at the table. She stood when she saw me.

"Hello, Eliana," she smiled.

"Fenna!" I said, running to her.

We embraced. The guard pulled us apart.

"No contact or you're going back to your cell," she said.

"Yes, I'm sorry," I said, sitting down.

Fenna sat as well.

"What are you doing here?" I said.

"I told them I'm your sister," she said. "I hope you don't mind. I needed to see you."

I smiled.

"You are my sister."

"I was here... testifying against Ziegler, during his trial..."

"Fenna..." I said.

"It's all right... I'm proud I had the courage to do it. After I was done testifying, your lawyer, Uzi, approached me, and told me what had happened to you... I couldn't believe it."

I looked away in shame.

"He asked if I would be willing to testify on your

behalf…"

"Fenna, please, you don't have to do that. I don't want you dragged into this…"

"I don't know how much good I'll be able to do." She smiled. "He says I'm your only witness, the only one who knows what you really did… the prosecution has dozens of witnesses… sworn statements… but I wanted to be here for you… and tell the truth, as I know it."

I gripped the table and began to cry. "Fenna…" I said, my whole-body trembling.

"What you did was incredible, Eliana… so much so, no one may believe it…"

"All these years and I'm still in the camps… I never got out," I said.

Fenna reached out and took my hand.

"God's test was never death," she said. "It is life."

35
Askel

Gregor found a pair of wire shears in the truck which we planned to use to cut through a remote section of the border fence separating German occupied Alsace-Lorraine from the Vichy government's Southern Free Zone. We abandoned the truck in a grove of trees, then waited until nightfall to cut through. We entered the Free Zone on the morning of 12 November 1942. The next day, the entire German Army came looking for us...

Four days prior to our nighttime crossing, American and British troops landed in North Africa, establishing the Allies' first tenuous foothold in the west. In response, German and Italian troops flooded across the lines of demarcation, seizing southern France. We were not to know of the Allies' invasion, prompting the Germans' response, for many weeks; we all presumed the German army had nothing better to do than hunt down four runaway Jews.

"They've sent an entire division after us," hissed Josef, peering out through the thicket we were hiding in, studying the long grey column of German troops and motor vehicles trudging along the road in the valley below.

"That's ridiculous," said Elijah, recovering but still very weak from his bout with dysentery. "A squad of SS, maybe, but an entire division... something else is going on."

"Doesn't change anything," said Gregor, sat in the thicket

shaking, still only wearing his striped camp clothes. "The weather's changing quickly to winter… we can't make a fire for fear of being seen, but we can't stay out here much longer."

Gregor clutched his arms together, rubbing them, trying to warm himself. I took off the German coat I'd been wearing and put it around his shoulders. He nodded a thank you.

"We move at night," I said. "After the column of Germans has passed."

"And go where?" said Josef.

"Doesn't matter," I said. "Just as long as we keep moving."

"We need food, water… a place to rest out of the cold… a nice barn house would do," said Elijah. I looked at Gregor, trembling in Hegelmann's coat.

"Perhaps the Germans' arrival can be used to our advantage," I pondered aloud.

"What do you mean… how are more Germans a good thing?" said Josef.

"Look at us," I said, opening my arms somewhat theatrically. "Before, we were in Vichy France… dressed in a mix of German uniforms and Jewish prison outfits, both of which would draw immediate attention if we were seen by local authorities or even a passing farmer. But now, the countryside is swarming with Germans. And we still own the rank of Captain," I said, nodding toward Gregor. "We carry on as before, two Germans with two Jewish prisoners. We search for a vehicle, anything… hopefully we come across a quiet farmhouse we can requisition."

"Requisition a farmhouse?" said Elijah, half smiling at the thought. "

What?" I said. "Is a farmhouse not good enough for an SS

Captain?"

"Just make... make sure it has... chickens," Gregor stuttered with chill. "I'd like... scrambled eggs for breakfast."

Everyone laughed.

"What will we do with the people living there? If we do manage to find a farmhouse," said Elijah.

"Tell them to leave," said Josef.

"Throw them out?" said Elijah, blowing warm air into his hands and rubbing them together.

"Wouldn't they go complain to the nearest German or Vichy official?"

"Tie them up..." suggested Gregor.

"Kill them...," said Josef.

"We're not killing anyone, especially a whole family," I said. "We're not the fucking Germans. They're occupied... prisoners, just like us."

"Really?" said Josef. "How many French Jews have found their way to the camps we've visited, the death camps too... the Vichy hate Jews just as much as the Nazi, and hunt them just as good... it's us or them, Askel..."

"There's no point in discussing any of it..." sighed Elijah. "It's all circumstantial. We must keep focus on what is immediately in front of us, and for now that's staying warm and finding shelter... whatever comes, we will face it together..."

We were in the woods another two nights, wandering, searching, for what, we didn't know. We'd escaped Germany with our lives, only to come to southern France and once again be surrounded by Germans. We skulked in the tree line near the roads, hoping they would lead us to something... an abandoned vehicle, a township, a warm barn, anything to get us out of the cold. Gregor was unwell, his eyes, nose, and mouth inflamed. He broke into fits of coughing every few steps, causing us to stop. Elijah was none the better still, weak, and possessing no stamina. It would be better to say we crawled, limped, and cursed our way through the forest, and its many tickets, groves, and underbrush.

I was accustomed to the beech forest surrounding Weimar, camping and hiking there as a child — taking the girls and Mira on picnics — but the autumnal woods of central France were far wilder. The sky was a depthless grey and the wind cut through us. One more night in the cold and I feared we might all freeze to death. The night before, Gregor begged us to make a fire using Hegelmann's cigarette lighter.

"Before... we... all... freeze!" he said, his teeth chittering inside his head like the coins in a beggar's cup.

"Someone will see!" hissed Josef, his hands tucked under his armpits.

"So, we either freeze to death, or get shot in the head by a German patrol... either way, we're dead, so we might as well be warm before we die."

"No one's lighting a fire," said Elijah. "We huddle together for warmth as we've been doing."

"Everyone try to relax..." I said, beseeching God to warm us.

"We haven't eaten for days... but, if I'm right, I think there will be a farm just over that next ridge." I pointed in the darkness to the south, to a purple ridge line populated by oak, beech, and fir trees.

"How do you... know there is... a farm on the other side?" stammered Gregor.

"Because... one more night out in the cold like this and

we'll freeze to death, and God wouldn't allow that; he's brought us this far…" I said.

"And if there's no farm or salvation of any kind over that ridge, then what? God has abandoned us?" said Josef. "I think he did that a long time ago, Askel… if you haven't noticed, thousands of Jews are being murdered every day and He does nothing to stop it, nothing."

"He's kept us alive this long…" I said.

"Say… that… again in the… morning… after one of… us is frozen stiff," said Gregor.

"Only God can protect my girls now," I said. "I have to believe he will, somehow, and that he might return me to them again in this life, if only for the briefest moment, so that they would know my love for them is undying."

"Well… what are we all standing around here for," said Elijah, pacing off toward the ridge line. "Let's see what God has in store for us."

Elijah climbed the ridge with an energy I did not know he possessed. We did our best to keep pace, but he was nearly fifty meters ahead of us when he reached the ridge line looking down into the next valley.

Elijah laughed and howled like a wolf at the moon. We all scrambled up, coming up beside him. "Oh my God," I said.

In the valley below was a lone farmhouse surrounded by trellised slopes of fallow grape vines.

Grey and black smoke curled upward from the farmhouse's two chimneys. "You see," smiled Elijah, "God hasn't abandoned us…"

"And he's given us much wine to drink…" said Josef, marveling at the sight of the secluded farm and vineyards covering the surrounding slopes.

We crept down the ridge in the moonlight. I could smell the farm's smoke... rich; they were burning oak. We stopped at the edge of the vines, looking through the dark expanse for any signs of life or movement, the hint of guard dogs.

"The barrel house," I pointed to a series of wood structures adjacent the farmhouse. "We get in there, we stay quiet... let the morning come and see what we can learn."

Everyone nodded in agreement.

I went first, moving down the slope through the vines, stopping every so often when I thought I heard a sound or when the wind picked up. I suddenly thought, if God can give me a farm, then he can return my daughters to me. He's kept me alive... he will keep them alive... we will be together again...

I stopped just before the vines ended and the farm grounds began, crouching low, listening. The others came up behind me. I could hear them breathing heavily. We were all exhausted, though the journey from the ridge had warmed Gregor up enough for his teeth to stop chattering.

I turned around and whispered, "I'll go in first... make sure its empty."

I kept low and dashed from the edge of the vines to the barrel house door. It was locked. I pulled on it as hard as I dare, trying to make as little noise as I could.

God, salvation is at hand... just open the door...

Perhaps there was another way in. I moved around to the side of the house, my eyes and ears always searching the darkness. I felt along the wall: nothing. At the back of the building there was a large gate, chained and locked. It must be the loading area for delivery trucks picking up the finished wine. I searched the next corner of the barrel house, nothing. I scurried back into the vines, taking a moment to catch my breath.

They were eager to hear what I had found.

I shook my head.

"A door and gate... both locked."

"We go inside the house then," demanded Gregor.

"And do what?" said Elijah.

"Steal food, clothes, drink... their truck, whatever we can find."

"We can't do that," said Elijah.

I was still breathing heavily. Having no food for the last week save berries and grubs, I became dizzy.

"Gregor's right," said Josef. "We've tried being cautious... we won't survive another day like this, Askel... inside could be Jew-hating Vichy, or they could be friends, willing to feed and clothe us, keep us warm and hidden... we won't know until we go inside. All that is certain is, if we remain here, we will die."

I was too weary to contest. I was hungry and cold. Josef was right; each of us was dying, some faster than others.

"All right," I wheezed, looking at Elijah, the last remaining hold out.

Elijah's young eyes, tinged with wisdom beyond his years, met mine. I could see he knew he was dying too, and so at last, relented.

We all stood up, helping one another walk toward the farmhouse door. "Does anyone speak French?" said Elijah.

We looked around at one another.

"How many degrees do we have amongst us... six? Two being doctors... and no one speaks French?" said Josef.

"I spent all my youth learning mathematics and physics,

the universal languages," smiled Elijah. I couldn't help but laugh.

"Think of it this way," said Gregor. "Maybe the winemaker speaks German."

We arrived at front door a stinking, wretched band of men; our bodies wasted, shivering, numb, diseased... outcast, prisoners, runaway... we were the lowest of the low, destitute; starving, thirsty, unwashed... there was nothing left of us. I didn't realize it until then, how diminished we were; that Gregor could hardly breathe, that Elijah was too weak to even stand, that Josef was shivering uncontrollably. We were nothing, we were Jews chased from one country to the next, hunted like animals... and yet, in our miserable state, we represented all that was good and Godly: a willingness to endure, to love, to seek my daughters, to sacrifice for one another, as Josef held Elijah upright; a bravery beyond anything I witnessed in the trenches... we were human, God's creatures, and retained our dignity, even if on the other side of the door, with its gnarled slats of wood, greyed by age and weathering, was a man who despised us, who would hunt us down and turn us over to the Germans...it didn't matter, not any more... we were unconquerable. And would remain so even in death.

I raised my hand and struck the door thrice.

We waited.

I arrived in Dover, England on March 2, 1945. Sighting the towering white cliffs on the horizon, I firmly held the ferry's railing. The wind whipped about, stirring my hair and scarf, which I reached up and tied more tightly about my neck. White-capped waves bore us into the harbor. The ferry's horn sounded as we approached the mole. I was going toward the only family I knew remained: my brother, Efrayim. Every chance I got, I checked the newspapers or listened to the wire service, waiting, wishing, to read or hear of Buchenwald's liberation. News of the camps was beginning to emerge, first from Russian news sources, which many in the west seemed to dismiss. I told my story to everyone I could, told them about the camps, the mass murder, and the crematoriums... the madness of it all... but few, if any, listened. I could see it in their eyes, the reality of what I was saying was taking hold, then a switch inside them would flip, an invisible wheel turned, more often than not they would laugh uncomfortably, no longer able to believe me. I was just another mad Jew spewing mad lies... no one could imagine the organized slaughter of millions, and so surely it couldn't be true... could it... surely not...

I presented my papers to the custom officials.

Status: War Refugee

I was bound for London, I told them. I had a brother there, a resident. They wanted his address, but I didn't know it.

"Efrayim Wasserman," I said.

How many Jewish tailors and dressmakers could there be in London, I wondered? I would go to the Temples, yes, one by one, asking about my brother; had they seen him, heard of him, did he worship here?

"How many... Jewish Temples are... in London?" I asked the custom official in broken English. A grisly old man, he spied me with his one good eye.

"Ho' fuck shood ey' know... move it on, Jew." He stamped my paper and waved me through.

So that's what I did. I went to London and began my

search. I was given accommodation in an area of London called Whitechapel, housed with a family that was willing to take me in for a month while I sorted things out... while I searched for my brother. From my temporary home on Vallance Road, I departed each morning with a map of the city in hand. I'd circled all the locations of Jewish Temples. One by one, I walked to them. There were nearly a hundred. I couldn't believe it. Before coming to London, I thought I would find Efrayim in a week, maybe less; but as the end of March approached, my search was no nearer its conclusion.

Then it struck me one night, lying on the cot my adopted family provided me: I was trying to find a Jew in a city still full of Jews... instead of going to Temples, I needed to go to tailor shops... *design houses*, as Efrayim had called them in his letters to me long ago.

In the morning, I asked the family where the most prominent tailors and design houses were located.

"Savile Row, Mayfair," they said, circling it on the map for me.

I dressed in my donated suit and combed my hair in the mirror. I had a strange feeling that I would find Efrayim soon, re-forging one link of my shattered family. It was nearly the same feeling I had when knocking on the door at the farmhouse in France, exhausted and cold. Whatever comes today, I will continue on, I will find Efrayim... and one day I will find Illa and Eliana too. I will continue to knock on doors, unafraid of what lay behind them. Love has made me unconquerable, in life, and in death, for if they're gone, turned to ash like the millions, then it will not be long until I am with them. Life is a short and strange thing, but ever so cherished. I hope wherever my daughters are, they know they are loved, and if they still live, that they find the happiness and grace that love affords. I am with them, no matter the bounds of time and distance... they would be grown women now, that I might see them and not even know it...

I smiled, put on my jacket and headed out into the street. I began walking west toward Mayfair. Suddenly, the air raid sirens began to blare. People on the street scattered, running for shelters. The Germans were sending the last of their rockets. I looked up at the sky.

What a lovely blue, I thought...

36
Uzi

Two days after I met with Elon Redlich, Tomas Ziegler, formally Dr Sascha Ziegler, the *Butcher of Buchenwald*, was found dead in his prison cell. The newspapers cited Zeigler's lung cancer, however a part of me will always wonder... what would Director Harel do, what would Prime Minister Ben-Gurion do, what would Israel do to keep its secrets safe, to keep Tomas's identity hidden?

Israel does not forget... it cannot forget...

Redlich had said that over and over, as though it were a trained response, like a beaten dog cowering at the slightest sound from his master's mouth. Eichmann and Ziegler, both within the span of a year, two of the Shoah's most infamous names: both tried publicly, both sentenced to death... one escaping the hangman's noose.

Eliana didn't bat an eye when I told her about Ziegler's death, as though she were expecting it, even surprised it had taken so long.

"We will have to be more efficient than that in the future," she said, referring to State Security. We sat quietly for a time.

"I'm sorry, Eliana," I said, my fingers instinctively playing with my wedding band.

"Don't be, Uzi... whether it was cancer or piano string around his neck, he got what he deserved... Butcher or no Butcher... he stood by and did nothing, went along as thousands died and burned, as his brother raped me in the next room... and I'm no different. The things I did to survive... the choices I made... I belong in a prison cell as well, perhaps even to stand at the gallows."

"I admit, I used to think that way, that anyone who cooperated should be strung up... I spent nearly a decade going after Kapos... and for what? I keep asking myself, what did I do, how did I fight back... I did nothing, day after day loading bodies into the flames... I did nothing. I hid in a world of ash."

Tears began rolling down Eliana's cheeks. "I want to plead guilty, Uzi," she said.

I shook my head in defiance.

"No... Eliana, no... look at me."

She looked up at me, her dark brown eyes-stained red by grief.

"What you did... of all the tales of courage from the camps, I believe yours the most astonishing... and my heart fills with such sorrow that so many others should think it otherwise... but that is what the madness of that time did to us... does to us... whether it is vengeance or grief that drives Israel now, I honestly don't know... I can feel my body starting to slip away from me... I will be with my wife again soon, after so many years apart... but I will not go until your story is told, until Israel is burdened by the truth of what you did... this I promise you."

"Uzi... what I did, they were terrible, unforgivable things... that I should play God, selecting those to be subjected to Ziegler, to die in excruciating pain... I did that, no one else. I made those choices... no one else. I have only my life to give in recompense and I wish to give it... I can never balance the scales fully, but I must give what I can"

"Choices thrust upon you, Eliana! You were only a child... a young woman by the end of the war. What were you supposed to do? You stayed alive, that is all any of us could do. It does no good adding you to the ash heap. Already six million... there need not be another."

"Then there will be a trial... and the judges will decide... let all the witnesses come forth and say what they wish, let them tell their stories... let the scales be balanced as best as we are able... I will not deny the grievance and suffering I inflicted on Ziegler's subjects... his survivors..."

The morning of the trial, I woke from a dream with my wife. We'd been walking on a beach. I did not recognize the shoreline. It was not the rocky shoals of Israel. Instead, the beach was long and misty. Cold tides washed over our feet. Further up the beach, sand gave way to smoothed stones; there was a bluff leading up to a rocky ridge line where the beach became a dense forest of beech and oak trees, their leaves turning ochre with the late season. Hanging above the forest were grey clouds, always shifting with the wind. I could see a light rain falling on the forest. Following the ridge line down the beach, my eye caught a few natural rivulets cascading from the ridge down to the beach where the fresh water pooled, then snaked its way toward the ocean.

I looked out across the ocean, which I suddenly realized was not an ocean at all, but a wide river, much of it masked by a rolling fog. I spotted an oarsman, his slight craft weaving in and out of view as he worked against the river's current, rowing toward the opposite bank. I did not recall it, but I knew the oarsman had just deposited me upon the beach and was now returning from whence he came. I felt my wife's hand slip into mine. She pulled me toward her. We walked along the shoreline, expecting to find others there too. But in all our searching, we only found solitude.

I sat up in bed, looking at my wedding band. I pulled it off my finger, studying it more closely; all the tiny abrasions, scratches, and marks… what a journey we have been on, I said to my wife. I put the ring in my mouth, picked up a glass water placed on my bedside table and drank, swallowing the ring.

I dressed as neatly as I could, paying extra attention to my tie, washed my face, and combed what hair I had left. My body had shed much of its weight; my suit no longer fit properly, like a child wearing his father's. When I was finished, I hardly recognized myself.

Not much longer now…

The courtroom in Jerusalem was empty, save the opposing lawyers and the three judges sat behind a raised podium. State Security ensured it would be a quiet affair. Eliana was led in by a female guard who sat her down in the glass defendant's box, the same cage where, only a few weeks ago, Ziegler had sat. Eliana's face was sullen and pale. She looked over at me. I smiled. She hinted at a smile. Her eyes studied the empty rows of seats behind me. I wondered for a moment whether she expected to see her husband with his family, but as I watched her a little longer, I realized the magnitude of what she beheld…

I turned and cast my eyes upon the seats, now suddenly full, overflowing with all those lost, their ashen faces beset with eyes full of yearning; for what, though, I could not answer.